THE
FÆ
AND THE
HUNTER

T. E. MOUNTAIN

THE
FÆ
AND THE
HUNTER

The Book Guild Ltd

First published in Great Britain in 2023 by
The Book Guild Ltd
Unit E2 Airfield Business Park,
Harrison Road, Market Harborough,
Leicestershire. LE16 7UL
Tel: 0116 2792299
www.bookguild.co.uk
Email: info@bookguild.co.uk
Twitter: @bookguild

This work is entirely fictitious and bears no resemblance to any persons living or dead.

Typeset in 11pt Minion Pro

Printed and bound in the UK by TJ Books LTD, Padstow, Cornwall

ISBN 978 1915352 675

British Library Cataloguing in Publication Data.
A catalogue record for this book is available from the British Library.

To my family and friends,
for all their love and support.

To Liz, who cannot read this book
but might try eat it.

Act One

The Natural

Chapter One

Grind

Ryheart stepped gingerly through the labyrinthine sewers that ran under the grand old city of Londaya, his balance only slightly hampered by the hand he had clamped over his nose. He did so to avoid the rotten stench emanating from the sewage that ran beside the walkway he was on. The hand's effectiveness was considerably lower than he would have liked. He could taste the filth as much as smell it. He could virtually hear it.

When he'd signed up with the Hunter's Guild, this was not what he had imagined. The desk for registration had glorious illustrations of proud knights, resplendent in armour riding into battle against vile fire-spitting behemoths. He'd imagined riches, carousing with the exotic Fae, being knighted and celebrated. And in fairness, all that could be true. If – the big if – you were particularly good at it. Beyond good, really. Exceptional. Unfortunately, Ryheart was not. Ryheart was okay at it. Middling at it. Generously, he might have described himself as competent, even, on a good day.

Taking the dangerous, glamorous jobs when you were only decent was an excellent way to end up dead, he had quickly realised. Even for the good hunters, it was fifty-fifty. So, these were the jobs the middling hunters got. The less glamorous ones. The unpleasant ones. At the point he had realised this, he might well have quit the post altogether. But what the smiling, chatty representatives who signed him up had glossed over, was the cost of hunting. First, there was the mildly extortionate fee for the licence that allowed you to hunt officially on behalf of the guild. That was essential because freelancers tended to go 'missing'. Then there was the fee for a weapons licence, and the mandatory training the guild made you go through, and the inflated costs for renting the equipment you couldn't afford to buy outright, along with a dozen other necessities like provisions for travel.

Helpfully the guild didn't take the money upfront; they deducted a fee from the payment of every bounty you handed in. A substantial fee. So, Ryheart had neither the money for provisions nor the skill for the big-paying jobs that might wipe his debt. That left the lesser jobs. The low-grade bounties. The ones that left him scarcely a handful of copper beggars after each hunt. If he was extremely lucky, maybe a silver noble or two. Barely enough to keep afloat. At the rate he was going, it would take him five hundred years to pay off his outstanding balance. He hadn't dared look at it for some time, but last he checked, it had been approaching a couple of hundred gold crowns. That was close to buying-a-house money. Or, in his case, owing-a-house money.

It was hard to keep motivated in a job he barely muddled through, and he had spent too long lounging and squandering the little spare he had left, till he had no choice but to take the first, quickest job he could get.

So here he was. In the city, in the sewer. Underground. Hunting a set of brownies who had blocked a drainage pipe.

Using his free hand to hold up the small lantern he unclipped from his belt, he surveyed the water – water being a generous description – and saw that it was lower ahead. Creeping along and lifting the lantern, he saw movement in the dim gloom.

Faintly he heard the unmistakable noise of brownies, a screeching, nonsensical chattering. Their low, misshapen bodies stood out in the gloom as they packed their nest with gleefully pilfered goods. They had managed to scavenge cutlery, a jug and what looked to be someone's underwear from what he could make out. They were dim-witted, gangly creatures, but quick. He could dimly make out that there were five or six of them, and he very much hoped to be able to corner them and at least get a few before they had a chance to flee. He was unlikely to get all of them, but he needed at least three to call it a good day's work.

The brownies were stupid and unsettling, but ultimately, they were just pests, more nuisance than a genuine threat. Ryheart didn't quite have the sustained, unyielding hatred for anything and everything magical that some of his esteemed colleagues in the Hunter's Guild did, and the guild taking virtually everything he earned didn't exactly help his motivation. The imminent threat of starvation, however, did. Consequently, as a fresh surge of stench hit him as he let go of his nose, he felt past the knife on his belt, and instead pulled out a small cudgel. He'd knock them out and drop them off somewhere outside the city limits. Luckily the one advantage of his lack of importance was that the guild didn't exactly do much follow-up work, and they'd practically take him at his word. If he took their horns, that would be enough proof for the guild he had dispatched them.

He crept slowly forward, keeping as quiet as he could. The brownies were still virtually oblivious to his presence, and they scampered on their gangly limbs, sharp little teeth glinting in the light. The tunnel ahead had a fence of iron bars, the bottom half solid with no gaps.

The brownie nest also sat ahead, built like a dam across the gate, blocking the grating that would have otherwise let through a steady supply of water, cutting its flow to barely a trickle.

Ryheart peered into the gloom past the gate, and his heart nearly jumped from his chest.

Stood behind them, dimly lit by a lantern of his own, was another figure. A human figure. To his side was an iron bar jutting from the wall, that Ryheart couldn't quite make out in the shadows.

The mystery person was covered nearly head to toe in a dark fabric, a cloth wrapped around his face, presumably a somewhat better solution to the stench than Ryheart's admittedly ill-conceived one.

Ryheart couldn't make out his features, but he recognised the smug voice that spoke to him.

"Ryheart?" the human asked in a surprised voice.

Ryheart put his finger to his lips and glanced at the brownies. The last thing he needed was them fleeing. Fortunately, they seemed so enamoured by their chatter that they were oblivious to the fact they were effectively surrounded.

Slinking as close as he dared, Ryheart whispered back, "Yeah, yeah, it's me. Why are you here, Harand?"

"Well, rumour has it, there are brownies around. You haven't seen them, have you?"

Ryheart glanced down at them. His rival might not have been able to see them at such an angle, but their chatter was loud enough that he had to have heard them.

"Maybe. I have it covered, though."

"Yeah? Are you sure you don't need help? Might be a bit much for a D-rank hunter."

Help. As if the man had any interest in helping. By Divana's name, Ryheart hated him. He wanted to punch him in his smug face. Instead, he answered. "I think I can manage, thank you," he forced through gritted teeth. While a hunter signed their name to proclaim they had taken a bounty, technically, nothing stopped multiple hunters from taking the same contract. With longer jobs, the idea someone had a head start on you, and you might be wasting weeks, tended to stop people from taking a duplicate contract. With such a small job, though, all that was left as a barrier was common courtesy. That was in short supply. Harand had stolen more bounties from him than he could count. That wasn't going to happen this time, though. The spoils went to whoever claimed them first and overt violence between hunters was prohibited, so all Ryheart had to do was grab them before Harand could find a way around to him.

"Well, I was going to suggest splitting the bounty, but if you insist on competing…" Harand said, almost managing to sound regretful.

Ryheart thought it more likely he was about to be crowned King of Brittaya than any hunter willingly sharing a bounty, let alone one who hated him.

"Yeah? Well, you're on the wrong side of the bars there," Ryheart gloated, "so, looks like I win this one already."

"That'd be a first," Harand snorted. Disconcertingly, he didn't sound concerned. "But I have a better weapon than you."

"Yeah. What's that?"

"I checked the layout of the sewer," he said, taking hold of the iron handle, "and I know what a sluice gate is. More importantly, I know you open it on this side."

There was a creak of rusty iron as he pulled the bar. The bar, as Ryheart shortly learned, was a lever. A lever to the floodgate Harand stood behind.

A stream came through as the gate started to creak open behind the brownies' dam, beginning to wash it away from the bottom up. It battered Ryheart's legs, and he staggered back with the current, barely keeping his balance.

With a laugh as he held the lever for purchase, Harand stooped down through the now half-open floodgate and flung a net across the top of the startled brownies now collapsing home, catching all of them in one go. With a wink, he pulled the lever the rest of the way.

The sewage took its newfound freedom in earnest and rushed forth, a torrent of black ooze. With an involuntary howl that filled his mouth with something putrid beyond mention, Ryheart was bowled over into the now-rapid flow.

He caught his last glimpse of the triumphant Harand's hand merrily waving goodbye to him before he was carried away by the deluge of filth, along with his hopes of claiming the bounty that he so desperately needed.

Chapter Two

Occurrence

Fali felt a tug upon her consciousness. A light tug, scarcely noticeable. But niggling. Persistent. She and her kin had existed only in spirit for a long time. Seemingly an endless time, even for her. And she was considered endless in some quarters herself.

Now, she didn't just have a spiritual feeling, though, but a physical one. A mundane one. She had almost forgotten she had those. The feeling was fleeting and so faint she feared she might lose it. Concentrating as hard as she could, she pulled at the magical thread and let it take her where it wished.

Olyra Holloway stood implacable, her eyes fixed solidly on the sky. She was a calm centre surrounded by a whirl of activity as wizards rushed around her and chattered excitedly, checking their magical sensors and conferring. Her armour was bloody roasting even in the ebbing evening heat of the summer, but she ignored it, preparing herself.

She was a Valkyrie agent of the OPMC, Operations for the Prevention of Magical Crime. Her job was to investigate and terminate any magical threats to His Majesty's land of Grand Brittaya. If it was too otherworldly for the guard or too criminal for the Hunter's Guild, an agent dispatched to deal with it. Magical creatures, even the intelligent ones, were dangerous. Even those tenuously allied with the King of the civilised lands – the human lands – needed an eye keeping on them.

Any form of magic, living or enchanted, was closely monitored within the city. It was employed primarily within the government's tight control and the agencies who supported it to benefit King and the realm. Only the extravagantly rich were able to keep even the mildest of magical items for purely personal use. Outside of that, you had to be obscenely stupid or obscenely criminal. Olyra wasn't sure which she was about to find.

The King's wizards, one of the rare and esteemed groups who were allowed to remain in the city while openly and unrestrainedly practising magic, had reported an unknown and outrageously robust source of magical power sparking onto their detecting maps. She found the wizards pretentious and insufferable with their trinkets and grandstanding, but they did give good intelligence.

She stood in an empty field, only a short distance from the grand walls that towered protectively over the capital city of Londaya, the mother of all foreign magic dropped right on her doorstep.

"You're positive this is the spot?" she called to the nearest of the universally bearded and balding wizards.

"Positive, ma'am. These readings are astronomical. In both senses."

"Origin?" she questioned laconically.

"Well, that's a tough one," the first replied.

"Something celestial? Demonic, perhaps?" a second chimed in.

"Anything certain?" Olyra queried. "Or just guesswork?"

"Well... all that's certain is that we don't know what it is, I suppose!"

"Superb," Olyra muttered. She was going to probe them further when a distortion appeared in the air. First, it was a faint shimmer, mistakable as only heat haze, but it rapidly grew more pronounced.

"Alright, clear out," she ordered curtly. The last thing she needed was a group of bumbling old men in the way of her operation.

The wizards looked like they were about to protest, but one sharp glare from her quashed any objections, and they scurried away. Technically the King's wizards outranked her for as long as this was a purely investigative matter. If this was a security threat, however, her military rank took priority over their civilian one. If it turned out to need further study, she could always call them back.

In the middle of the seemingly breaking sky, a strange glyph formed in the air. It flared brightly, and then a figure blinked in and out of existence around it, slowly becoming more robust. It almost seemed like the world couldn't quite make up its mind about whether they existed or not.

Mundane monsters were terrible enough, but the supernatural ones could be devastating. Olyra had to be ready for immediate battle, the second whatever it was appeared. She cleared her mind and prepared for the mission at hand. Removing her newly created blunderbuss from its strapping, she aimed at the disturbance. There was a final violent flickering, and then with a blink, the figure truly appeared. Far from an immediate fiery battle, they instead fell a good twenty feet to the ground, immobile.

Olyra lowered her weapon ever so slightly as the being hit the ground headfirst with a crunch and collapsed in a heap. Hellcana's bells, that was a fall, even for a monster.

She froze again as the figure suddenly sprang to her feet.

"Dear me!" the mysterious creature proclaimed, picking a bit of dirt from her hair as if the would-be neck-snapping fall she had just been through was at most a minor inconvenience.

Olyra studied her cautiously, scanning for any details of interest. She was a small woman. Compared to Olyra's muscular build, she was positively delicate. Her red hair flowed like a river of blood, framing her face. Strange triangular markings sat against either eye, and some unknown magical glyph shone upon her cheek. An enchantment, perhaps?

She was also, well, naked. Completely and entirely. Olyra noted that the skin was perfect. Flawless. There wasn't so much as a single wrinkle or scar. It almost looked new.

She had completed her initial assessment when her eyes seemed to tingle, and she noticed two bright wings stretched aside the creature. Every feather seemed to shimmer with all the colours Olyra had ever seen before, and many she had never seen. Somehow she had completely missed the wings, despite them being in clear view. Even now she knew they were there, she had trouble focusing on them, only truly aware of them in her peripheral vision. She was not one to get nervous, but she felt a slight tremble in her legs when she saw them.

"I am Olyra Holloway," she declared, lifting her weapon, "Valkyrie agent of the OPMC. I am detaining you on the authority extended to me by the King of Brittaya. Identify yourself and come with me without resistance, or I will view you as hostile and terminate you as such."

That should be authoritative enough, she thought. The creature positively radiated peaceful intent. Despite her evident durability, surely she wouldn't be any trouble.

Chapter Three

Arrest

Fali regarded the human who was currently aiming at her with one of those dreadful metal tubes they had become so enamoured with in recent years. She was tall, muscular, dark-skinned and virtually encased in metal. Her bright hazel eyes were narrowed into an intense stare. A warrior. A confident one, to judge by her demands. This wasn't the most gracious welcome she'd ever had upon a visitation, though it wasn't the worst, either.

"I see your manners have not improved much," Fali directed to her host.

"Have we met?" the soldier asked, only the slightest curiosity carried in her otherwise measured tone.

"Humans, I mean. Such impolite creatures."

"Identify yourself," she affirmed.

"My name? Fali. The rest is irrelevant because I do not make a habit of following the orders of children. Especially rude children."

"Children? I'm twenty-six."

"Scarcely a babe," she sniffed.

"Look, you have two options. You can come with me, alive or dead. I recommend the former, but it's your choice."

Fali couldn't help but laugh at that.

"Well, how friendly. May I ask why I am being detained or murdered?"

"You're an unknown magical entity, and you're directly outside the biggest city in the lands. Magic must be controlled. If we can get you assessed and catalogued, I'm sure we can find something useful for you to do in the city. Or you can be on your way to the Fae-lands if you're deemed safe."

"I will pass, thank you."

Olyra shrugged at her, and then with no further hesitation, the soldier fired. The buckshot parted violently from the barrel with a furious roar. Fali was in the air before it even finished. She leapt gracefully over the scatter, and then just for a lark, she kicked two of the pellets back towards the soldier where they pinged off her armour. Fali landed in front of Olyra before the soldier could react, waved like she was greeting a friend and then slapped her. The soldier crashed to the floor and bounced twice with a clatter, then pulled herself up onto her feet, staggering, but upright.

Fali was impressed by her tenacity, if nothing else.

"Son of a goblin!" Olyra proclaimed, spitting a small globule of blood to the floor, steadying herself. By Divana, that stung. She adjusted her mental assessment of the creature from 'not much trouble' to 'quite a bloody lot of trouble, probably be more careful next time'.

She was remarkably powerful and extraordinarily swift. Olyra's considerable height advantage and musculature should have given her a clear physical edge, but that was bloody magic for you. Still, given the creature was utterly naked, unless she had something hidden between her buttocks, there was at least one advantage Olyra still had on her – technology. Tricks. She was not above using them.

Alright, alright, you win," she intoned, mollifying, before whipping a small sphere from her belt and launching it at her target.

The creature slapped it to the floor in front of her. "Look, I am trying not to kill you here, but you are making it bloody awkward!"

her foe intoned, stamping her foot. Evidently, she didn't even consider it a threat. Good.

The sphere exploded into large orbs of crackling energy that surrounded and hemmed in her foe. Weaponised magic, contained in enchanted casings that kept the power contained until they were physically shattered. The government-sanctioned Fae provided them to be used to capture their less reasonable kin. The creature reached out and touched one gingerly, and it exploded around her, causing her to flinch back. Again, Olyra saw her fortitude. A human would have been unconscious at this point. It had harmed her, though, so she had a vulnerability. Good. She'd still rather have the target alive now she was effectively immobilised, but dead would do if necessary.

"You're fast, but all the speed in the world won't do you much good if you can't move. Stay still. I'll restrain you, and we can do this somewhere more pleasant."

The creature didn't reply, so Olyra got her restraining sphere from her pocket, feeling the wind brush against her still-smarting cheek. Something was off about that; it had been a still day. She narrowed her eyes. The orbs. Are they separating? They should hang entirely still unless blown away. Can the bloody creature control the wind? She launched her restraining sphere, where it caught in a violent gust that sent it careening off target and to the floor. It exploded into enchanted iron ribbons that snatched angrily at the air, then collapsed when they failed to find anything to wrap themselves around.

Olyra discarded the blunderbuss and raised her rifle, this time using her ace in the hole. A band she wore on her arm, enchanted, injected magic into her artificially. It was a rare and expensive contraption used exclusively by the Valkyries to allow them to dispatch magical foes that couldn't be killed by conventional means. It taxed her physically and mentally to channel something entirely foreign to her body and took a significant toll upon her. Nevertheless, with effort, she began focusing the magic into the weapon as quickly as she could manage. The spheres were less affected by the wind than physical objects, but they were parting now, a clear gap forming between them.

"Fine. Dead it is, then!" Olyra warned. Her gun crackled with the magic artificially pouring into it, and she fired.

Fali's skin rippled with alarm as a flash of light streaked towards her, cutting the air. Her wind hadn't entirely separated the semi-intangible orbs, and she had barely any room to manoeuvre. With no other option, gritting her teeth, she jerked her head sideways into the sphere beside it. Her body wracked with pain as the strange artificial magic disrupted her own, and she felt a burning pain as the shot tore her open.

A splash of effervescent colour, her magic-filled blood, painted the air and evaporated into the ambient magic of the world.

Her eyes narrowed into deadly slits. By the Twin-Divinities, the shot had only skimmed her cheek. She had expected nothing more than parlour tricks from the human, scarcely taking her seriously. But that shot had thrummed with power. If she had been just a touch slower, it would have done more than embarrass her. It might very well have ended her short visit to the mundane, newly formed as she was. She hadn't felt quite so fragile for a very long time. She wasn't thrilled about being reintroduced to the feeling, and cold anger gripped her.

By this point, the rest of the spheres had drifted considerably. Fali spread her wings imposingly, and she marched towards the soldier, who stood panting. Whatever artificial means the human had used to empower herself with magic, it had taken quite a toll. The soldier raised the gun weakly and fired, this time unpowered. Not bothering to deflect it back at her this time, Fali slapped the bullet away and then slammed her head into the soldier's face. There was an unpleasant crunch as the cartilage of the nose moved somewhere it shouldn't be. Before Olyra could fall, Fali caught her and lifted her with two fingers under her chin.

The soldier's eyes glazed over, unfocused but conscious. If barely.

"Child, I could unravel you in a heartbeat. Tell your ilk that if they try to cage me again, I will end them."

Olyra responded with a weak cough, and with a laugh. From delirium, perhaps.

There was a faint click, and Fali looked down and saw an explosive in Olyra's hand. Ah. Not delirium, then.

She dropped the soldier and jumped backwards. Olyra covered her head with her armoured fists as she hit the floor, and an explosion tore the world apart with a deafening blast.

While metal encased Olyra, Fali had no such luck. All she could do was let the explosion take her.

Olyra blearily opened her eyes, unfocused and seeing double, half-cooked in her armour. Despite the pain rankling her face, she couldn't help a faint smile as she saw feathers raining down to the floor, stained with blood. She had only one thought before she fell back into unconsciousness.

Dead it is, then.

Chapter Four

Meeting

Ryheart climbed out of a manhole, having been washed through the sewer until he had managed to grab an outlying stone, pulling himself out once the surge had subsided. 'Washed' was probably not the best term, given the dubious cleanliness of the waterway he had emerged from. He was extremely thankful that night had fallen, and the streets were mostly empty by this point. He wasn't exactly the most avid of bathers, but it had gone past luxury and into an absolute necessity at this point.

"I hope a harpy feeds your bollocks to their young," he cursed at his long-away hunting nemesis, now that he could open his mouth without the risk of sewer contamination, "I needed that bloody bounty."

The city of Londaya was split into sections that divided the five districts, giving both physical protection with stone and magical protection with the warding the walls' pentagram shape afforded. Fortunately, he had come up in the residential district. That was at least a small mercy.

His hand stung slightly along with his battered pride, and he found his glove torn. Underneath, his palm was grazed and bloody. It must have ripped when he was grabbing for the stone edge of the sewer bank as he desperately tried to stop himself from being carried away. Bloody great, he thought. A potential infection was just what he needed to make his day that little bit better.

Thoroughly depressed, he set off towards home. Another failed bounty really wouldn't do his already patchy competence rating within the guild any favours. He needed to pay off at least a token amount of his ever-growing debt. He had heard all sorts of tales about the unpleasantness that occurred with hunters who failed to pay off their debt fast enough. All of them involved legs. More specifically, legs breaking. He was rather keen to keep them intact.

Not too far away from Ryheart's contemplation of his financial woes, too quiet for him to hear, the patter of tiny feet rang across the cobblestone floor.

Fali, now about the size her hand had been a fleeting time ago, ran along the pavement. She had determined it best if Olyra – and equally importantly, the government she represented – wasn't aware she was alive. So, she had shrunk herself and fled as the explosion went off.

In what she felt was a minor stroke of genius, she had also shed her wings and allowed their charred feathers to suggest her demise. On the downside, the loss of wings was not a pleasant experience. Further, it limited her connection to her realm, which was a large part of the source of her powers. On the plus side, their disappearance, along with her reduced size, would limit her magical signature while she stabilised her form. This would make her harder to detect by whatever sensors Olyra had access to until she devised something better. She didn't intend to stay shrunk in the long term. Her legs were short enough as it was.

Fortunately, she already had a solution. If she could find a human, one entirely unremarkable and without any Fae ancestry or artificial means of magic, she could mimic their life signature. As far as any detecting device or even other creature could tell if they sensed her, she would appear as unremarkable as whomever she mimicked. She could do little about the glyph and markings upon her face, as they were quintessential to her being. They bound the magic her body formed from together, but she doubted anyone would recognise them. Many cycles ago, the barriers between the realms had been sealed as the last resort to guard against a terrible cataclysm, and her people had stopped appearing physically within the mundane. The knock-on effect was that the humans had all but forgotten her kind existed, and never remembered their brief spiritual visits clearly.

She wiped a small bead of the magical blood that had formed on her cut cheek away with her palm as she reasoned out her plan. She would simply need to make a minor magical contract with a human, to perform some trivial spell for them in return. Creating a magical contract wouldn't be detectable the way using magic more directly would be, and then she could be on her way. The bargain would allow her to retain their life signature – their aura – until she no longer had use of it. She just needed someone unremarkable enough to copy.

Fortunately, she had just spotted someone slinking along the street. And by the Twin-Divinities, was he unremarkable – not even the slightest spark of long-forgotten ancestral Fae within him.

She watched him for a moment, pondering. He was a tall man, though not overly. His brown hair was plastered to his head, and he was filthy. In fact, he absolutely reeked. Thankfully, she didn't have to copy his smell along with his aura. Aside from that, he was about as plain as plain could be, other than his eyes being a not-unattractive jolt of green.

Given humanity's evident lack of trust in magical beings, she had some misgivings about propositioning a stranger, and she mused how to approach this. With a smile, her size gave her an idea. If she said she was a fairy, if he were clueless enough, she would be able to convince him. Fairies, at least the last time she had checked, were one of the few Fae somewhat widely spread through 'civilisation'. This was due partly to their general harmlessness, and more importantly, she thought – given the human's avarice – due to the good fortune they often brought with their blessings.

19

That gave her an idea of how to propose her deal.

"Lo, greetings fair traveller! I require respite," she called. "Might I perhaps trouble you for shelter for the night?" Technically, she reasoned, it was shelter she wanted. Sanctuary within his aura. She didn't have to explain that small distinction to him. And, since she was the only magical party within the deal, she would be the one to dictate all the terms.

What a nice, easy fix this would be!

Chapter Five

Oath

Ryheart snapped out of his moody reverie when a small, melodious voice called out to him. He turned towards it but couldn't see the source. With a shrug, he started forward again.

"Halt, please! I would rather like not to be stepped on today!"

He stopped once again as the voice piped up, and this time saw a small creature on the ground before him.

Squinting into the gloom, he peered at them. Was that a fairy? If it was, she was an unusual one. First off, she didn't have the butterfly wings they always had. Or indeed, any wings at all. He didn't know of any other creature so small and human-like, however, let alone one that would be walking around the most magically warded city in the land unimpeded, unescorted or lacking clear government affiliation.

Also, she was absolutely bollock-naked. While Fae weren't exactly known for following all of civilised society's little quirks, even for them, this seemed to be pushing the limits of modesty to the extreme.

He crouched down and questioned her, straining his hearing to try to catch her tiny voice. "Can I help you?"

"You can pick me up for a start. Carefully!" the fairy squeaked as Ryheart bowled her off her feet as he scooped her up in his hand. He stood up, holding his palm flat at eye level.

"Clumsy oaf!" she proclaimed as she found her balance, giving a stomp of her tiny foot. She at least had the grace to avoid the wound on his palm.

He moved over to the light of a hanging lantern on the edge of the street so he could see her a little better. Whatever she was, she was extraordinarily beautiful. She was like a statuette of a goddess with her tiny size, though decidedly warmer in his hand.

"Sorry. I'm not used to handling, err, tiny people."

"Okay. Now that we are treating each other with a modicum of respect," the Fae intoned haughtily, "perhaps we can talk?"

"I can hear you properly now, so shoot."

"I was wondering if you might perhaps offer me sanctuary. In return, I could offer you some magical assistance."

"What kind of magic?" he said, eyes narrowed. The last thing he needed on top of his other issues was a government investigator banging his door down and arresting him for illegal use of magic, let alone potentially unregistered magic.

"Oh, just some small magical trifle. Fairies perform them all the time."

"And you're a fairy?"

"Why, of course! What else would I be?"

"Where are your wings, then?"

"A... bird ate them," she said, after a brief moment's hesitation.

"A bird ate them?"

"Yes, a bird. Look," Fali said, turning her back to him, "see the scars?"

There were indeed angry-looking marks on her back that he could make out in the light of the flame.

"Gods, I'm sorry. Don't you need medical help?"

"No, no. They will grow back." She waved it off dismissively. "I only need sanctuary. Shelter. Just for a brief time."

"I don't know..." he said. It wasn't that he didn't want to help, but he'd heard enough horror stories about magical things forcibly being taken away from people to be wary.

"I will not be a bother, I promise. And if you are worried about engaging in magic," she said, seemingly picking up on the reason for his hesitancy, "it is purely benign, natural bargaining magic, centred within the sanctity of your domicile. Undetectable. Fairy promise."

"So, it's a deal, then? What exactly do I get?"

"As I say, just some minor charm. For luck, perhaps? Help with money?"

That caught his interest.

"Help with money?"

"Absolutely."

"So, if I had debts, say…?" he asked, feeling a spark of hope.

"Oh, I could help pay them off, absolutely."

He weighed the options, deciding his fear of maybe being found guilty of a magic misdemeanour was less than his fear of definitely having his legs broken. Finally, a way out of the deepening hole he was in.

"Alright, I'm in."

"Marvellous! We need to seal the contract, then. I will help with your debt once your end of the bargain is upheld."

"So, what do we do?" he said, furtively checking no one was watching.

"Well, generally, we would shake hands, but it is the physical contact that is important. Given my tiny size, bring your head nearer," she commanded imperially. He did so, casting her into near-total darkness as he blocked the light. She laid her tiny hand on his nose. "Now that we have that, we just need to make our offering to one another formally."

"Alright. I offer you sanctuary?"

"And I…" She paused, and he felt strange electricity in the graze on his palm, under his torn glove.

"What's the matter?"

"Nothing, sorry," she mumbled, wiping something from her cheek. "And I offer you help with your debt."

"That's it?"

"That is it," she agreed.

"Well, when humans make deals, we give each other our names. I'm Ryheart, a hunter."

"You shouldn't give your name so casually to a Fae, Ryheart," she tutted. "You give away some of your protection against them."

"Oh. Well, you have it now." He laughed nervously. "What do I call you if not your name?"

"You may call me Fali. Fali Lightflower. Now then, let us proceed home! You will hardly notice I am there."

Chapter Six

Payment

Fali looked around the home her host had presented to her. Hovel, she would have called it, personally. Even with her diminished size, the room she was in looked tiny.

Generously the living room and kitchen might have been called 'open plan', though she thought that was likely a matter of necessity rather than style. Two doors lead to what she presumed was a bedroom and a bathroom, and that looked to be the limits of the abode.

"Charming," she murmured to herself, stepping over unwashed clothes that were piled haphazardly by the door. Clearly, he was not a tidy man. Fortunately, she didn't intend to stay very long.

"So, I've got a bottle somewhere," he said. "You can sleep in that for the night if you want. I can put some cotton in it or something for you."

"A bottle?" she exclaimed, outraged.

"Yeah, don't fairies love them?"

"Not this one," she said, narrowing her eyes.

"Alright, a pillow then?"

"Adequate, I suppose." It wasn't like she planned on sleeping in it anyway. On principle, she was simply offended that the human's first solution for her was to stuff her in a bottle. Still, it was better than trying to murder her on sight, she supposed.

"Do you not have any family?" she asked, curious.

"No," he said flatly, evidently not something he wanted to discuss further.

"Ah. My apologies," she said, sincere.

"Alright, well, I'm going to go wash this crap off of me, make yourself at home," he said with a vague wave around the room.

Given he'd been carrying her, she hoped 'crap' wasn't literal, though, given the smell, it might well have been.

"That might be a good idea, yes." She bounded up onto the chair, to the table and then to his shoulder, wrinkling her nose in distaste. "Don't forget to wash behind your ears. Inside them, too."

"Err, yeah. I won't."

She patted his cheek fondly, taking an echo of his life essence as she did so and wrapping herself in it, cloaking her own much more vivid, noticeable aura.

With that, she hopped off his shoulder, and he left the room. It wouldn't harm him, and he wouldn't even notice it was gone.

She listened as water started running, and then traced a glowing series of intricate lines in the air. After about fifteen minutes of work to weave the exact pattern of the spell into reality, she double-checked everything was accurate and then poured her magic into it. A small hole opened like a tear in the world, and she stuck her hand inside. She couldn't create true physical objects from nothing, but she had a survival chest of sorts and could pull things she had already placed into that magical storage through to the mundane.

Retracting her hand, she pulled out a gold coin. It came from an old society that had been lost to the sands of time – literally, in this case, buried under it. While it was certainly no longer recognised currency, it was still gold. Probably purer than most modern money, too, so often padded out with lead or other less valuable metals.

Hopping up with the coin held over her head, she placed it on the table, where he would see it. She had said she'd help pay his debt, after all, not all his debt.

Not that she had any more to give him anyway; that was all she had. She wasn't exactly one to care for currency. While she had vaguely remembered having the coin in her storage, she couldn't even remember why she'd been given it so long ago.

Besides, she had more important things to do. Years ago, the mundane had almost been swamped with corruption from the void, eroding the barriers between realms severely as it did so. Her people had had no choice but to seal the various domains off from one another completely. This had stopped the barriers shattering irreparably and all the realms collapsing in on one other, along with stopping the flow of corruption into the mundane. However, it also had caused a cataclysmic break in the flow of magic that had driven many creatures attuned to it insane, creating a flood of monsters that had nearly overrun the humans and forced them to retreat into concentrated populations. In response, they had formed the beginnings of the Hunter's Guild, initially a loose coalition of defenders that had become gradually more formalised. Eventually, they managed to drive back the monsters enough for them to create the shelter of civilisation, growing into towns and cities. While the human's desperation had been understandable, in their zealous push to protect themselves, Fae had often been treated with suspicion and downright hostility, driven from anywhere the humans settled and into the wild.

The barriers had sealed the corruption, but in doing so, had sealed her own people as well. Only the loosest of spiritual visitations remained possible.

Now, though, for unknown reasons, she had fallen through that barrier of realms. Through walls that had been impassable for hundreds of years. She was now physically in the mundane.

She had, to be perfectly honest with herself, absolutely no idea why, or even how, that had happened. But if the shaken foundation of the realms had settled enough, and she could find out how she had got here, perhaps she could even bring her people back through. Then they could purge the leftover corruption, and the barriers could be restored to their original state to allow the natural passage of magic between realms again.

With her deal made, she turned and went to leave. Only, she couldn't. Two steps beyond the door of the human's tiny abode, she was yanked back nearly off her feet. Like some tether was holding her back. Tying her to the place. Or... tying her to Ryheart. That wasn't a pleasant train of thought.

Why, though? Magical contracts could be extremely binding. This one shouldn't be, though. As the only magical participant, she should have controlled all the rules. Besides, she had fulfilled the contract, hadn't she? She had made sure she only said she'd help pay off the debt he had. Not pay it entirely. She must be mistaken.

She walked back into the room, and what she found wasn't reassuring. The house had the distinct magical feeling of the sanctity of a home to it. The kind that stopped vampires entering uninvited. Not just of a home, though. Of her home. This was her sanctuary now, as powerful as if it was the home of her kin.

Evidently, something had gone terribly wrong. For some reason, Ryheart's offer of shelter had applied far more powerfully than it should have.

So had her tie to him. She tried to leave again, but as hard as she pushed, she couldn't break the bonds holding her to him. Now she was aware of it; she could feel the power of vow chaining her to him.

Given that she considered herself fairly paid, that meant it had to be her end of the deal that was yet unfulfilled. Clearly, Ryheart did not.

Oh, but of course! That was it. He hadn't seen the coin yet, had he? Whatever had amplified the power of the spell, he would consider himself paid once she gave it to him, surely?

Chapter Seven

Remodelling

After a vigorous scrubbing of his every body part and orifice, clothes now resigned to the rubbish pile, Ryheart returned to find the fairy sitting patiently upon his table.

"Ah. Now that is an improvement! Both to sight and smell," she commented on his clean visage.

"Yeah, thanks. What's that?" Ryheart asked, pointing at a gold coin next to her.

"It is for you," she replied sunnily.

He picked it up and stared at it dubiously. He didn't recognise the currency. He didn't even understand the language.

"And it is?" he asked.

"It is a Kemetayan gold coin," she explained, but Ryheart just stared at her blankly, so she elaborated, "It is your payment. My part of the bargain?"

"Okay? Is it magical, or?"

"No? It is just a coin."

"Why are you giving it to me then?"

"Why, to pay your debt, of course," she said, pursing her lips as if that was apparent.

"Then what use is it to me?" he asked bluntly. "I can't pay my debt with this. I can't even buy a bloody loaf of bread with it."

"But it is gold," she restated, looking displeased.

"What am I going to do with it? Melt it down? I'll barely end up with a tooth's worth."

"Well, I do not have anything else!" she said, stamping her foot. "This is all I can pay you."

He felt a flash of anger at that.

"So you tricked me, is what you're saying?"

"I never said I would pay all your debt!" she protested.

"You haven't paid any of my debt!" he exclaimed hotly. "I should have known not to help a bloody monster."

"Monster?!" she shouted, her voice raising an octave.

"Fae, whatever," he corrected dismissively. "If you aren't eating people, you're tricking them. No respect at all."

"Respect? Your first offer of hospitality was a bottle! You just called me a monster!"

"Know what?" he said, throwing the coin across the room, his head pounding. "I'm not dealing with this right now. You can stay the night, since I take promises seriously, but if you're going to break your end, fine. You can get out in the morning."

"I cannot—" she started to protest hotly, but he stuck his hand out to silence her. Fuming, he walked to his room, slamming the door behind him, and climbed into bed.

He awoke the following day, feeling like his skull was full of sand. He could usually sleep at the best of times, but his mind had been racing. He had slept in to try to compensate, but if anything, he just felt even worse for it.

Maybe I was a little harsh, he thought, but having a brief glimmer of hope only for it to be quickly dashed had stung.

Dressing in a plain brown tunic, he opened his bedroom door and immediately locked eyes on the letter lying upon his doormat. It was a letter from the guild, judging from the envelope.

Groggily and with a dreadful feeling in his stomach, eyes fixed upon the letter like it was a deadly naga that might bite him, he walked across to it. It faintly registered in the back of his mind that the walk to it had seemed strangely far. He picked it up and turned around to face his tastefully decorated drawing-room. It took him a moment to register that he didn't have a tastefully decorated drawing-room. Or indeed, a drawing-room.

Forgetting the letter momentarily in bewilderment, he surveyed the room. It was about five times larger than it should have been. It was larger than his entire home should have been. Luxurious carpets, oak furniture and plump stuffed sofas dotted the room, which might have been a palace. There were also multiple doors with wide arches scattered through the place.

"What the Friggana is going on?" he exclaimed, struggling to rationalise the situation. Had he woken up somewhere else, somehow? He walked back to his room. It was identical to how he had left it. Proceeding to the bathroom, he found it too was now palatial. A grand freestanding bath with ornate golden taps stood in the centre of a marble floor. He didn't dare try any of the doors to rooms that shouldn't have been there at all.

"Fali?" he shouted, panicked. Was this somehow the fairy's doing? He was aware his knowledge of magic was at best patchy, but this was well outside of even the wildest stories he had heard.

"In here, Ryheart," a voice came from one of them. "Fourth one on the western wall."

He walked over and opened the door tentatively. Whatever he had expected, it wasn't the sight that greeted him. A vast, open plain of rolling grassy hills stood before him, and a sparkling stream merrily tinkled as it weaved its way across the room and into a brook that bathed in warm sunlight. Despite seemingly being outside, however, the field stopped with a razor-straight edge, a perfectly cuboid chunk of nature.

The fairy reclined in a minuscule lounge chair, where she greeted him merrily as if they were dear friends, and this was a casual meeting.

"Morning, Ryheart. I hope you slept well?"

"What? How?" he managed to stammer out, shocked beyond words.

"Hmm? Oh, this," she said with a careless wave of her hand. "This is just a little magic. I decided I would improve our home."

He skipped over her use of 'our' in favour of the more pressing. "This is magic? You know how restricted its use is, don't you? The King's soldiers could kick my door down at any moment!"

"They cannot possibly know about this," she soothed, looking at him with bright eyes. "I swear on my heart."

He breathed in deeply. "Alright then, if you can make all this, entire bloody fields, why don't you make me a pile of money? Why are you mugging me off with an old coin?"

"Because," she said, gesturing with her hand as the chair she was sitting on dissolved, "none of this is quite real. At least, not entirely."

"So you weren't even going to give me a real coin?" he accused flatly.

"No! The coin is as real as you are," she assured him defensively.

"Alright, explain," he said wearily, massaging his temples.

"Within the mundane..." She paused at his evident lack of comprehension. "Within what you would call the real world, there are layers of reality. The purely physical exists within the lower layers and the supernatural within the higher layers. They intersect, though often imperfectly. All this exists only within the higher levels. This domicile is currently my place of power, so within it, I can blur the lines and give all this physical form to any who share the sanctuary. But only within the confines of said sanctuary. You could not take anything here outside the house because strictly, none of this exists within the same reality."

"And that's why it's undetectable?" he asked, thinking he had at least a vague understanding.

"Yes. Even within the house, none of this exists for other humans. At least, not in a state they can see or sense. It is undetectable to anyone who does not consider this home. Anyone else would see it as it was previously. We are in just about the safest place in the world, as is, from magical threats."

"And the coin?"

"I have a small storage chest, here in the mundane. I can pull things out of it from here, but only things I already own. Money is not exactly a concern of mine generally, so I do not have any. Nothing else in there is valuable. At least, not to you."

"Well, look. I have enough to deal with without all this," Ryheart said, gesturing at the air around them, "so, if you want to leave, leave. If you can't pay me back, I guess you'll have to break the oath."

She looked at him for a moment, then sighed. "I cannot."

"Can't?"

"The deal we made was stronger than anticipated. My obligations are much higher than they should be."

"And what's that mean, practically?"

"I am tied to you, spiritually, by my debt. I cannot leave your presence, seemingly, until it is paid."

It was maybe a little cruel, but he couldn't help but laugh at that.

"So, you're saying you tried to trick me, and instead of screwing me over, it ended up backfiring on you?"

She looked decidedly unimpressed by that. "Look, I need you to feel paid back!" she demanded. "I have duties to fulfil!"

"Well, that's an issue, because I don't feel paid back. This stuff," Ryheart waved at the surroundings, "is all useless to me. I need money, not make-believe furniture."

"How much money do you need, then?"

He sighed and took up the letter from the guild. He had put off reading it for long enough with all these magical shenanigans.

"Let's find out, shall we?"

Chapter Eight

Debt

"Dear Ryheart of no family name,

"We have recently received concluding paperwork of bounty filing 90032, filed by Harand Smithe. Given your failure to complete this job, the board of competence review has adjusted your reliability score from a D-rank certification to an E-rank certification. While D-rank hunters are allowed a maximum amount of 200 gold crowns debt to be outstanding, E-rank hunters are only allowed a maximum amount of 100 gold crowns worth of debt.

"Given this, as your total outstanding debt is 148 gold crowns, 2 silver nobles and 5 bronze beggars, you are now above the ceiling of acceptable debt allowed to you. Consequently, you must immediately make the minimum payment of 49 gold crowns, 2 silver nobles and 5 bronze beggars to bring you back within the acceptable range of liability.

"The guild will allow a grace period of two weeks to either pay a minimum of 49 gold crowns, 2 silver nobles and 5 bronze beggars, or to successfully achieve a bounty of a high enough calibre to increase your ranking.

"Failure to do so will be met with your contract and debt to us being passed on to the Grand Brittayan salt mining association, which will expect you to work off the debt within the salt mines.

"Kind regards,
"Anford Boudaine, Guild Secretary."

There was a long pause before Fali commented.

"Well, that is not very good, is it?" she said somewhat dryly.

"No. No, it isn't," Ryheart replied flatly.

"I am presuming you do not have some hidden fortune?"

"I don't have any fortune. Open, hidden or metaphorical."

"What is the plan, then?"

"Spend the rest of my life in a salt mine? I have no gods-damn idea."

"That would be a problem for me, given I seemingly cannot leave your sight," she said, shaking her head firmly.

"Oh, it would be a problem for you, would it?" he said irritably. "I'm not exactly fucking ecstatic about it. What else do you propose? You've already said you don't have a single bronze beggar to your name, let alone forty-nine gold crowns. That's a bloody fortune!"

"But they said they would allow you to take a bounty to pay off your debt, did they not?"

"Yeah, but I can't hunt a bloody monster worth enough to pay that!" he scoffed. "I can barely hunt enough to pay for my food! Annual fees aside, they take a twenty per cent cut of all earnings to account for your interest and the admin cost of collating and posting the bounty. So for a pay-out of forty-nine gold crowns plus change, I'd need a bounty of about sixty gold crowns. Not a chance I can deal with that."

She pursed her lips for a moment. "No, but I could."

He couldn't help but laugh. "You could? You're a fairy. What are you going to do, put magic dust in the monster's eyes?"

"Hypothetically, if I could, would you consider my debt paid to you? If we made enough to clear at least the unacceptable debt?"

"What's it bloody matter? You can't!"

"This is very important, Ryheart," she said sternly. "Would you consider our debt repaid. Truly?"

"Fine, sure," he said, throwing his arms up in the air. "I will consider your debt repaid."

"Alright. I give you my word. I can fight anything your guild might have posted."

"Forgive me if I'm not reassured," he intoned in a dry voice. "I suppose it couldn't hurt to at least look at bounties. Being eaten by a monster is probably a better way to go than dying of exhaustion mining salt, I suppose."

"What are you mining salt for, anyway?" she asked.

"They make salt-brick with it. Mix it into the stone for cities. It's supposed to keep monsters away. The supernatural ones, anyway."

"Deter, perhaps," she murmured.

"I suppose it's win-win for you, anyway, right?"

"How so?"

"Well, if we somehow perform the impossible and kill this thing, which would require a miracle, by the way—"

"I am good at those," she interjected.

"...If we pull that off, then you'll be free from me. If I die, then you'll also be free. So why would it matter to you one way or another?"

She stared off into the distance for a while before replying. "I am not so sure about that," she murmured.

"What do you mean?"

"Well, as recent events have shown," she said wryly, "symbiotic magic can be very tricky. Normally, even the most powerfully sworn spoken oath would, at worst, cast a vague penance upon its breaker. Bad luck, maybe. But this power of this oath is staggering."

"So what's that mean, practically?"

"Well, aside from being chained so tightly to you that I cannot even leave your presence, if you die, maybe my obligation stays with you, and I end up tied to your ghost. Maybe I die with you."

"Die?" he exclaimed.

"I am so tightly bound to you, we are virtually one spirit. And with my spirit so tightly bound to yours, my mortality may be, too."

He couldn't help but feel a pang of sympathy for her at that, but what could he do? If she didn't have any idea how to free him aside from paying her debt as he initially understood it, nor did he.

"Alright, so what are you, anyway?" he asked bluntly. If he was going to risk taking her to the guild, he at least wanted to know that much.

"What do you mean?"

"Look, I freely admit I know absolutely pag all about magic. But I do know fairies can't do all this. And I don't think they could fight a cat, let alone a monster with an A-rated threat level."

"A-rated?"

"That's what we're going to need to get sixty gold crowns from one bounty."

"Alright, well, I perhaps stretched the truth a teensy bit," she said.

"Oh, you have? You mean you've lied about something else? Or everything you've already said?"

"Not lied," she corrected, slightly snappily. "Anyway, look. I suppose if we must do this together, we should be honest with one another."

"Okay. So what are you?" he repeated bluntly.

"Well, alright. I am not just a fairy. I am the Queen of the Fairies," she said.

"Just my fucking luck. I have a queen indebted to me, and it's one with no bloody money," he said, and he couldn't help but chuckle bitterly about it. "So how does that help us, other than that I'll be dead and in the presence of royalty, rather than just dead?"

"Well," she said, "queens have a few perks that normal fairies do not."

"Like?"

"This, for one thing," she said, and a bright light engulfed her. Ryheart closed his eyes instinctively and then opened them to find the fairy stood before him, considerably larger than she had been before. Though still on the short side, admittedly.

His heart hammered in his chest. The creature before him had an almost glowing sun-drenched colour to her skin, and aside from a small cut on her cheek that sparkled ever so slightly, her skin was flawless. Long crimson hair ran down her back like a flaming sun rising to meet the sky.

Strangely, he couldn't figure out her age. There was nary a wrinkle to her skin, and she was positively overflowing with vitality. Still, her eyes seemed to carry that wise, somehow slightly distant look that he had sometimes observed in the elderly.

It was now also vastly more difficult to ignore the fact that she was still utterly naked, given he could see her properly.

A deep flush came to his cheeks, and he turned his head.

"So, err, might a fairy queen deign to wear clothes?" he questioned.

Despite their current plight, she seemed amused by his reaction and evidently couldn't help a little entertainment.

"Why, am I unpleasant to behold?" she asked, looking down at herself.

"No, no, everything's… just lovely," he said flustered, blushing even harder. "It's just a bit distracting."

"Oh, it is the impropriety that bothers you!" she said, as if she had only just noticed. "Honestly, you humans are so preoccupied about that. Especially in Brittaya."

"Well, since we're trying not to get arrested, it might be a good idea to wear something."

"Oh, go on then," she said like it was a minor inconvenience, "if it will make you happy."

Chapter Nine

Hansom

Fali sat in a small horse-drawn cabbie opposite Ryheart, ruminating as they travelled through the city towards the guild.

Aside from everything else, she wasn't overly fond of being cooped up in the small cabin. She'd have preferred riding on one of the horses, rather than towed behind them.

The prospect of spending what minuscule amount of change Ryheart had left given his spiralling debt seemed somewhat counterproductive to her. She had offered to carry him, given she could move faster than the carriage, but through either disbelief or pride, he had declined. He had insisted that given either he got the gold from the bounty, or he was done; he may as well spend what little he had. Perhaps that's a small insight into how he got himself into such a situation in the first place, she thought.

Ryheart sat flipping idly through a book on monsters she had given him. He was reading it incorrectly, of course, but given he was so skittish about magic, she figured he'd probably burn it if he realised its nature before they left the city.

"Are you sure you can't cover up your… whatever those are?" he asked, pointing at the glyph, her sigil that sat on her cheek and the green triangular markings beside her eyes.

"Do not point, Ryheart," she chided. "It is rude."

He rolled his eyes but stopped.

"Well? Can you?"

"With what?"

"I don't know. Makeup, or something?"

She laughed softly at that. "Do you have any makeup I could use?"

"No, of course not."

"Then no, I cannot," she said with a small smile.

"Well, at least you've covered something up, I suppose," he said, waving at her dress. "It's not exactly hunting-appropriate, though, is it?"

He had dressed in a very hodgepodge set of leather armour, with mismatched and rusted panels of metal laid over it. Fali didn't think the effect was exactly impressive. She, meanwhile, was dressed in a simple white dress, wide enough at the skirt to be manoeuvrable without being so full that it might snag, though the protection it offered was non-existent.

"If I am going to get eaten by a monster, I am going to at least look good doing it," she said with a shrug.

"Wow. That really fills me with confidence. Do I even want to ask about the empty scabbard you have?"

"What about it?" she asked innocently.

He sighed deeply. "Why is it empty?"

"It is not." She shrugged.

"It isn't?"

"It is not," she reaffirmed.

He looked like he was about to argue, then he shook his head and evidently decided it wasn't worth the fight.

"And you're absolutely sure your weird fairy queen monster magic can't be traced?"

"Fae," she said flatly. If he didn't want disembowelling by a touchier species for discourteous behaviour, she was going to have to break him out of that.

"Alright, Fae, sorry. Monsters are related to Fae, aren't they?"

"Are humans not related to apes?" she asked bluntly.

"Okay, point taken."

"Well, then. Besides which," she said primly, "not all Fae are. Fairies are old magic. They are not related to any genus of monster."

"Old magic?"

"There are three categories of magic. Old magic refers to the ancients. Fairies and such. Beings that generate their own power, independent of outside sources. Middle magic is used by creatures and Fae that use energy to control other sources of magic, external to them."

"What sort of stuff does that?"

"Dryads and such. They use their energy to call upon nature spirits to perform magic for them. They are creatures with power over magic, but they are not, in the truest sense, magical creatures themselves."

"I presume new magic is the last lot then?"

"Yes," she muttered darkly, and Ryheart looked shocked at the venom in her voice. He probably also had been surprised as her eyes had inevitably muddied with red as she spoke of it. It always seemed to captivate humans that her irises changed with her emotions. "New magic involves unnaturally forcing magic into something that should not possess it. Vampires, that sort of thing. It almost inevitably corrupts both host and practitioner. It is vile."

"Oh. So, sorry to go back to this, but your magic can't be detected? This is important. We'll end up in more guff than just the salt mines if someone finds out about you."

"Magically, I may as well be one of your body parts. I am as mundane as you are. I did mean to ask about that, though. I am not exactly up to date on current events, but Fae are allowed within the city, are they not? You used to tolerate at least the ones who could work for you."

"They are, yeah. The recognised ones. They need to register, though, and honestly, it's rare to see any who aren't employed directly within the government. Unless they work for someone wealthy, anyway."

"I do not think we could get away with that pretence," she murmured, with a glance at his ramshackle armour.

"Fairies are the most commonly seen, but even then, given you aren't exactly typical of a fairy, you might want to just go with human. Say you're a Fae-kin, maybe?"

"Fae-kin?" she asked. She could perhaps hazard a guess as to its meaning from the evident etymology of the word, but it wasn't a term she had heard directly.

"Humans with a bit of Fae ancestry in them somewhere. They're pretty rare, honestly. It isn't exactly common practice. Sometimes they don't quite look human. You could probably get away with that if anyone asks."

"At least you consider them human now, I suppose."

"Of course. Some folk aren't exactly... predisposed to liking them, though. You might want to try to keep your head down."

Fali sighed sadly. "I would like to say I was surprised."

He looked at her, seemingly sympathetic. "We barely survived when so many magical creatures and monsters went insane. I know it was a long time ago, but people are still wary."

"Most of the Fae were affected even worse than humans, you know. They are the ones who lived right amongst the other magical creatures, after all. And they did not have 'civilisation' and walls to hide behind."

"I know," he said. "I'm not saying it was their fault."

"Perhaps do not call them monsters, then."

"Alright. Look, I'm sorry, okay? Maybe I was a little gruff. A lot of stuff on my mind, you know?"

"That is alright," she said, touching his arm softly for a moment, then grinning. "Perhaps we will make a gentleman out of you yet."

He blushed slightly at that. "Let's settle for not being eaten, for the time being," he replied with a nervous laugh.

Chapter Ten

Guild

The new pair of tentative allies stepped from the cab as it arrived at the guild. Ryheart shifted the uncomfortable weight of the travel bag on his back. The bag that Fali had insisted he both pack and carry.

A large stone building towered before them, a grand arched gateway standing imposingly in front of the entrance to the courtyard and hall of the Hunter's Guild.

Ryheart's heart pounded. Time to see if Fali was at least telling the truth about being undetectable as magical. If not, they were probably about to be arrested. Even had she been recognised as magic, it might have been fine if – and it was a big if – she was registered correctly and catalogued already. Given the somewhat circumspect situation he had met her in and her behaviour so far, he highly doubted she was.

A metal bracket jutted from the gate, upon which hung a lantern. Inside the lamp, rather than flame, was a fairy, sat behind a doll house-sized desk. Sitting on a pile of leaves, she was around six inches tall, with vibrant orange wings like those of a butterfly. Her hair was piled in an ornate bob, held in place with a drawing pin.

"Hi, Willathena," Ryheart said, waving. Fairies made great gatekeepers for official government buildings, given their ability to see through most magical trickery and uncanny remembrance of people.

"Ryheart, hi!" she said with a warm smile. The other reason those who could acquire a fairy loved them, was their always sunny disposition. Which, now Ryheart thought about it, was strangely absent from Fali.

"I have a plus one," Ryheart informed her. "That's alright if she stays with me, isn't it?"

"Of course, just let me get a look at her. Just in case you're trying to smuggle in any spooky magic!" She wiggled her fingers as she spoke. "You know how the guild is about that."

He did, unfortunately.

"Fali?" He gestured.

She walked forward with a benign smile and curtsied extravagantly.

"Greetings, little one."

"Greetings," the fairy said merrily, seemingly impressed with the extra flourish. "I didn't know you had a sister, Ryheart? She's just like you!"

Ryheart had to assume she was entirely oblivious to physical features and judged purely on whatever magical feeling she had. Given the red hair, sometimes blue but occasionally not eyes, and the golden tone to her skin, not to mention her somewhat formal speech, they certainly didn't compare otherwise.

"Oh, yeah," he lied, "she's just visiting. I'm alright to show her around, aren't I?"

"Of course! Have a wonderful day, and may your bounties be fulfilled." With that, she waved her hand, and the gates creaked open before them.

"Is that why you thought I would like to be in a bottle?" Fali leaned in and murmured into his ear as they walked into the courtyard.

"Don't all fairies? Also, my sister?"

"I told you we were nearly spiritually identical," she said with a grin, "with enough little tweaks that we are not completely the same, of course."

"Well, if you can fool her, I suppose you can fool anyone. One thing, though. If you're her queen, why didn't she recognise you?"

"She is a fairly young fairy, I think. Besides, I am not exactly someone you would expect to see walking around. What is the plan then?"

He wasn't entirely convinced, but he left it at that for the moment and addressed her question instead. "Let's go get a bounty, and then we can get straight to hunting. We don't exactly have a ton of time."

"You do not want to say goodbye to anyone before we depart?"

"There's no one to say goodbye to," he said a little bitterly. He hadn't known his father, and his mother had died when he was a teenager. At that point, he'd been stupid enough, and desperate enough, to find the guild recruiters' stories of heroics and, more importantly, money, enticing enough to take their apprenticeship. A barebones course of training, loaned equipment and a mountain of debt later, here he was.

"Well," Fali commented lightly, "I suppose it will save us a trip back in one of those horrible little cupboards on wheels if nothing else."

He was grateful she hadn't pushed any further about his lack of family. He wasn't exactly in the mood to get into it.

Through the gate was a large courtyard in which dozens of market stalls sat.

"What is all this, then?" she asked curiously.

"Since the rent for equipment from the guild is astronomical, people buy it if they can. Plus, there's a lot of weird creatures that need something particular to kill them within higher bounties. Wood from an Acer, that sort of thing. So, hunters tend to trade the more niche things between each other, since it's a waste otherwise to buy something you might never use again."

45

"Ah. And the guild's fine with people undercutting their business on their doorstep?"

He laughed at that. "Oh, they rent the space out, and they take a cut of any sales made here, so they win out either way."

"Why do people not just sell elsewhere and not have to pay tithes?"

"Well, for starters, there's a lot of stuff that you need a hunting licence to be allowed to use, so this is about the only place you can guarantee passers-by might be able to buy your stuff legally. Secondly, you need a licence to sell anything regulated anywhere else. Here, the guild provides that for you. It's worth paying what they take to avoid the astronomical fee, and the scrutiny that getting a licence to sell elsewhere would take."

"They certainly have things sewn up."

"That's what happens when you're the only hunting guild in this half of the country," he said with a shrug. "Maybe the Northies have it different. I don't know."

Leading her through the throng as discreetly as he could, he led her through a series of corridors. They stopped at a small circular pool, which bathed in sunlight streaming from a glass skylight.

"What is this?" Fali asked, cocking her head and staring at it as if she was puzzled.

"Oh, that's just the hunter's fountain. Legend is that it was built by Divana, the goddess of the hunt. Its waters are supposed to be blessed to give success to any weapons submerged in it. I could probably do with some of that, actually."

He was going to unbuckle his short sword when Fali stepped ahead of him and dipped her hand in the pool. She raised it to her nose and sniffed delicately, then erupted in a peal of laughter.

"I would not bother, dear-heart."

"Why?"

"Smell," she commended, holding her hand to him.

He sniffed tentatively, and the distinct scent of apples infused his nostrils. "What's that about?"

"The water's enchanted, absolutely. It is enchanted to perfume skin, though."

"Why would Divana want to do that?"

She leant over to whisper in a conspiratorial fashion. "I think some Fae probably played a trick on whoever they built it for, my darling," she told him, and then gave a fresh peal of musical laughter.

He couldn't help but laugh in sympathy with her. "At least I'm not the only dupe to get played by a Fae, I suppose."

Chapter Eleven

Bounty

After a few more corridors, they found their way to the heart of the guild, the bounty room.

"You are sure I can be signed up for a hunt? Did you not say you need licences and such?" Fali asked Ryheart.

"To take a hunt yourself, yes. You can accompany me as an assistant, though," he explained.

"Is that not somewhat exploitable? Why does everyone not do that rather than paying fees?"

"Well, because if you aren't registered with the guild, it means you also aren't protected by them. I could promise you half of what we earn, and then turn around and take every bit of money we make down to the last bronze beggar, and you'd have absolutely no protection against it. Plus, you couldn't take any bounties by yourself. It's good for experience, but not much else."

"Ah. It is fortunate I am not interested in money, then."

Walls covered floor to ceiling in papers stretched before them, separated by the ranking assigned to the expected difficulty of the task. While any rank hunter could theoretically take any rank bounty, taking one higher than your competence was generally an excellent way to end up dead. The wall by the entrance had a desk with a clerk, at which a bounty could be formally registered.

He walked to the D-rank section, and without a word, Fali walked straight past him towards the highest rankings available.

"I'm only a D-rank, you know," he called, before adding somewhat grudgingly, "E-rank, now."

"I am not," she replied with a shrug. Ryheart was still hoping that somehow, with the right combination of bounties, he might manage to accrue the amount he needed from various more maintenance-based, less dangerous jobs.

"What are these?" she asked, pointing to the opposite wall. Bounties were laid out there too, but each with a rune above them.

"Hmm?" he asked before he saw what she was referring to. "Oh, gods no. Those are supernatural postings. Swords won't kill them but condiments will, all that sort of crap."

"Oh, those are much more interesting than mundane monsters, are they not?"

"They're also much more likely to murder me," he responded. The last thing he needed was more magic he didn't understand inflicted on him. "Absolutely no chance."

"Fine, fine," she sighed. "We will do a boring one, then."

"I'd hardly call being disembowelled by a monster boring," he muttered, shaking his head. He skimmed the lowest rank filings and clenched his fist impotently. The absolute highest-paying bounty left there was worth a measly three crowns and would take the better part of two days. Even if he didn't sleep, he wouldn't be able to come close to the sixty gold crowns that he'd need to earn to pay off his outstanding forty-nine gold crown debt after deductions.

His situation grew worse when he realised he couldn't even take half a dozen C-rank, or even a couple of B-rank bounties to pay the debt. The two-week window didn't give him enough time, since the amount of tracking and travel time needed increased with the task's difficulty.

He would need to make enough money from a single bounty to cover his costs, to give him enough time to get the job done.

"Well, if I'm going to drown, I guess it doesn't matter how deep the bloody lake is," he scowled, resigning himself to the fact there was no clever way out of this. He walked over to his diminutive companion. "Anything there's a remote chance we won't get horrifically killed by?"

In response, she closed her eyes and stood silent for a moment, and then her hand shot out. She tore off a copy of one of the bounty filings from the wall and held it to him.

"This one," she intoned calmly.

"Are you out of your fucking mind?" he exclaimed, lowering his voice when his outburst drew the attention of some other hunters in the room. Was this some bizarre fairy humour he didn't understand?

"Excuse me?" she asked archly, her eyes blazing.

"Did you even look at that? This is serious, we can't just leave such a choice to luck!"

"Luck does not shape me. I shape it," she replied stubbornly, shaking the paper at him.

"Oh, of course. You've sure been lucky so far since I've known you."

She scowled darkly at that but remained implacable.

"Leviathan's balls, fine." He gave up and snatched the paper from her hand. "Filing 89050. A Nemean lion has passed the outer forest on a heading towards the inner barrier of the Weir Wood to the south of Londaya. Extermination is required to protect the Fae who are allied with the government of Brittaya and minimise potential future danger to Londaya. This request is direct from the King's estate and has a bounty of sixty-five gold crowns and three silver nobles. Details of the monster's last known location attached."

"Well, what do you think?"

"I think I'm going to get eaten by a lion," he said bluntly, "though the bounty's at least high enough. And it's near enough we should just about be able to get there and back, at least if we're lucky finding its trail. It's been sat here for a little while unfulfilled, though, judging by the filing number."

"Perhaps no hunter cared enough about it since it is 'only' Fae being threatening currently?" she suggested.

"Or maybe there's just been no one stupid enough to take it."

Fali looked like she was about to argue when a voice called out, "Ryheart? Fancy meeting you here."

Turning around, he scowled. Harand. Again. "Yeah, shocking finding a hunter in the Hunter's Guild," he said dryly.

"Well, it's been so long since you've managed to finish any bounties, it's hard to remember you are a hunter," Harand taunted, and Ryheart tried and failed to stop himself grinding his teeth. "What are you doing over here in the big-boy section anyway? Daydreaming you were competent?"

"If you don't mind, we were just discussing something private, actually," Ryheart said as civilly as he could manage.

"Oh, well, I have to see a hunter daft or desperate enough to take you with them." He moved to look around Ryheart as Fali sheltered behind him, and let out a hiss of surprise. "Is this a half-breed?"

"'This' is someone who you would be better off not bothering," she replied haughtily with ice in her voice, her eyes flinty.

"Ryheart, pal. I know we aren't exactly best buddies, but business is just business. This, though? Their kind can't be trusted. They bring ruin wherever they go."

"Who I associate with is nothing to do with you," he replied flatly. "Regardless, she's not magic. If she were, she'd hardly have been able to stroll in here, would she?"

"She's clearly got monster in her somewhere," he hissed, pointing at her. "If she isn't magic, her family are. I know you're just a dumb city kid, Ryheart, but I lived out in the sticks. We trusted one of them, and they burnt our farm down."

"My memory must be somewhat foggy in my old age," Fali interjected.

"What?" Harand asked, clearly stumped by her meaning.

"Well, I certainly do not remember having set your farm on fire."

"No, one of your kind did, though."

"If you like, I have a litany of sins others have committed that I could ascribe to you," she said with a sniff.

"Fae-kin are citizens just like we are," Ryheart reminded him. "So are some Fae, for that matter."

"Only because the monarchy went soft. Not too long ago, she would have been one of the bounties on that wall," the hunter raged. "I'm telling you, Ryheart, they aren't to be trusted."

"Well, as highly as I regard your advice, I think I'll keep my own companions, thanks."

"I'll be watching you, monster," the enraged hunter said, poking Fali's chest.

As his finger touched her, she turned her gaze fully upon him. Ryheart couldn't quite see her face given the angle, but Harand stumbled back like he had been physically hit, face pale. He looked like he was about to faint.

Violent disagreements in the guild between hunters were not technically allowed, if not actively discouraged. It was only at the point an injury hampered a hunter's ability to make money for them that the guild tended to get involved.

"Come on, Fali," Ryheart whispered. "Let's go before we do anything that draws too much attention, shall we?"

Fali's gaze lingered a moment, and then she turned to Ryheart. Whatever in her visage had unsettled his rival so much, he couldn't see. As he led her away, she let out a harsh, guttural sound that Ryheart was surprised she could even make.

He ushered her towards the guild counter. Signing both their names to the bounty and filing the paperwork with the clerk, he rushed them out.

"What exactly did you do?" he murmured.

"Looked at him," she said with a shrug.

"Just looked?"

"Just looked."

"Well, I suppose I did tell you to try to keep quiet," he said. "What was that noise you made?"

"Oh, well, that was a curse word," she said with a sniff.

"What language?" It was unlike anything he had ever heard. It was more noise than a word, like two rocks grating together.

"Troll. Ghastly, is it not?"

"What did it mean?" he asked, curiosity burning.

"I am not going to repeat it, Ryheart!" she said, sounding scandalised. "If I had wanted you to understand it, I would have said it in Anglasa."

"Aww, come on."

"A lady of my standing does not simply speak with such vulgarity in pleasant company," she said with an indignant toss of her flaming hair.

"Alright, alright."

"…It is rather satisfying cursing in troll, though," she said with a mischievous grin. "Maybe I'll teach you when you're older."

Chapter Twelve

Familiar

Olyra sat mulling over reports, having earned a slight reprieve from fieldwork. Her nose still ached, irreversibly crooked now, and her cheek still rankled with burns. She skimmed through the files before her, mainly reports of suspected unregistered magic, to see if any were worth the OPMC's time. Anything that wasn't would be delegated to lesser agencies.

She picked up the next in the batch and skimmed over it. It was a filing about a trivial encounter with a Fae-kin from some minor hunter within the guild, one Harand Smithe.

She might have disregarded it, as hunters were famously eager with suspected magic. If the Fae-kin was within the guild, she must have been checked and registered. But the description of the individual sent a shiver down her spine: red hair, the name Fali, and strange markings on her face.

None of these things was worth note by themselves; red hair wasn't unusual – at least if they meant 'red' and not red – some of the allied Fae and even some Fae-kin had various tribal markings on their faces, and all sorts of wild names existed. But all three together?

Though, surely, it couldn't be the creature, could it? Olyra had seen her die. It had to be a coincidence. Unfortunately, her job didn't allow for dismissal on mere coincidence. At the very least, this bore further investigation. She put the remaining files to the side for the secretary to look over in the absence of any agents.

Her first order of business was finding the hunter who had filed the report, to question him further.

Ryheart and his new hunting companion found themselves stood in front of a nearly solid barrier of trees, the edge of the Weir Wood. They had taken a short carriage to the far side of the town, which Fali had made quite clear she was distinctly unpleased with.

While he hadn't any money to rent one anyway, he was glad that he didn't have a horse. The woods were so thick they might have found them near impassable while riding. A primordial forest had a romantic sound to it, but the reality before him was a tangled, thick mess of vast trees and roots. Despite its intimidating nature, there was a majestic beauty to it, and even Fali seemed awed by it.

"Okay, now that we are well out of the city, give me a moment. We need a guide," she suggested. "It will give you time to eat before we start in earnest."

He shifted the uncomfortable weight of his pack off his shoulders and dropped it to the floor. The one Fali had stuffed with gear. She took her relatively small bag from her back and took out a tiny seed packed in a clod of dirt.

"Is that all you're carrying?" he exclaimed, incredulous. It was bad enough his new partner had rammed his bag full, let alone that she had barely anything herself.

"We will redistribute." She waved dismissively. "This was too delicate to pack with anything else."

He watched, bemused, as she kneeled and carved a hole in the ground with her bare hand, then packed the seed into it, laying her hand on the soil above it. There was a spark of light, and the grass grew up around her, then a white rose-like flower grew before her. It was substantially larger than a typical rose, and it had a slightly ethereal quality to it.

"What did you need a flower for?" he asked.

"It is not a flower. It is a rabbit," Fali informed him.

While he wasn't quite sure exactly what type of flower it was, he was entirely convinced that it was not a rabbit.

"I, err, I think you have your Anglasan mixed up," he informed her. "A rabbit's a hoppy thing that eats carrots."

She fixed him with a profound look of disapproval at that. "Yes, thank you, Ryheart. I am aware of what a rabbit is," she said tartly.

"Well, why did you call it one, then?" he asked, exasperated.

"Because it is one," she insisted adamantly.

He sighed a long-suffering sigh. "Fine, I'll bite. How is it a rabbit?"

"Give it a minute, and you will see."

"Alright," he said, taking a small piece of dried meat from his pack and offering her some. "Want some?"

"I already ate." She dismissed him with a wave of her hand.

He hadn't seen her eat, but she was clearly distracted by her little project and barely paying attention to him. He chewed in silence as she sat daintily waiting, then she sprang up. The plant glowed for a moment, and then the petals unfurled to reveal a rabbit sat upon it, looking regal upon its flower throne. It had soft ashy grey fur, and ears that flopped down either side of its head. Curiously, it also had green triangular markings by its wide black eyes, like those upon Fali's face.

She let out an exclamation of delight and picked up the rabbit, and Ryheart caught her eyes as they swirled with pink.

He briefly felt jealous of the rabbit being looked at with such evident love, then felt silly about it.

"Oh, so it was a rabbit," he said calmly. Two days ago, he might have found that miraculous, but given how upheaved his life had been recently, he was almost numb to it.

"Is he not wonderful?" she asked joyously.

"It is quite regal," he admitted. "Can I pet him?"

"No, you cannot."

"Why?" he said defensively. "I won't hurt him."

"You can try," she sang with a knowing smile.

Tentatively he reached out to pat the rabbit, dubious, only to find his hand passed clear through it. He recoiled in shock, and Fali chuckled.

"Why's your rabbit a spooky ghost?"

"He is not spooky," she protested in an affronted voice, "nor is he a ghost. He is my familiar. I do not originate from the mundane; I am from the realm of magic. He is still mostly back there, but he can tether himself to me to be here, albeit in an astral sort of manner."

"Like a witch familiar?"

"Hardly," she said in an offended tone. "He is a part of me."

"So, if he's tethered to you here, are you tethered to him back, well, wherever he is?"

"Very astute." She smiled. "There might be some hope for you yet. My wings are my tether back home. Currently, though, I am, well, disconnected."

"Is that a fairy thing? It lets you travel back to magic fairyland?"

"Along those lines, yes."

The rabbit was staring at him with unblinking black globes in a manner that made him feel uncomfortable, and he shifted slightly.

"So, what's he do exactly?"

"He is my secret weapon."

"How? He can't touch anything, can he?"

Fali looked at the rabbit a moment as if she was determining something, then nodded.

"Well, humans have your DNA and a dozen quirks and foibles that keep you grounded. For me, born in 'magic fairyland', as you put it, I am not subject to the quirk of genetics. I would, theoretically, be perfect. Perfect is very dangerous. Nothing other than the Twin-Divinities is perfect. Not even other gods. Instead, we are born with one specific physical imperfection. Our familiar is born to cover that weakness."

"You have an imperfection?"

"Yes. My designed foible, if you will, is my eyes. You might have noticed they change colour. You have probably put together by now that they change with my emotions?"

"But they're beautiful. How are they a weakness?" Ryheart blurted, blushing once he realised what he had said.

Fali smiled warmly, and her eyes flooded with purple. "Thank you, dear-heart. Though I might not look it, I am, by design, a warrior to the very core of my being. It is, quite literally, why I was made. Having my emotions read so easily can be dangerous if the wrong people can use them to predict my intent. My little friend here helps me see their hidden character, and judge their trustworthiness." She paused and smiled fondly. "On top of that, he comes in handy in all sorts of ways. He can pass through things, scout my surroundings, and people tend to pay less attention to him. You can learn all sorts of interesting things when people don't think anyone is listening."

"How does he tell you all that when he's a rabbit? Twitching his nose?"

"Well, since he was born from my essence, we have an intrinsic spiritual tie that lets us share our senses through a multispectral dimensional tether."

She looked at his uncomprehending face, and then gave a little weary sigh. 'Magic," she said, waggling her fingers.

Chapter Thirteen

Woods

After a short break in which Fali ate absolutely nothing, the unlikely duo set off through the dense trees, following behind the grey rabbit as it found the path of least resistance for them. The fact the little familiar seemed to flicker in and out of existence didn't exactly help Ryheart keep track of him. Still, fortunately, Fali seemed acutely aware of its position even when it wasn't visible.

"So how do we find this bounty? Wander about until we hear an angry monster?" he asked. The majority of hunting he had done had been within the city, or occasionally within smaller settlements that orbited Londaya. He had minimal exposure to this sort of wild hunt.

"Hardly," Fali chided. "The bounty said a naiad colony reported it, did it not? We find the lake and ask them."

"They'll be friendly?" he asked nervously.

"Of course they are. They are just about the gentlest species on the planet. I am rather fond of them, actually."

"Oh, good," he said, relieved.

"Of course, there might be other things in the forest."

That tightened the knot in his stomach back up. "Wonderful."

"Say, do we get paid for killing any other monsters we find?" she asked.

"Not if we haven't taken a bounty for them, no."

"Ah. We should probably avoid them, then," Ryheart's guide said nonchalantly.

"Wait, you weren't planning on avoiding them already?" he asked, incredulous.

"Not if it meant detouring considerably. We are on a schedule, are we not?"

"One monster trying to eat me is enough as it is, thanks."

"Oh, alright, if it makes you happy, I suppose we will do so."

Disconcertingly, he couldn't tell whether she was just winding him up or not.

"It should be clear, anyway, right? Isn't there a shield or whatever to keep monsters out?" he asked.

"Well, yes, but it is not infallible. Besides, the shield can only keep things out, not get rid of something already in here. There should not be anything too strong, or your guild would probably have eventually posted a big enough bounty for someone to deal with it. Even if it is 'only' a Fae enclave."

"Phenomenal," he said, decidedly nervous.

"Ah. My familiar has found a marker," Fali exclaimed, gesturing towards a small clearing. Her mood at least seemed to have perked up considerably since they had got to the forest, which was frankly the most fairy-like behaviour he'd seen her exhibit since he had met her.

He watched curiously as she approached an enormous tree, stood on her tiptoes and then, with a genteel stretch, stuck her head into a hollow inside its trunk.

"There is a path of sorts this way," she reported triumphantly.

"Did you just smell where it was?" he asked curiously.

"The tree was a territory marker; it points over that way. Whoever made it marked the path for travellers, how nice of them."

"Oh," he said, scrunching his nose up in disgust, given how animals usually marked things.

She stared at him coolly. "They marked it magically, Ryheart. I would hardly stick my head inside something's toilet, would I?"

"Oh, yeah. That's what I thought," he bluffed none too convincingly. "Do you know who marked it?"

"Not a clue," she said, sounding way too merry about that lack of knowledge for his liking.

"So they might be dangerous?"

"They have made a path specifically to make travel easier, and I doubt they need it themselves given any Fae are unlikely to leave their territory. I think we are fine."

"Let's hope so."

"I think we can get to the lake within about three days if we make good time," she declared. "From there, we will have to see what we can find. It might be a little tight, but as long as it does not take us too long to track it down, we should be able to get back before your deadline."

"We better, otherwise there's no point going back at all," he murmured.

"It will work out," she said with a reassuring smile, squeezing his shoulder lightly.

"Yeah, thanks."

Some hours into the walk, Ryheart's feet were aching, then his back, then his entire body. Fali's pace was unrelenting despite her stride being nearly half that of his own.

By this point, monotony had overcome both wonder and caution, and he trod along, focusing on nothing but keeping pace.

He was semi-aware of a slight movement, and he stopped in his tracks. Off in the distance, just barely visible, was a set of globe-like eyes staring at them.

"The Friggana is that?" he whispered to Fali, pointing.

"Not Friggana," Fali said calmly, seemingly already aware of it. "Dryad."

"What do we do about it?" he asked, panicked.

"Her," Fali corrected mildly. "And we do nothing. Is she really the first one you have noticed?"

"Err, yeah? There's been more of them?" he said, eyes fixed on the creature as they walked nearer.

"We have passed thirty-seven of them, dear-heart. This one is a bit younger, so she is not as adept at blending yet. I am surprised you have not noticed any of them."

As they passed by, Fali gave a small wave at the creature, and it ever so slightly tilted its head to her.

He couldn't help a not-so-subtle stare as they passed. The strange Fae had slightly rough-looking skin, the brown of a tree and a large pair of amber globes that stared at him. She was about his height, but everything was elongated, her gangly arms hanging down nearly to her feet. A mossy mess of hair hung down her back, and vines tied all manner of accoutrements to her. Her toes burrowed into the soil like roots, and she carried a bow, many jointed fingers wrapping several times around it. He took his eyes off her briefly, and when he looked back again, he couldn't see her at all.

"What in the gods' names was that about?" he exclaimed.

"As I said, that was a dryad. They are quite remarkable creatures. Born with seed in their hands that they plant at birth. Their health and life are intrinsically tied to that of the tree."

"Why was she just staring at us? Can't they speak?"

"Oh, they can speak. Far too well, in fact. Dryads have a minimal concept of time beyond seasons. She would have chatted for days, weeks. All of them would. Given we do not have that much time, I asked the trees to convey that we were on the King's business. The treaties they are bound by say none of the King's men can be molested on their travels, so they are giving us space. That was the easiest way, given you are male."

"Why would that matter?" He frowned.

"Well, dryads are all female, and they rely on travellers, to, ah, 'fertilise' new growth. They can be quite persistent."

"What, they'd just consider me a resource?"

"Why, imagine treating something different because you do

not understand it," she murmured wryly. "That is something humans would not do at all."

"Not like that, we don't! Not like you're just tools for us to use!"

She stared at him for a long moment. "Is that not how you viewed Fae?" she asked.

He stared at her for a moment, then flushed. "Maybe, I suppose. Isn't that exactly what you did, though?" Ryheart accused, partly to deflect his embarrassment.

"Excuse me?" she said, raising an eyebrow.

"Didn't you make your little magic deal with me to get what you wanted? Knowing you didn't have anything to pay me with?"

"Yes, but the thing I wanted was negligible," she protested. "You wanted a fortune in return for something you barely even noticed!"

"If you didn't have anything to give, you could have just asked!" he said hotly.

"You would not have helped," she scoffed.

"Who knows? I didn't get a chance to, did I?" he retorted. "Your go-to was trickery. You purposely let me think you could help me and dangled hope in front of me to manipulate me into getting what you wanted. You didn't even think about asking."

There was a long silence between them as they stewed in their recriminations.

"I did not realise you were so desperate," Fali half apologised. "If I had have known—"

"It's fine," he said with a sigh. "Maybe I didn't exactly treat you as graciously as I would have if you were human."

"Perhaps we could both stand to treat each other with a touch more consideration," she acquiesced.

"From now on, then," he said, holding out a hand.

She stared at it a moment, then laughed. "I agree, but given how we got into this mess, perhaps we should avoid shaking on any promises we make?"

"Shall we carry on, then?" he asked.

"Why, absolutely, dear-heart. After you," Fali said with a gesture.

He bowed as grandly as he could manage with a grin, then led the way.

Chapter Fourteen

Camp

After a long walk, Fali finally, joyously, declared it was time to stop and camp for the night. Tired past pride, Ryheart dropped his pack where he stood and let himself fall to the floor. He felt drained, entirely and utterly, his clothes soaked with sweat from the exertion. Fali, meanwhile, somewhat annoyingly, looked as fresh as she had when they set off. She even still had the light scent of freshly bloomed flowers that he caught whenever she brushed by him.

"I think we are making quite good time," she said with a smile. "You are fitter than you seemed."

"Cheers," he said wearily, pulling off his boots and throwing them across the clearing.

She wrinkled her nose in distaste but didn't say anything.

"I suppose we ought to have supper before we sleep," he said, getting back up despite his protesting body.

"I will dig the supplies out," she said, rummaging through the bag he had dumped. While she searched, he gathered up a small pile of dried twigs for kindling, layering them over some larger chunks of wood. Sparking his flint together, he set a fire ablaze.

She turned around at the noise, the colour draining from her eyes. "Ryheart, what are you doing?" she half-shouted.

Proud of the blaze in the manner men usually are of things they've set on fire, he looked at her, confused and ever so slightly irrationally offended. "It's fire. It's for food. What's wrong with it? I can't expect you to eat cold, can I?"

"Well, that is very nice of you, Ryheart," she said in a level tone, "but you remember the dryad we met a few hours ago? I do not think she is going to be very happy if you have just snapped off her cousin's finger."

"I only used dead wood off the floor. That's fine, isn't it?" he asked worriedly, hoping very much so that it was.

She exhaled with relief, and the tension left him with it.

"Yes, that is fine. Just do not start snapping branches off any trees. As a rule of thumb, ask me before you do anything irreversible."

"I'll be careful," he assured her. "Look, I made a ring of stones and everything."

"Well, that is alright then," she said, seemingly appeased, handing him a small pot with ingredients to stew piled inside. "I do not want any, by the way."

"I'm a decent cook, you know," he said defensively. "It'll be edible at the very least."

"I am sure it will be, dear-heart," she soothed, "but I ate already."

That puzzled him. He hadn't seen Fali eat, and he had been with her all day.

"When?"

She pursed her lips a moment as if she were considering. "Last night. I had a small bit of food from your pantry. Well, the shelf you have in lieu of a pantry."

"That's ridiculous, aren't you starving?"

"No, I have barely used any magic all day," she said simply and, seemingly to Ryheart, irrelevantly.

"What's that got to do with it?"

"Everything. I only eat to break down energy to replenish my natural well of magic, if I have put enough of a drain on it that it has not refilled naturally," she explained, adding in a musing voice. "I will have to use some soon though, or I will get hiccups."

If anything, that only confused him further. "Hiccups?"

"Yes. My heart regenerates and refills my magic reserves, but I have a maximum capacity. Hiccups vent the excess when I am full to bursting."

"Huh," Ryheart said. Knowing he shouldn't, but unable to entirely stop himself, he added a follow-up question: "Do you, well, trump out magic as well?"

"Ryheart!" she exclaimed, sounding scandalised. "I do not 'trump'."

"Why, because you're magic?"

"No, because I am a lady," she said, with the hint of a smile belying her offended tone. "Ladies do not 'trump'; they break wind. But, as it happens, I do not do that either. My conversion of matter is perfect. That is because I am magic."

"Oh. That's good. The conversion thing, I mean," Ryheart clarified, "not the trumping thing."

"If we meet any other Fae on our trip," she cautioned in a light tone, "please do not ask them about how they expel gas."

"I wouldn't," he said defensively, grinning, "but you did bring it up. Kind of."

He ate while she busied herself preparing a camp, which he felt a little awkward about. Frowning, he realised that while she'd packed all manner of camping paraphernalia, maps, provisions and clothes, she had only packed his single, one-person tent.

"Where's your tent?" he asked.

"Hmm?" She glanced back at him. "Oh, I do not have one. You should have realised by now I have little to no possessions besides my boots, my scabbard and a few clothes."

"Isn't that one a bit small, though?" he asked, gesturing at his threadbare tent.

"No?"

"But we won't both fit," he said, apparently needing to clarify.

"We will not need to," she said, looking over to him. "We are going to take shifts keeping watch, are we not?"

"The forest's peaceful, isn't it?"

She sighed exasperatedly. "Ryheart, there is an angry rampaging lion somewhere in this forest. I have experienced being eaten, and I do not like it very much."

"Yeah, but it's behind the barrier, isn't it?"

"Okay, I will give you that," she conceded. "However, even if these woods are absolutely, utterly free of monsters, a bear is just as capable of eating you in your sleep."

"Yeah, I didn't think of that," he said, scratching the back of his head in embarrassment.

"So every time you go on a hunt, you just sleep without any sort of protection?" she asked, sounding incredulous. "How are you still alive?"

"Well, I'm usually in the city," he said defensively.

"By the Twin-Divinities, this is the incompetent I have to babysit," she murmured, before sighing in a long-suffering way. "Alright, well, let us chalk it up to inexperience."

"Sorry," he murmured with an embarrassed laugh, "I'm a tad out of my depth here."

"That is alright," she said primly, before perking up, seemingly to signify her point had been made, and it wouldn't be dwelled on. "Now, if we sleep until dawn breaks, we should still have a good eight hours or so," she said, looking up at the sky. "Fortunately, we are still in Junicana's time, and we still have a lot of light in the day."

"Junicana's time?" he asked.

"The month of Juma, to use the colloquial language. It is what you used to call it before you forgot the god you named it after in the first place."

"Oh. Do you want me to go first, or second?"

"If you could go first, that would be delightful. If you cover the first half-hour for me, I will take the rest."

"What? That's not fair," he said, confused.

"Well," Fali said a touch on the huffy side, "I suppose I could

68

only sleep for fifteen minutes, but I think it is rather rude of you to demand it."

"No, Fali," he said with a sigh. "I mean, we should both have four hours each."

"Oh," she said with a laugh, "well, that is very kind of you, but there is no need. I only need to sleep to allow my thoughts to sort themselves out and regenerate magic if depleted. I do not even need it, strictly, but it helps me stay sparky."

He gaped at her. He could accept strange psychic rabbits, size changes, even lack of food. But no real sleeping was insane. He loved to sleep.

"Well, I'll still feel bad," he said. "How about I just take four hours, and I'll at least keep you company for the rest if it's too dark to set off straight away?"

"Alright, fine," she said with a warm smile. "Just see when you wake up."

Her rabbit scampered into the camp. It sat before her, grey nose twitching, and she crouched down to it and stroked between its floppy ears lovingly.

"How are we looking?" she asked. The rabbit didn't answer, at least as far as Ryheart could tell, but she carried on as if it had. "Grand. Keep an eye out anyway, will you? Let me know if anything comes close by."

"How's he keep up with us?" he asked. He hadn't seen the rabbit ahead of them for quite some time.

"Well," Fali pondered, "do you want the long or short version?"

"Short, please." He laughed.

"Magic," she said, wiggling her fingers again as she had once before. Despite her warm temperament, she seemed to have a degree of reserved formality and wariness about revealing any more than she needed, Ryheart noticed. Little by little, though, she seemed to be relaxing the walls around her. However, her speech remained resolutely formal in its lack of contractions.

"Well, I best make preparations and burn off this magic before I sleep," she said, standing gracefully.

She walked around the camp, tracing a wide glowing circle around the clearing, then drew in a series of intricate lines intersecting each other. He tried to fix on one end and follow its path all the way around, but found his eyes kept getting lost and jumping to another line. She stood in the centre, her eyes glowing with a bright blue light, the air around her crackling.

"This is a little gauche," she said apologetically. "All the light and sparkle is the result of inefficiency in this case. But, well, the point is to burn off magic, so I may as well let loose. No one is going to pick us up out here."

She placed her hand on the ground, and a small pentacle appeared around her, then blue fire burst alive through the lines she had drawn as they raced to the outer circle, five further pentacles spaced evenly along its length. A translucent sphere grew over them, casting the air in a blue hue, before fading until only the slightest tinge of colour suggested it was still present.

"It is nothing too powerful," she said modestly, "but it will give us a heads-up and a chance to prepare if anything tries to get in. Just in case."

"Oh. Is that tiring?"

"A little, yes. I will take my nap now, Ryheart. Goodnight."

She put her hand on his shoulder briefly, then retired into the tent. Evidently, she wasn't quite prepared to leave her safety entirely in his hands. In fairness, he didn't blame her.

Chapter Fifteen

Tome

Ryheart sat on a stump at the edge of the camp and rested his lantern by him. The shield made him feel somewhat redundant, but he kept his sword ready at the belt. If there were any indication something hit the shimmer of magic that guarded them, he would be prepared.

He fished through his pack and picked up the small leather tome Fali had given him. A Complete Study of the Creatures of the Garden and the Other Realms. It was catchily titled. The author was 'Lady Dolati'. Fali had told him to study it if he wanted to avoid being killed. Given the barrier shimmering between him and the outside world, this seemed as good a time as any.

He opened it to the glossary and frowned. It didn't have any page numbers in it. Just a list of monsters and Fae. He wasn't exactly the most avid reader, but he was reasonably sure that was a flaw. Scratching his head, he flicked through the pages, but if anything, that was even more bizarre. The entries weren't alphabetical, nor were they grouped by category. At least, not any he could determine. There was an entry on pixies, followed immediately by an entry about a spider-like creature called a jorōgumo which appeared primarily far off across the ocean in Nippaya. Apparently, it seemed to be a handsome woman and lured people into waterfalls to drown, which was a lovely thought.

The following entry was about an albino troll only found in the mountain ranges of Nordaya. He could not for the life of him figure out any order to the pages.

"How in Divana's name am I supposed to find anything in here?" he muttered.

"Well, you are reading in a very inefficient manner, you know," a rich voice declared, startling him so much he threw the book on the floor. Looking around, he found he was still very much alone, and Fali was soundly asleep, so far as he could tell.

The voice had seemed to come from the book. Deciding that if he was going loopy and hearing voices, he might as well see what they had to say, he picked the book back up.

"I'm, um, reading it wrong?" he asked, feeling like a buffoon for talking to himself.

"I have a name," the book replied haughtily. "Calling me 'it' is most discourteous."

Oh, great, he thought. Not only is the book talking to me, but it's also giving me sass.

"I don't know your name?"

"Dolati, dear," the book sighed wearily, apparently not impressed with her new charge's intellect. "It is on the cover. You have read a book before, have you not?"

"Sure, ones never talked to me before, though."

"Ah."

"Well, I'm Ryheart," he said, feeling very odd introducing himself to a book.

"Dolati. Charmed, I am sure," the book said cordially. The voice carried an exquisite grace and courtesy to it, at least now it wasn't insulting him. "And what do we wish to study today?"

"First, can I ask, well, to put it bluntly, what in the gods' names you are?"

"I am a book, dear," the book said tartly. "I would have thought that rather self-evident."

"Yes, but books aren't usually vocal like you." Or as lippy, he might have added.

"Oh, that. Well, simply put, I have my author's personality imbued within me, along with her knowledge of the subject matter I was created to impart," she said, further elaborating. "In this case, her knowledge of Fae, monsters, spirits, magic, realm-dancers and empty-ones, and everything else that either lives in, or visits, the garden."

"The garden?" he queried.

"Ah. A rather romanticised colloquialism for the land of mortals, or more expansively, the physical realm."

"Oh. Well, Realm-dancers and empty-ones are nonsense," he argued. "Hunters would know about them. Someone would, anyway. No one's ever seen either."

"That is nice, dear," the book replied so agreeably it almost sounded affirmative. "What did we want to learn about, if not the truth?"

"Nemean lions would be a good start."

"Now that we can manage," the book said, flipping open to a page with an illustration of the beast, along with text about it. At a glance, the creature might have simply been a lion, but further inspection showed subtle differences. The teeth were longer, claws thin and razor-like, with a spark of cruelty to the eyes not present within its mundane counterpart.

Fortunately, beyond its origin, it wasn't supernatural in ability. It didn't breathe fire or shoot lightning from its eyes, and it didn't require magical items to kill it. If you stabbed it hard enough, it would die. Ryheart started to feel a glimmer of hope that with Fali's magical assistance, he might be able to maybe, just maybe, kill the thing.

"Okay. Could you maybe tell me what species my friend is?" he asked, glancing towards the tent to check it was still quiet. It wasn't that he didn't trust Fali, exactly, but he wasn't entirely sold on the Fairy Queen's fairy-ness, nor for that matter, her queenliness.

"I am sure we could elucidate what she is for you," the book replied cordially.

"Alright, great. Well, she's over there," Ryheart said, pointing towards the tent.

"I cannot see her," the book said after a long pause. "I somewhat lack the optical functions to do so. If you are trying to identify something you do not recognise, perhaps describe her to me? Or I can provide a blank page, and you could draw her?"

"Oh. Well…" Ryheart pondered, stating the first thing that sprang to mind when he pictured her, "she has red hair. Not like, ginger. Red. Bright red."

"That is a fair start," the book said approvingly, flicking through its pages until it landed on a list of creatures, all of which typically had red hair. Ryheart was sure the book hadn't been ordered in such a manner before, nor had enough pages to contain such specific groupings.

The list was relatively short, and nearly all of them were either fire elementals or particular creatures during the autumn.

Fali's personality is fiery, at least, he thought.

"Could a fairy make a magical deal?" he asked, a sudden thought entering his mind. Perhaps abilities were a better identifier than looks.

"Oh, yes. Any creature of old magic could."

So much for that, then. Ryheart thought about going back to descriptors, deciding the marking on her cheek might be a good shout. Really, though, he was only incidentally curious about what she was. The strange magic tying her to him, though, that he was interested in. Especially since his reluctant ally had been somewhat reticent with some of her explanations.

"Could they make it powerful?" he queried instead.

"Fairies, you mean? Modestly so, I suppose," the book replied after a moment of contemplation. "What do you mean by powerful, exactly?"

"So strong she literally can't leave my presence until her bond is completed."

"Possibly," the book mused. "Who was the other party?"

"Me."

"Oh," the book said as if that changed things, "and you are not magical in any capacity?"

"No, just a regular human."

"How was it made? Do you remember how you phrased it?"

"'I offer you sanctuary', I think I said."

"Peculiar," the book murmured. "Offer is such a weak term, it should carry barely any weight. Did the other participant say 'offer' as well?"

"Yes. She said, 'I offer to help with your debt.'"

"Well, if only one magical party were involved, they would have nearly all the control over both the power of the spell, and how strict its terms were as to what constituted its fulfilment. Perhaps they might make it so strong to absolutely ensure that you must fulfil your end of the bargain?"

"I don't think so," he contemplated. "I mean, all she wanted was a shelter, and she seemed surprised herself by how strong it was. Besides, she seems tied to me, rather than the other way around."

"Aside from an external modifier, I cannot think of any reason that might be so."

"An external modifier? Like what?"

"Some extreme ritual significance to the deal, or a blood pact, or if it was made somewhere holy. Something along those lines."

A sudden spark of clarity hit him with that. A seemingly insignificant coincidence suddenly taking a new meaning. He knew, he thought, what had happened. And he was sure Fali would know how to fix it if he told her.

He jumped with a start as he heard movement from the tent. He had been so enthralled reading he had lost track of time, but her half an hour must have passed. He shoved the book into his bag quickly, his heart hammering.

He just had to tell her. If nothing else, it would be good to see her face when she found out he was the one who knew something she didn't know for once. He could hold that over her for the rest of the trip.

Except... would there be a rest of the trip? She was here to help him, yes, but only because she had no choice. Once he told her, would she just leave him? What if she could immediately fix it, and she just left him here? Doubt started to creep into his heart. He needed to pay his debt. He needed to kill the Nemean Lion to do so. He needed her to do so. Without her magic, without her guidance, he wasn't even sure he could find the damn thing. Let alone kill it.

She clambered from the tent and stretched delicately, her golden skin glowing softly in the light of her shield, and she walked over to him.

"Morning, Ryheart," she said with a smile.

His gut twisted, and he smiled back weakly. "Hi. Did you, err, sleep well?"

"Adequately," she said. "How was the watch?"

"Oh, fine, yeah. The shield kind of did my job for me," Ryheart said, trying to avoid looking directly into her brilliant eyes.

"Well, do not worry," she said with a laugh. "As soon as we get this deal done, I will be out of your hair. Then you will not have to put up with me forcing you to keep watch and being so demanding of you."

"Yeah. You must be sick of babysitting me as well, I guess," Ryheart replied, trying to return the humour.

"Oh, we all make sacrifices," she joked, then tilted her head. "Are you alright, Ryheart? You seem a little peaky."

"Just tired," he lied.

"Well, do not let me keep you. Sleep well, dear-heart," the Fae said graciously.

"Yeah, goodnight," he said, turning away, gut wrenching even harder. He had to tell her, but he couldn't. Besides, he'd only be delaying her by a week, anyway, he justified to himself. As soon as they got the monster, they'd be clear either way.

Chapter Sixteen

Shield

Ryheart woke up feeling like his eyes were full of sand. His exhaustion had overtaken his conscience, but his sleep had been fitful. Judging from the sun streaming through the tent, he'd had more than his allocated time.

He got dressed quickly and climbed out.

"Ah. Morning, Ryheart," Fali greeted him. "I was about to wake you. I figured it would not hurt for you to get a little bit of extra sleep, but we probably ought to set off before the moon says hello again."

"Yeah, sorry. Rough night," he apologised. As he drew closer to her, he couldn't help but notice that despite their long hike and their sleeping in the woods, Fali still carried the scent of flowers. He, on the other hand, wasn't quite so fresh.

"Same plan as yesterday?" he asked.

"More or less. If we make good time, we should hopefully reach the naiad lake the report mentioned today. They can point us in the right direction, and then we can go a-hunting."

"Great. The naiads are friendly?"

"If they were not, I would have picked somewhere else," she informed him, handing him leftovers to eat and pouring some tea from their beat-up teapot. "I suppose this old thing will have to do, till we get somewhere more civilised."

"What, you like sitting around drinking tea with little porcelain cups and all that?" he asked.

"Why, yes," she said, smoothing her dress down, "I do, as a matter of fact."

"Oh. I didn't peg you as that type."

"What are you suggesting, Ryheart?" she asked with a hint of danger in her voice.

"Just that, err, you'd be a coffee person?"

She stared at him a moment, then laughed. "Well played, Ryheart," she murmured. "Actually, to tell the truth, it is really my sister's hobby, but some of her idiosyncrasies have rubbed off on me."

Both his tea and meal were hot, but curiously Ryheart couldn't see any sign Fali had lit a fire.

He had a quiet breakfast, Ryheart subdued somewhat by the moral quandary he was having, and then they packed up the camp.

"Come along then, Ryheart," she demanded, and he followed her lead immediately. Strangely he found himself carrying out all of her little commands without question, and he didn't really mind it. She was never outright demanding, but despite having only known her a short time, he had a strange compulsion not to disappoint her. The knowledge he was keeping from her probably didn't help with that.

They set off once again, Fali unerringly following her ash-grey wraith-like familiar's lead. They made good progress, and by the end of the afternoon, they came to a vast meadow within the woods, a rolling landscape of hills leading down to a lake with a small island in the middle of it.

The air past it shimmered with a sapphire glow, a wall of magic protecting the Fae territory, keeping it clear of monsters. It wasn't entirely dissimilar from Fali's little campfire shield, though stupendously broader in scope.

"I've never actually seen a barrier," Ryheart exclaimed in amazement. "It's huge."

It towered higher than the walls that protected Londaya, and it curved into the sky.

"Yes," Fali agreed absently, seemingly lost in the unending dance of its surface, "there is the magic of about a dozen species worth of Fae mixed up in there. It is beautiful."

"It is," he agreed. "What's powerful enough to make that?"

"By themselves, perpetually? Unless you happen to have a very popular god handy, nothing," she mused. "Not individually, anyway. No one mortal could permanently sustain something that large. The basic framework is the same as my somewhat modest campfire spell, but it has had entire generations of Fae pumping magic into it. It can keep itself running as long as it does not overreach and they keep topping it up. I could make a stronger shield myself, but nowhere near that scale, and it would need near-constant attention. The one I made at our camp burns itself out in about eight hours or so unless I replenish it. And that is if nothing touches it."

"Is it circular like yours then?" he asked. "Why didn't we go through it?"

"Oh, they are, yes," she said with an approving smile. "Well noted. Given the hostile territories to this end, and humans are at least somewhat welcome, I daresay it is heavily front-loaded." She gave him a sidelong glance. "I imagine it is designed to be able to distribute the magic more evenly, though, just in case any humans think the woods might be a nice logging resource and decide to ignore the Fae treaties."

"And the Nemean is approaching it?"

"Apparently," she conceded. "I am not sure why, though. It presumably had quite a lot of territory, and a Nemean is not one of the monsters that have to eat humans specifically."

It wasn't like he had expected it to be a herbivore. However, the confirmation that they did indeed eat humans, even if not exclusively, still brought a slight twinge of apprehension to his already thoroughly twisted gut.

"So what's the plan to find it, then?"

"Why, we go and ask the locals, of course," she answered with a smile.

Chapter Seventeen

Break

The pair carried on down the gently sloping clearing until they reached the lakeside, which stood glassy and still.

"Isn't the lake a bit quiet?" Ryheart asked.

"It is rather sleepy," she agreed. "I would have expected more naiads than this in a lake so large."

"More? It's empty," he said, baffled.

He admittedly wasn't any sort of expert on naiads, or on many things for that matter, but he was reasonably sure they weren't supposed to be invisible.

"Oh, you just need to look correctly," she said with a mysterious smile that he found simultaneously both endearing and frustrating.

"Well, how should I be looking then?"

"Oh, just look a bit closer."

He frowned at her dubiously, then bent down to peer into the water. There was a ripple, and then an icy splash hit him in the face as something erupted from the lake. He let out a not entirely manly yelp, as much from the chill as from surprise. The water congealed and formed something human-like in the shape of a child. However, the sun shone lazily through its midriff as it simply melted, rippling into the water at the waist.

"Wotcha doing there, mister?" the creature, he presumed a naiad, asked him curiously.

He flushed slightly at his less than heroic reaction and scowled at Fali, whose only response was to beam at him innocently.

"I was just looking at the water. Both kinds, evidently."

"Oh, that's nice. It's lonely here since nearly all our siblings left."

"Left?" Fali chimed in. "To where?"

"To the shield. It's our time to tend it."

"You have a schedule between the different Fae?" Fali said, sounding impressed.

"Yeah, we look after it during Maian and Junicana's time," he explained. As he spoke, a small number of other watery children sprang up, flocking around Fali, a single red flower in a pool of water.

"Are you a fire sprite?" one of them asked her, seemingly enraptured by her hair.

"No, dearest."

"You have red hair, though," the child pointed out.

"Yes."

"And it's not on fire?"

"No."

"But you aren't a fire sprite?"

"No, young one. It is just red."

"Are you sure?" another asked, seemingly genuinely concerned she may be on fire and somehow unaware of it. "We could water it, just in case."

"I am quite sure, thank you. I do appreciate the concern, though."

"Well, if you're sure," the naiad said, still sounding dubious.

"How come you all stayed here?" Ryheart asked.

"We can't hold our form yet," one explained.

"Yeah, Flow here still dries the bed on a night!" another teased.

"Do not!" the youngest exclaimed.

"Now now, I am sure you have all done it at one point," Fali chided, before turning to Ryheart to explain. "Naiads can stay somewhat solid outside of the water for a time, but it is something they develop. These precious little ones are not a day over thirty, by the look of it."

"Thirty?" Ryheart exclaimed in amazement. They looked like little children. Apparently, they were older than him. "That's young?"

"Why, yes, of course that is young," Fali said, splashing water at one of them playfully. "They are practically babies."

"Compared to what, other naiads?"

"Well, yes. And to me, for that matter," she said with a smile.

"How old are you then?"

"Why, Ryheart," she protested mildly. "What a thing to ask a lady."

"Why are you both here?" one of the naiads asked.

"Well," Fali said, crouching down to one of them, her tone light, "there is something terrible in the forest, and we are here to find it."

"Oh, is it the stompy one? Daddy said it's really big, and really upset, but it doesn't even know why it's so angry. Isn't that sad?"

Fali's eyes took on a sombre blue, and she sighed softly as if remembering something. "It is sad, yes. Once upon a time, such creatures were peaceful."

"When they say it's big…" Ryheart asked, trailing off nervously.

"Oh, I have fought a few before," Fali said with a dismissive wave of her hand. "They are not all that much bigger than regular lions. They will just kill anything living that they come across for fun, rather than for food."

"That's a cheery thought," he murmured.

"At least it cannot paralyse you if you look at it, or turn you into a chicken with its scream," she said. "Anyway, between us, we shouldn't have any—"

Whatever she had been about to say, she was interrupted by a monumental, catastrophic sound. The blue shimmer in the air flared brightly, then blinked. Then it vanished altogether.

"What in Divana's name was that?" Ryheart shouted, half deafened by the thunderous crack.

The impact had thrown him from his feet, and he scrambled back up. The naiads had dealt with the issue by simply collapsing in on themselves, and a couple of the braver ones now poked their heads out of the water, surveying the situation curiously.

"Ekkksllpth!" Fali cursed, evidently another troll epithet. Her tone was slightly wild, even her usual self-assured demeanour seemingly rattled. "The barrier just shut down!"

"The Nemean?" he asked, wide-eyed.

Fali nodded her head. "Yes. It is through the barrier, I can feel it." She made another harsh, guttural noise. "And it has not just pushed through it. It has broken it. The shield is gone."

Chapter Eighteen

Decision

"Gone?" Ryheart gasped in disbelief.

"Gone. Shattered," Fali confirmed.

"How near is the monster?"

"Close," she said, her eyes distant.

"What's the matter?" he asked, glancing towards the now-clear sky. "Besides the giant angry monster, I mean. We were going to kill it anyway, right? This just means we find it earlier."

"Ryheart, the barrier is at the edge of wildlands, remember?" she said. "All sorts of filth could make a break for the border now the shield's down. Any of them can get into Fae territory now."

"I mean, that's bad and all, but the Fae can repair it, can't they?"

"I do not know that they will have such an easy job. The things relatively efficient once it is up, but the initial power needed to start it is huge. Besides, the longer it is down, the more things can pass through it. If we do not get that shield restored, they now have a direct path to Londaya, and all you have to stop them is stone and salt."

"It'll be enough, right?" he asked, feeling a chill pass down him.

"Who can say?"

"Well, we go fix the shield, then go get the monster," he decided. It meant eking away his precious time until his deadline, but the monster practically throwing itself into their path had made things considerably more straightforward. Quicker, anyway.

"That would be the best option, but why is it coming in this direction?" she asked herself aloud. "It will instinctively work its way towards the biggest source of pure magic it can sense near to it to consume it. I would be the strongest, but it cannot be me that it is picking up on. I am masked. So why is it… oh," she said, and her tone of voice made him decidedly worried.

"What?"

She glanced at the apprehensive-looking naiads, then leaned into him and lowered her voice. "It is after them."

"What?" he asked, looking nervously over to them. "They're the strongest thing in the forest?"

"The lake is. It is what gives all naiads life. It is where the collective power of all the naiads comes from. Magically it is tremendous. It will be what everything else that passes the barrier homes in on too."

"Can they use that power somehow?"

"They are too young. Besides which, it is strong, but it is not offensive. They do not stand a chance."

"Gods. Can they run?" Ryheart asked, his mind racing.

"They cannot even leave the lake."

"What can it do to them? I mean, they are just water, aren't they?"

"If it was purely a physical threat, nothing. But a naiad's entire spirit is dependent on the purity of the water. The Nemean might be mundane, but it is still a monster. It still has a touch of the corruption within it. The children's spirit is still only fragile. If it tears them out, they could lose their ability to manifest altogether. If it pollutes the water, it could well kill the entire colony."

"So, we fight the monster first, then."

"Then anything else will be free to get in. Other creatures are just as likely to be drawn to the lake as the lion. And the longer it takes to fix, the harder it gets. By the time we kill the monster, it might not be fixable."

"Then what do we do?"

"I do not know," she exclaimed, her eyes a conflicted mix of colours. "There is no clever way out of this. We can save the children from the Nemean, or everything in the forest from the unknown. We could try both if not for this bloody chain tying us together!"

The immediate danger had pushed all else out of his mind, but her comment snapped his discovery the night before back to him.

"If we could separate, I could fight the monster while you fix the shield," he clarified.

"If being the problem, there," she said distracted. "We do not have the time for hypotheticals anymore. It is starting to pick up its pace now. We need to stop it before it gets here."

"I know why you're bound to me," he blurted. He felt a strange clarity given the imminent peril of what he was about to do, and the knot of tension that had plagued him disappeared.

"What?" she exclaimed, her eyes wide. "How?"

He looked at the naiads huddled together. Only a matter of days ago, viewing the Fae as some strange abstract entities, his fear over facing the monster alone might have held his tongue even in the threat of danger to them. But now, seeing them, hearing them, knowing how human they were. Or, rather, how alive they were. There was no longer any way he could put himself first.

Taking a deep breath, he plunged into it. "It's a blood oath. Your blood got into me, and that's what's tying you to me," Ryheart explained as succinctly as he could. "Your blood dripped into a cut on my hand as we made the deal."

"A one-way blood oath," she hissed, and her eyes smouldered dangerously as they bored into him. "That is why I am so strongly tied to you. I gave my blood as a guarantee."

"Can you break it, now you know?"

She took one long breath as if she were suppressing her emotions, then held her hand out with a look of concentration. A bubble of fractured colour welled up from her palm as if punctured, sparkling in the sunlight.

"You have to 'return the blood', symbolically. To release your claim over me," Fali said in a clipped tone, extending her palm to him.

He pricked his palm with his knife, then held his hand above hers.

"I renounce my claim to you helping with my debt," he intoned, and he squeezed his palm. A drop of blood beaded then dropped. It hit Fali's blood with a plop, and he felt like something he hadn't even been aware of was lifted from him.

"I'm sorry," he said simply. He wanted to explain, to rationalise, to apologise. But now wasn't the time. He just had to hope that when – if – he got to talk to Fali again, she would forgive him. "Go fix the shield, I'll do what I can to stop it and protect the children. At the very least, I can buy you some time."

She stared at him for what seemed like a long moment. "After I fix the shield, I will come to help you if I can," she said solemnly. "Keep the children safe."

Without another word, she turned on her heel and ran, leaving him alone to face something that would likely kill him.

Chapter Nineteen

Barrier

Fali raced through the trees like a wraith on the wind, homing in on the feeling of sputtering magic that signified the damaged part of the spell that made the shield. Created from multiple nodes connected like spokes on a wheel, all of them joined the grand central reservoir, the magical weir that had likely given the forest its name. Most likely, the feedback from the break had disrupted its flow, and without a complete circuit, the entire thing fell.

She could feel the suddenly displaced magic from the break dissipating into the ether, but even through that, she could feel the leaking power at the broken node, calling her like a beacon.

Worryingly, the next beacon also felt slightly wrong, but she couldn't determine why through the pervading fog of magic in the air. She pushed the worrying niggle from her mind. Fretting over it now wouldn't do much good.

She could also faintly feel Ryheart's life force moving steadily towards the far greater life force of the Nemean. She currently had several emotions directed at the young hunter, not least of which was pure unbridled anger at his keeping her prisoner when he could have released her from the oath. Despite all that, she still had at least some fondness towards him. She certainly didn't want him to die. And not only because he needed to protect the naiad children.

Fortunately, while fierce, Nemean lions weren't beyond the realms of capability for a lone human to fight. And if Ryheart had displayed one talent so far in her limited observation, it was bumbling his way through situations beyond him.

The slight hiccup in that analysis was that even if the lion had been fortunate in hitting an exceptional weak spot in the shield, the Nemean shouldn't have been able to break it. Worm its way through, perhaps. But not break.

That too, however, was all out of her hands now. Approaching the node, she cleared her mind of all extraneous concerns.

The node was a tiered platform of ancient stone that dominated the circular clearing of trees it stood within. The groove of three lines of entrenched magical spell-work ran out from it, one to the grand reservoir and the others to adjacent nodes.

A weathered flight of stairs carved into the side made a path, but she ignored them and leapt up tier by tier.

Nearly two dozen naiads were either frantically conversing with one another, or crouched over the large intricate pattern of magic that sat upon the summit, a pentacle at its core. It pulsed with energy, but it was pale and had an almost sickly pallor to it as the power built over centuries gradually seeped away.

Several naiads yelped in alarm as she shot over the edge, and the two tallest, bulkiest members surged towards her with bottom halves of rolling surf. They had a sun-blessed tone to their skin, but it rippled slightly, belying its less-than-solid nature, and their hair still flowed freely like a waterfall. At seven foot they positively towered over her, but as they levelled their spears at her, they looked decidedly unused to wielding them. In fact, Fali noted, one of them had the business end of the spear pointed at himself.

"Stop and identify yourself!" he demanded, jabbing at her threateningly with the blunt pole.

"Oh, do not embarrass yourself," Fali chastised impatiently, swatting the weapon away and sending it pinwheeling off the edge of the platform. "We do not have time for silly games."

"Identify yourself," the still-armed naiad demanded, his hairs flow faltering nervously.

"Child, you are too young to recognise me, or you would have already, and it is frankly unimportant. What is important is that we fix this spell-work before your forests swarmed with monsters, or did you want Ginny Green-teeth infecting your lake and poisoning you all?" Despite her declaration, the naiads held their place, and she snapped at them, stamping her foot imperiously. "Alright, if it is so important, who is the eldest naiad here?"

They looked hesitantly at her, then called out, "Laaké, can you come to identify this guest?"

The naiad who answered his call had no age to her face, but the water of her hair had a silvery tinge to it, and it flowed with a steady, methodical speed rather than with the exuberant rush of youth.

"Alright, do you recognise what I am?" she demanded, the glyph on her cheek blazing with her fervour.

The matriarch's eyes glanced at the green pattern by her eyes, then stared at the glyph upon her cheek, and her eyes widened.

"Goddess?" she exclaimed in a startled voice. "Let her through, let her through!" She ushered frantically to the younger naiads. "Apologies, Goddess, but we haven't had a visitation in a long time, and it's rather a dire situation. How can we help you?"

Evidently, the naiad didn't just recognise her people but knew of her specifically. Grand. That should speed things up considerably. The naiad would be accustomed to doing as she was told, knowing who Fali was. Technically, 'Goddess' wasn't strictly accurate, given there were no pantheons left for her to be considered a part of, but now wasn't the time for an extended lesson in theology.

"I am here to help restore this node. With my help, we should have this empowered in no time."

"If it was just this node that needed restarting, I'm sure you could, Goddess," Laaké informed her, "but the opposite node was broken by the feedback as well, and they both lost a considerable bit of power in the hit. It would take us days to build enough power to restart the flow over two nodes distance, and we'd need to sustain it the entire time to stop it pooling back out of the broken ones!"

"Unacceptable." Fali shook her head. "The place will be swamped with black-jacks and all sorts in that time, and even if you do get both individual nodes repaired and working, there is no guarantee they will join back together over that distance just by their power alone."

"We don't have any other options, Goddess," the naiad informed her apologetically.

"Fali," she corrected absently while her mind raced to find a solution. She could add the amount of lost power back to the node herself. But both nodes would need restoring, and she could only do one at a time. Even then, she would only be able to sustain it a short time before her reservoir of magic ran dry. And every second passing, the broken nodes lost more of their accumulated power, making the jump start harder.

"Alright," she said decisively, "I presume you have communication with the other nodes?"

"We have mirror pools, yes."

"Alright. I want you all to add as much power as you can manage to the two nodes on the hour. Then let it flow."

"But there's not nearly enough power built up yet to restore the two nodes and let them run independently!"

"No, but I am going to stand in the middle of the two broken nodes and act as a temporary one myself. You might not have enough power to recharge the nodes fully, but since the magic will only have half as far to travel, it will only need half the push."

"But the nodes don't have enough power stored to self-sustain yet!"

"But I can act as a conduit and pull the two streams of magic together, forcing them to reconnect. If I knit them together into one continuous flow, even if only for a few seconds, the grand reservoir in the centre will refill them, and they will be able to sustain themselves again."

The naiad's eyes widened as she thought over the ramifications.

"But you'll die!" she exclaimed. "Back when we were in Elladaya moons ago before we flowed here, Zuthan tried to take the full force of a grand node exploding to win a bet, and he was unconscious for a month! He was very drunk at the time, but still!"

"Oh, I have a lot more subtle hand than he did. I will not take the entire force head-on; I will be channelling it."

"What about when it converges! All those streams together could rip you asunder."

"Well, I am not really dressed for it. But I do know a thing or two about magic, and I rather hope I can avoid that," Fali said in a deprecating manner, before giving the slightest hint of a mischievous smile. "If you are worried about the responsibility, I can make it a command, if you like?"

"I will do as you ask, of course," the naiad bowed in respect, "but are you sure you only want an hour? It's the best part of five hours' travel to the next node."

"Well then," Fali said, dusting off her dress lightly, "I had best be off then, had I not?"

And with that, she was gone.

Chapter Twenty

Nemean

Ryheart crouched on top of an outcrop, puzzled. He could hear the creatures' stomping feet. He could feel them, even. He didn't like that he could feel them.

Peering through the trees, he swore when he spotted movement. The Nemean was somewhat larger than anticipated. The thing was about the size of a barn. Fali had said it was a bit larger than a regular lion, not that it was bloody massive.

He swore. He didn't know how to fight something the same size as him, let alone ten times larger. He had a brief glimmer of hope that, at the very least, its testicles might be an easy target if all else failed. Then he noticed it didn't have a mane, so even that small mercy was robbed from him.

Well, he thought to himself dryly, at least I'd die as a real hunter and not a glorified rubbish collector. He'd even go out saving innocents. Strangely the biggest regret that flashed in his mind was that he wouldn't get to properly apologise to Fali for his selfishness.

He drew his short sword and examined it one last time. Its heft didn't inspire much confidence in him. His Fae guide had demanded he sharpen it, but it was still decidedly underwhelming in the face of the creature before him.

"Well, I best not keep it waiting," he murmured to himself. "That would be bad manners, after all, and I am Anglasan."

He moved forward softly, every crunch of leaves hanging in the air, his heart pounding.

Now, all that separated him from the creature was a small thicket, and as it bullied a way through the trees before it, each step sent a slight tremor under Ryheart's feet. If anything, its bulk seemed even vaster up close, its golden coat pale, with a strange pattern of black spirals across it.

He was going to step forth when a whistle rang through the air, followed by a soft thump as a javelin pierced the creature's flank. Amazed, he whirled to see the mystery attacker. For the first time in his life, he was pleased to see Harand Smithe. His rival hunter burst through the trees and launched another javelin.

It too lodged in the creature's flank, and the beast turned clumsily, enraged if not harmed, the projectiles barely piercing its thick coat. It let loose a furious ear-splitting roar, angry froth flecking its mouth.

The creature swatted its massive paw at its attacker, catching a tree and splintering chunks of bark. Harand flung himself back, just barely avoiding the razor claws that tried to pierce him. The creatures size made it slow but also meant the sheer bulk gave it a massive reach.

All thoughts of bounty aside and with all but the beast wiped from his mind, Ryheart ran forward and slashed at the now-exposed back leg, gouging through its red flecked fur. The creature whirled furiously, giving Harand enough time to climb to his feet.

Harand followed suit, attempting to distract the creature with a volley into its flank. This time, though, the beast realised that the assault wasn't life-threatening. It swiped at Ryheart with its claws, and he was too slow. A jolt of pain shot through his arm as the nail shredded his light armour like parchment, ripping his arm open underneath. The sheer force knocked him off his feet; his sword dropped in the assault.

He hit the ground with a thud, arm wet with blood. Without time to react and adrenaline racing, the Nemean's head loomed over him. Its gaping mouth opened, the stench sickening, and it snapped its jaws at him as he scrambled desperately back. In a blind panic, he fumbled for the knife in his belt and thrust it up, the blade sticking between two of its massive teeth. It screeched in pain and reared back even as he still held the knife. His blade pulled free, giving him a short respite that he so desperately needed.

Harand had abandoned his useless ranged assault and had flung himself into its flank, hacking furiously, barely keeping his grip on its blood-slicked fur. Ryheart scrambled to his feet, panting and coursing with the electric thrill of adrenaline. His arm was slick with blood under his armour and burned with pain, but blessedly he could still feel and move it.

The creature swung its back end, then slammed itself into the ground, crushing its attacker beneath its bulk.

Harand's armour was far better quality and much more substantial than Ryheart's own, saving him from the otherwise crushing weight. However, even with its protection, the titanic blow still left him stunned and gasping for air, struggling to gain his footing. Ryheart took off towards his once bitterest of rivals. As he did so, the beast ripped its paw along the ground, showering Ryheart with splinters and rocks before he could reach them, stopping his charge. The blow caught Harand and swept him up, flinging him clean through the air. He slammed into a tree with a bone-shattering impact and fell to the floor, unmoving.

The beast snarled triumphantly and stalked towards its fallen foe, seemingly savouring its victory a moment, then raised its paw to crush him.

Ryheart swept his dropped sword from the ground and ran forward with a spark of inspiration born from sheer desperation. If he weren't strong enough to do any real damage, he would have to use its own power against it. He dived through the air, holding his sword directly upwards, arms outstretched. The paw slammed down towards him, directly onto his blade. The creature felt the shock of pain too late, the metal connecting with the softer, vulnerable pad of its foot, burying the sword to its hilt. It gave an ear-splitting howl and jerked in pain, shaking its paw to try to dislodge the terrible metal splinter.

Ryheart slammed into the ground, panting and covered in sweat, saved from its crushing blow by the desperate gamble. He got to his feet, mind racing even faster than his heart. He had bought himself a precious few seconds, but all he had now was his little knife. Somehow, he needed to stop the creature before it recovered, or he was done.

He glanced to the sky, praying he would see the shimmer of blue that meant Fali had managed her side of their gambit, and he could attempt to retreat and regroup with her. No such luck. That was it. There wasn't going to be any last-minute backup. Either he did this alone, or he didn't do it at all. He took a deep breath, then made his play.

Chapter Twenty-One

Flood

Fali stood in the middle of two dying streams of magic, petering out before they could reach her. If she couldn't even get them to touch, let alone crash together with enough force to merge into a continuous stream, they were in trouble. Angry crackles of magic snapped at her outstretched palms, stinging violently, but they were only flickers of power.

Exasperated, she took deep breaths to replenish herself as much as she could with the ambient magic in the air. Pulling out a message bottle she had swiped from the naiads, she emptied the water onto the ground. The water smoothed itself into a glassy puddle, then the head and shoulders of Laaké formed from it, defined but clear.

"Goddess?" the messenger asked, polite despite the evident concern in her rippling features.

Fali spoke as calmly but commandingly as she could manage, even as her mind raced. "There just is not enough power coming from the nodes, even with me central. Is this the absolute most you can manage?"

"We're giving it our all, ma'am. Some of us are starting to flag, too. We're going to start drying out soon if we keep this up without replenishing ourselves at the lake."

Fali considered her options in silence, each potential path weighed then disregarded until only one remained.

"Alright, Laaké. Here is the plan. Slow your pace down, but keep the flow steady. I am going to hold either side up like a dam, so it builds itself against me. Once it is as much as I can hold, I want you all to push with everything you have left. As your wave meets me, I will drop my resistance and let everything flood through me. If we do this right, it will be enough of a connection for the circuit to complete and the grand reservoir to reconnect the nodes."

"If it doesn't work, we won't have anything left to try anything else," the naiad cautioned.

"We already don't have enough left to try anything else," Fali corrected. "We can either piddle what we have left away in little fits and spurts, or we can commit it all to one last-ditch effort and make this work. Besides, you know what they say, 'Put all your basilisk eggs in one basket, so they're easier to step on.'"

"Okay, but that's an incredible amount of magic that's going to be crashing against you. Are you sure you can handle it long enough to knit them?"

"For both our sakes, we better hope so," Fali said softly after a moment's silence.

The magic built up and swelled either side of her, the weight of its pressure steadily growing as she held it back.

She held until there was a thunderous storm of roiling magic on either side of her, desperately trying to force its way beyond her. She repelled it, only for it to re-join the ever-growing stream to crash against her once again.

"Now!" she commanded, her arms shaking from the pressure. She heard the thunder of all the magic the naiads could muster raging towards her, then dropped her barrier and let the torrent in.

She inhaled sharply as the magic flooded through her, the excess she couldn't channel battering against her violently. The sheer force nearly overwhelmed her, the foreign power threatening to drown out her own. Her body wracked and spasmed as it raged through her, crushing her, enveloping her.

The connections joined, and the circuit completed, the grand reservoir flowing to the damaged nodes and flooding across the broken lines. Fali shrieked as her entire being electrified with the burst. All manner of Fae had filled the magic pool over the long years, and fire raged in her veins, water surged against her, the wind tore and vines lashed as the supernatural magnet she had made of herself attracted every node to focus on her.

Her mind burned, and sharp needles stabbed at her core, trying to overwhelm and claim her heart of magic. She focused as hard as she could, fighting off the creeping darkness that threatened to rend her unconscious. It had been a long time since she was so overwhelmed, and only the fact she was channelling the bulk of the flow through her was keeping her standing.

Even then, she was still only going to last seconds.

It wasn't enough. It still wasn't enough.

The nodes must have lost more power than she had realised. Magic was flowing from all corners, but it was still flowing as separate streams; it wasn't genuinely joining into one unending loop. If she left it at this, the magic would simply falter and fail once again, and all their effort would be for nought. She needed to keep herself going, just a little longer. Unfortunately, at this rate, a little longer might be more than she could manage.

A voice pierced her swirling thoughts, and she looked up through bleary eyes to see the naiad still watching her through the message pool, panicked.

"Goddess, you're being overwhelmed! You need to save yourself!"

For the briefest of moments, she considered it. As her eyes burst with bright spots of white and she felt her physical form starting to tear, she thought of retreating. Then she remembered the children.

"I can hardly leave you defenceless, can I?" she forced out through gritted teeth. "Tell me your sibling's names, Laaké."

"My siblings?" the naiad exclaimed, clearly taken aback by the out-of-place question.

"Their names," Fali demanded more firmly. "Despite my position, I was never good with abstracts. I need something personal. A face and a name."

"There's a lot of them," the matriarch supplied obediently. "There's Torena. And little Flow."

Fali concentrated everything she had on the innocent face of the naiad, the focus keeping the pain from overtaking her.

"Lovely names, child." She let out a gasp as a fresh wave enveloped her. "How many?"

"A couple of dozen. We're quite a big lake, really. We flowed here from Elladaya."

"I am glad. I was always fond of naiads," Fali said, her blood boiling. "The first time I met some of you, you saw a sword and asked what the point of making a walking stick sharp was."

"Well, we've never really needed them. Why would we go off fighting when we have a perfect lake here?" the naiad asked with absolute sincerity.

"Where did the boys get those spears?"

"Oh, well," the naiad said, sounding embarrassed despite the situation. "Some dryads visited and gave us them as a gift. We don't have any need for them, but we didn't want to be rude, so we let the boys play with them."

Fali chuckled through the pain, and then her head snapped up.

"That is what I am fighting for," she murmured. With a deep breath, she marshalled every bit of magical power she could muster, and with a roar of effort, pulled one last colossal surge of the shield's energy into her. The streams churned against each other, then with a burst of power, they simultaneously both gave way and enveloped each other. They realigned themselves into one continuous stream of shimmering magic, without end or beginning, and the shield established itself, filling the sky with a blue glow.

Caught in the middle, there was a shattering crack that seemed to split the sky as Fali was engulfed in the re-established shield.

She was tossed violently across the forest, crashing limply with a muffled thud into the leaves carpeting the floor. She laid there unmoving, illuminated softly by the shield's glow.

Chapter Twenty-Two

Hunt

Ryheart ran towards the monster as it stumbled and picked at its injured paw, its final attacker temporarily forgotten in its pain.

He had to give credit to his fallen rival. What precisely he had planned, Ryheart wasn't sure, but the javelins he had thrown were spaced almost evenly apart in the beast's flank. They climbed up the bulk of the creature, giving Ryheart his last hope. He had to be quick, or the creature would simply roll as it had before, only, unlike Harand, his flimsy protection would do nothing to stop it.

He took a breath, then ran alongside the distracted beast and leapt onto the first javelin. It sprang under him but held his weight, the added momentum boosting him along the protrusions like stepping stones, scaling the creature. His foot slipped on the last one, and he grabbed desperately at the beast's fur, feet scrambling. Kicking out, he found the weapon beneath and pushed himself up, scrambling onto its back. If he could get to its head, maybe he could at least blind it with his knife before it inevitably dislodged him and took him out.

He braced himself for the last charge, then froze as a voice bellowed to him. "Ryheart!" his bitter rival-turned-ally bellowed, staggering to his feet and swaying. "Kill that fucker!"

The hunter drew his last javelin and launched it through the air, then fell back to the floor, the final effort depleting his last reserve.

Ryheart steadied himself. Heart ringing like a starting gong, he burst forward. The desperately thrown javelin was going to go wide out of his reach. He ran, barely keeping his balance in the rugged fur below him, then leapt.

Catching the weapon in the air, he pivoted it around and down towards the creature's neck. He thrust and felt a surge of electrifying power ripple through him as he slammed down with everything he had. The javelin drove deep, between the creature's skull and its neck. It gave an anguished scream of pain and stumbled, jerking violently before crashing to the ground. He was thrown clear, rolling desperately to avoid the falling wall of muscle threatening to crush him.

All the wind left him as he hit the floor, and he lay panting. The creature pawed at the ground, tearing deep gashes, unable to gain any footing with its failing strength. Its mouth foamed bloody, and its growls became weaker.

Feeling a twinge of guilt as the creature writhed, he climbed wearily to his feet and gathered his wits. Spotting the other hunter's weapon, he picked it up. Despite the necessity of the situation, he felt no malice for the creature.

Steeling himself, he cautiously approached the Nemean, but its eyes were glazed and unfocused, and it no longer seemed aware of his presence. He stroked its fur soothingly, then drove the sword up through its neck to the brain. It shuddered for a moment, then its twitching and writhing ceased, forever falling into silence.

As his heart stopped trying to force its way out of his ribcage, a silence fell across the glade. It felt strange and out of place after his ordeal. He pulled the sword from the now-still monster, the sickly blade red with blood, and he collapsed, exhausted. The adrenaline keeping him on his feet suddenly gone.

That was it. An A-rank hunt, done. Not a bad day's work for an E-rank hunter. What's more, while yes, terrifying, and true, he had barely scraped through by the skin of his teeth: this was the first time he had ever felt anything while hunting beyond boredom. The first time he had felt a drive, a need, for what he was doing, besides dull necessity. True, he had the debt pushing him, but during the fight, it had been more than that. He hadn't just felt he was doing something he had to. He had felt he was doing something right.

The thought of the debt brought him back to reality, and he glanced at the fallen hunter. If he had to share the bounty, he wouldn't have enough to get back under the threshold he was allowed. He didn't want Harand to be dead, mind, but, well… the darker part of his thoughts contemplated that it would be easier if he were. Not better. But easier. From a purely clinical standpoint. The hunter had helped him, though. Without him, he would have had little chance of victory.

He pulled himself up, muscles protesting that they had to work once more, and walked over to the collapsed figure.

Despite his animosity to the hunter, he was glad when he saw signs of life under the armour, albeit faint.

"Well, we got her," he assured him by way of greeting, prying the hunter's battered helmet from his head.

Harand's head was bloody and his eyes glazed, and he coughed in spurts. He clasped Ryheart's arm, dragging himself half upright against the tree he had collided with.

"Hunters have to be tough," he forced out between coughs, wincing. "Better those who can't hack it quit before they end up food, or worse. Didn't think you had what it takes."

"Neither did I," Ryheart murmured, too tired to argue.

"I was wrong," Harand said, breathing heavily. "You just needed the right push."

Ryheart was taken aback. That was almost an apology.

"Well, I couldn't have done it without you here," he admitted, exhausted into honesty. "I need the money, but we should split it."

He still had no love for the hunter, but his pride wouldn't let him take something he wasn't due, even when he needed it so desperately. He would just have to hope that having finished a bounty for a monster with such a high difficulty classification, his competence score would go back up to a D-rank. He would still be in debt. Heavily in debt. But he would at least have breathing room.

"No," Harand said firmly, "consider my half repayment for saving my hide. That's us even, though, clear?"

Ryheart had various conflicting feelings about both the man before him and the idea of taking money from him, but he swallowed his pride. "Why were you here, anyway? I know I was well out of my league, but I was fucking desperate. What's your excuse?"

Harand laughed, then winced as he wracked with a fresh fit of coughs. "Didn't want that Fae-kin getting her hands on any money from the guild. Didn't want you helping her."

"What's your problem with her, seriously?"

"She's magic, Ryheart. I don't know to what extent, but I know. They're dangerous. Even the half-human ones."

"She's out here fighting monsters, same as you. In fact, she went to the shield to fix it, specifically to stop monsters from getting to Londaya and harming innocent people. The same job we're doing, just a different approach."

"I'm not from the city, you know, originally. I'm from a little village to the south. They're soft like you out there, too. We had a Fae in our village. Orphan. We took him in. He was like a brother to me. One day, he lost control of himself. Now I'm an orphan, too."

Ryheart closed his eyes and sighed. "That's awful. But it doesn't sound like they meant you any harm."

"That's my point," Harand said bitterly. "Even when they're trying to help, all they do is make things worse. Magic is a blight."

"I can't judge her based on someone else's mistakes," Ryheart said firmly, "or on her own mistakes, for that matter. I've made enough of my own."

"Just keep an eye on her," Harand begged. "Keep people safe from her magic."

With that, he slumped back down and fell unconscious again, leaving Ryheart in silence once more.

Chapter Twenty-Three

Reprieve

Feeling somewhat weak and bemused, Fali felt herself lifted and then steadily carried along with a rhythmic bobbing. She could barely even feel her own magic, let alone that of other people. Fortunately, the faint flicker she was picking up seemed benign, its presence soothing. For a brief time, she focused on nothing but the feeling of her depleted heart gradually revitalising her with the flow of magic through her veins. She allowed herself a moment to simply be.

Then, with a sigh, she opened her eyes blearily. She was greeted by the sideways view of trees and smiled softly as she saw her familiar padding alongside her, one eye fixed on her, ears alert. Realising the world had not fallen over, and she was simply laid on her side, she lifted her head to find she was being carried by a group of naiads, aloft on a viscous pool of water.

"Where?" she asked, her tongue heavy in her mouth, before coughing delicately and trying again with more of the grace that fit a lady of her station. "Where are we?"

"In the forest, on our way to the lake, Goddess. We were out purifying some water for some harpies when the shield broke. We were going to help at the node, but we were asked to find you instead. We owe you a debt."

"Oh, do not bother about that." She waved dismissively, then the thought of the shield brought everything else racing back to her. "The hunter? Is he alright?"

She could no longer sense him. Admittedly she could detect little right now, but the thought still clawed at her.

"Hush now," the naiad crooned reassuringly, pushing her back with rippling hands as Fali attempted to climb off the watery stretcher. "He's fine; they both are."

"Both of them?" Fali asked, frowning. "I only remember having one."

"My brother definitely said two," the naiad said. "One of them is severely injured but stable."

"And the Nemean?"

"Dead," the naiad said, making a sign of cleansing. "May it finally rest. Your servants are quite remarkable."

Sighing with relief, the feeling of pixies in Fali's stomach calmed down. She was still decidedly miffed with the unruly hunter at his keeping their blood oath secret, and he most certainly wasn't out of the goblin house with her yet. He had come through when it had counted, though. More, even. He had not only delayed the beast but killed it. That was about as strong a redemption as he could have achieved for his transgression against her. Perhaps how easily she forgave him would depend on how injured he was.

"I do not suppose you know the names of the hunters, or who was injured more heavily?" she queried.

"Couldn't say, I'm afraid. We can stop and make contact with one of my sisters if you'd like?"

"No, that is quite alright. I suppose I will find out shortly," Fali said, letting herself sink back. If she relaxed a short while, she would be able to refill herself with magic quicker, and the faster she would be fully battle-ready again. The place was most likely peaceful once more, but the instinct to prepare was so ingrained she didn't even consider it consciously. She just did so. Fortunately, her life force itself was intact, and she had simply drained all her reserve of naturally stored magic. That would fix itself with the simple beating of her heart, each beat generating a new flush of power, along with what ambient magic she could gather from the world around her.

After a brief while, she felt markedly better and tried to prop herself up on the spongy water beneath her. At this point, some exercise wouldn't harm her. Indeed, her magic supply wouldn't be in any way affected by simple physical activity. She could walk for a thousand years, and as long as she didn't actively use any magic, she would be no worse for wear. Such were the advantages of not being made of actual flesh and blood.

"Alright, you can put me down now, children," she commanded. Despite her station – or perhaps because of it – she was distinctly averse to being seen to rely upon anyone.

"Oh no, that won't do," the naiad fussed, gentle but unrelenting. "You'll heal faster if you rest, will you not?"

"I am fine," Fali sniffed, downplaying the affair and smoothing out her red locks. "It was only a small explosion."

"I think it would be best if you stay put at least until the lake," the matron reinforced. "I really have to insist."

While her tone was gentle, it carried the same hint of steel hidden underneath it that Fali herself used when she 'suggested' things. She wasn't used to being on the receiving end of it.

"Oh? And if I demand otherwise?"

"Well, I respect your wishes, but I must do what's best for my patient, Goddess or no. You can go back to gallivanting around saving the world after you're better."

Naiads! Despite their gentle demeanour, they could be one of the most stubborn species on the planet when it came to insisting on helping someone.

Fali looked at her indignantly, then sighed and laughed softly. "Alright, since I admire your dedication. You are fortunate I know how oblivious you are. Some gods wouldn't even dare talk to me so demandingly, you know."

"Even the strongest need help now and then," the naiad informed her sagely. "Often they're the ones who least recognise when they do."

"Alright, alright," Fali acquiesced. "So what is your name, dear jailor of mine?"

"Reeva, Goddess."

"Tell me," Fali asked with a questioning look, "does everyone in this colony have names related to water? Does it not get hard to think of them after a while?"

The naiad looked like she had to genuinely ponder the question. "Florence. That's not related to water, is it? I think there are even some humans called that."

"Why, Reeva. Are you suggesting it is just accidental that Florence is commonly shortened to Flow?"

"Well, no," the naiad said innocently, "but it's not technically connected to water, is it?"

Chapter Twenty-Four

Insight

Ryheart sat overlooking the lake, his entire body sore but surprisingly unscathed. After washing away the blood soaking his undershirt, the cut on his arm was long but blessedly shallow. His hunting counterpart had not come out of the situation so well, ribs broken and battered. The rival hunter had yet to regain consciousness, but the small horde of naiads who were fussing over him had assured Ryheart he would recover in time with their care.

He watched the naiads lazily. Several of them had returned from the shield, depleted as they were. He had been given some cooked fish and sweet nectar-like drink, and after a few sips, he was positive it was alcoholic. The lake Fae had absolutely fawned over him, and he had to admit hunting where there were people to be immediately thankful for your work was certainly gratifying. People, he mused, was likely not how he would have described the naiads only a day ago.

He watched as some of the younger ones played a game, firing a ball towards each other with water sprays. It struck him as odd, particularly compared to the extremely aggressive combat sports humans played. After every goal scored, the opposing team paused to celebrate, congratulating the others on their point well won. They seemed to have taken the friendly part of friendly competition to an absolute extreme.

Hearing a mild hubbub, he looked around to see a group of naiads carrying his flighty Fae companion upon what appeared to be a throne made of water. She sat cross-legged upon it, and she seemed decidedly huffy about it.

"How much do I owe you for the fare?" she asked her escort dryly as she climbed down and brushed herself off.

"Begging your pardon, Goddess?"

"Never mind, Reeva. Thank you," Ryheart watched her say with a slight bow of her head. Hearing her referred to as a goddess was new.

Fali turned to look at him and her eyes flooded with a swirl of conflicting colours, then settled on a rich, if slightly marred, purple.

"Before I got here, I was not sure if I wanted to hit you or hug you," she informed him.

"And now?" he said nervously.

"I will settle for a warm greeting," she said with a laugh, crouching down and examining him. "Are you hurt?"

"I'm good, surprisingly," he said modestly, before pointing at Harand. "Naiads helped heal me a lot. I'm a lot better off than he is, for sure."

She looked over, clearly surprised by the other hunter's presence. "What on earth was he doing here?"

"He wanted to stop you from getting any money."

"Oh?"

"He's a top arsehole, but I'd probably be dead if he hadn't turned up."

"Oh. Well, I suppose I am glad he did, then," Fali said with a grin.

He laughed at that. "I doubt we're ever going to be best friends or anything, but me too."

"And the bounty?" she asked, sounding genuinely concerned with his plight. "Is he not going to take half?"

"He says not. I think he just hates the idea of being indebted to someone as lowly as me." He breathed deeply and looked across at her. "Look, I'm sorry about the oath. About not telling you."

"When did you find out?" she asked, staring at him, unblinking. His heartbeat was even faster than it had been when the Nemean was staring him down.

"Last night. I happened to figure it out with the book you gave me. Well, guessed, really. I would've told you, just… I was terrified you'd abandon me."

She stared a few moments longer, then sighed. "I cannot entirely blame you for thinking so. I perhaps was not the most gracious about your needs when we met."

He felt a wave of relief, along with a twinge of guilt. "It's still not an excuse. I'm sorry."

She stared at the naiads a moment. "I think, perhaps, your view on Fae might have been coloured somewhat by having been told your entire life they are one step away from monsters. Look at them," she said, gesturing towards the naiads playing. "Do they seem like monsters?"

"No. They don't. And for the first time, I felt something while I was hunting. More than just a necessity. I felt like I had an actual purpose. Something, someone, to protect," he said, glancing at her. "And someone to not let down."

"Alright, I forgive you," she said with a small smile. "Just tell me next time. I would have helped you. Most Fae would, most likely. And I am sorry I was so flippant with you when we met. I did not realise you were in such a bind. And I did not know, because I did not ask."

"Will there be a next time?" he asked, feeling a pang of regret at the idea they were done. "You aren't bound to me anymore."

"Well, perhaps. But I did say I would see your emergency debt paid. I will see you back to the guild, and then I will have to go my own way. I can at least do that part voluntarily," she said with a small smile, which broke into a grin. "Besides, if I do not babysit you, you will probably get eaten by a wolf on the way home."

He laughed. "Yeah, maybe. Well, it'll be nice to travel together without the threat of a giant monster to kill, anyway. We can travel as friends, this time," he said, holding out his hand.

She eyed it, then laughed, laying her soft palm on top of his hand. "Do not think me impolite, but given how we met, I think I will forgo actively shaking anyone's hand for a while," she said with a tinkle of musical laughter. "Now, I am going to go bathe in the delightful water. I suggest you do the same."

"I am a tad dirty," he admitted.

"Ryheart, dear, you absolutely bloody stink."

"Alright, promise. Soon as I get my paperwork done."

"Paperwork?"

"Yeah. Just my 32-b."

"Ryheart, I have not the foggiest idea what you are talking about. What on earth is a '32-b'?"

"Oh, I guess you wouldn't know at that," he mused. "They're so commonplace I hardly think about it. It's just a form to process the fact we completed this bounty. It documents what occurred, any outside help, any guild equipment damaged, all that stuff. We submit the forms along with proof of kill, either witness statements or a claw or something."

He thought he had explained reasonably simply, but she looked incredulous. "You bureaucratised fighting monsters!" she exclaimed.

Ryheart couldn't help but chuckle. Time to get a little payback for her winding him up so much. "Speaking of which," he said in an offhand manner, sifting out several sheets and holding them out to her, "since you're just an additional member of my hunting party, you avoid most of these, but there are a few pages you'll have to fill out. Just a dozen or so."

She gave him a long, level stare, then took them disgustedly. "You have to do this after every hunt you undertake?"

"Yep."

"Every single time?"

"Yep."

"Even though there is an entire lake full of naiads who will testify you did indeed kill the monster?"

"That's right."

"And I have to do so even though I did not even participate in the kill itself?"

"Yeah. You were still officially on the hunt, after all."

"And I suppose you do not get any sort of accolade for me having repaired the shield and stopping Londaya getting overrun with monsters?"

"Wasn't in the official brief, was it?" he said with a grin and a shrug. "I'm sure they'll be very grateful to you, though."

"But not enough to pay you extra, I gather," she said dryly.

"I think they'd rather be overrun than pay someone something they aren't contractually obligated to," he said with a slightly bitter laugh.

She let out a deep, mournful sigh and then held out a hand in defeat. "Alright, hand me a quill. But I want it on record that I am very disappointed in you," Fali said, seemingly talking about his whole species rather than him specifically.

"Welcome to the modern world, Your Majesty," he said with an overly exaggerated flourish of a bow.

Chapter Twenty-Five

Mail

The next day Ryheart awoke with his entire body sore from his trial, nevertheless having slept blissfully from utter exhaustion. He climbed from his tent to see Fali surrounded by a gaggle of naiads, all fussing over her.

"Morning," he called, rubbing his eyes.

"Oh, good morning, dear-heart," she greeted him. "I am glad you are awake. I wanted to go check the Nemean over, but I did not want to leave until you were up and about."

"Why?" he asked, curious. "I got its claw for proof of the kill."

"Something about it felt strange, and I am intrigued. Besides which, a Nemean really should not have been able to break the barrier."

"Oh. Well, will it take long? I do need to get this bounty back and paid before they decide I'm taking up a new, exciting career as a salt miner."

"It will not take long at all, dear-heart, do not worry. I will be back by midday, and we can get on your way. Then I can get back to figuring out why I am here rather than back home."

"What's it like?" he asked, suddenly curious.

"My home?" she asked, with a smile. "Bright. It is positively brimming with magic."

"Sounds nice. Maybe I could visit one day?"

She seemed slightly taken aback by that and took a moment to respond. "I rather suppose you will, yes," she said with a wry smile. "Hopefully not for a while, though."

He wasn't sure exactly what she was implying, but for some reason, the thought made him decidedly nervous.

"Well, do you need a guide to the monster? I think I can just about remember where it was," he offered.

"Oh, I felt where it was, and I am sure with my familiar, I can find it easily enough," she said, giving him a self-confident smile. "Besides, you could not keep up."

She waved merrily, winked, then took off at an astonishing pace towards the area he had found it.

"Show-off," he muttered, watching as she disappeared into the trees at the edge of the lake clearing.

He bathed in a small inlet in the lake that was somewhat secluded. As he was relaxing, one of the naiads surged over to him. "Excuse me, hunter, but you're wanted."

"Oh, is Fali back?" he asked. She had said it wouldn't be too long, but it had scarcely been half an hour.

"No, there's a gentleman here to speak with you. He said he was a royal messenger, whatever that is."

He looked at her, wide-eyed, a strange mix of both anticipation and panic filling him. That was one of the King's personal messengers, travelling far and wide through the wild territory to deliver his summons to otherwise inaccessible people.

"Is it just him, or is he with guards?" he asked in a panic, heart pounding.

"No, just him. Well, and a dryad."

The dryad's presence confused the matter even more, but he breathed a sigh of relief. If this pertained to illegal use of magic, there would be more than just mail. But if not that, what? What would they want with him? Had they somehow heard about the repairing of the shield, and so fast?

He dressed as quickly as he could, and the naiad led him to the far bank by his tent.

The man was immaculately dressed despite the journey he must have made: pressed red uniform and gold highlights, moustache pristinely groomed. Stood beside him was a dryad, her skin a chalky white with grey rings like that of a birch tree. She was even taller and more elongated than the previous one he had seen, nearly ten feet tall but skeletally thin. They both strode over as they spotted Ryheart, the man's stride imperious and self-assured, the dryad's languid and casual.

"I found this guy in the forest," the dryad informed Ryheart in a bored sort of manner. "I thought he'd make a decent mate, but the orchard mother said we absolutely must not impede him in his journey. Further, I had to ensure his successful passage because we have some sort of treaty with your King."

"Yes, quite," the man agreed with her somewhat babbling statement, holding his hand out to Ryheart. "Greetings, I am first-class postmaster Edward Nathaniel-Abingdon Rackersby II. I remind you that to lie about your identity would, in this case, constitute treason, as I speak on direct behalf of His Majesty. Do I have it on your honour as a Brittayan that you are Ryheart of no surname, hunter of the Londaya branch of the Hunter's Guild?"

"Yes. Yes, sir," he replied, sweating as the man clasped his hand and shook powerfully. He didn't know what this was about, but this was potentially huge.

"Grand. And you are currently in a hunting party with a 'Fali', of no given formal rank, are you not?"

"Err, yes?" he said, blood running cold. Did they know his tumultuous companion had performed unregistered magic somehow?

"Excellent. Is she here?"

"Not at the moment, but she'll be back in a while."

"Very well. Then I present this letter from the King's hand to yours."

"Do you know what it's about?" Ryheart asked, examining the thick paper of the envelope and the wax crest of the kingdom.

"I'm not privy to His Majesty's dealings," the messenger said with a sniff, "but I believe he wishes your help in some small matter regarding your companion. I must attend to my other duties, but this dryad will remain with you for the moment. If you have a reply, give it to the dryad, and she will ensure it gets to their grove, and from there is dictated to the King via magical channels quicker than I could return it by hand."

The dryad blinked her globe-like eyes once, seemingly in acknowledgement, but otherwise remained silent.

"I will." Ryheart nodded.

"Marvellous. I inform you that the letter will set both itself and the opener aflame if opened by anyone other than you. I bid you a good day," the postmaster said, bowing his head respectfully and then marching away after Ryheart returned a somewhat more clumsily delivered bow.

He stared at the letter in his hand. What in Brittaya had Fali got him into this time?

Chapter Twenty-Six

Purpose

Fali followed along behind the grey loping run of her familiar, weaving between trees and over roots. She had earmarked a rough location for the Nemean before she had contested with the shield. Now they were near, and the creature's life signature lost forever into the ether, her companion's more earthly senses suited better to pinpoint it.

They came across a fresh scar in the forest with a bit of searching, trees splintered and knocked over, and then to the creature.

She stared in shock. Ryheart had said the creature was gigantic, but she had presumed he was exaggerating in the way humans often did. It certainly wasn't the biggest creature she'd ever seen, not by a long shot. But it was far larger than any Nemean should have been. Abnormally so.

She approached the still creature and inspected its hide. There were faint markings ethereally upon its fur that were also unnatural. In fact, they looked distinctly like the shadow of some kind of curse. Even dead, the creature carried the ghostly feel of malodorous magic.

She swore, not bothering to disguise it in troll. Something had warped the creature, significantly increasing the corruption of the monster to the point it was physically manifest. Unfortunately, the pattern in its fur was merely the shadow of the spell-work cast upon it. It wasn't the spell itself. Consequently, it didn't provide anything she could read to reason as to its source. The feeling she had, the aura as humans generally envisioned it, was also long faded and scarcely a flicker. Not enough to give her a solid idea as to its origin. It certainly hadn't come from anything pleasant, though. However, the evident curse upon it explained how it had got through the barrier around the woods. Such a concentration of corruption, channelled properly through a spell, could pierce the shield, disrupting its flow as it did so.

She bit her lip. In company, she would have never shown such a sign of nervousness, but she allowed herself the small comfort in the absence of people to potentially perceive the weakness. When she had been pulled to the garden, she had assumed, or perhaps hoped, that it was because of something good. That the general corruption in the mundane had subsided enough that her presence had been drawn there. Potentially, to cleanse it altogether.

This, though. This was the opposite. In all her time, Fali had never seen a monster corrupted in such a manner. Had the ambient corruption in the realm become worse? So much so that even mundane creatures were warped? Surely, her people would have realised it even barred from physical entry if that were the case. And besides, the ambient eddies and flows of magic and energy around her, while limited in their ability to travel between realms, still felt relatively healthy.

The corruption of the void was still there, certainly, marring the perfection of creation. But it was a tint. A shade. Not a dominance. So, not an environmental change. At least, not a widespread one. Which meant the corruption of the beast had to be of an intent. Malicious. The remains of what seemed to be an engineered curse upon the creature lined up with that. And that did explain why she was here. Something purposefully marring creation in such a way would be enough of an affront to the fabric of reality that her heart would feel it.

While she and her people had been restrained almost exclusively to their own realm for so long, visiting the garden only in spirit, her physical core had remained in the world, hibernating, split from her soul.

She wasn't truly a creature of flesh and blood but of pure magic creation. The core that had remained was her true physical essence. Upon feeling the tug and reuniting her spirit with that core, it had formed her heart, her true sigil, and pulled magic to it. That solidified to shape her and give her physical presence. That heart showed its existence as the sigil on her cheek, a visible manifestation of the core within.

While disconcerted for various reasons, she had her first real idea as to what she should do. Why she was here. It seemed the fates had led her to pick out this specific hunt for a reason. She had presumed at the time that it was merely because it was the most expedient way for her to resolve the silly binding to Ryheart she had accidentally made. However, it seemed it was because the monster was her first step to finding why she was here.

What she didn't know was where the corruption was coming from. Fortunately, if she remembered the map they had looked over previously, she knew someone not too far away that she could consult. They had a far more down-to-earth feeling of the realm than she did. If she had felt the corruption when she was so detached, they must have noticed something too.

She sighed. It seemed she wasn't going to have time to see Ryheart home through the forest after all. Every time they had things resolved, new unseen complications were popping up.

Olyra Holloway rubbed her nose gingerly, now set thoroughly crooked where the creature had broken it. Her armoured gloves and helm had fortunately protected the best part of her skin during the explosion she had used as a last-ditch bid to kill her target. The other visible sign of their encounter that remained was her cheek. It remained pocked and still burned faintly at the thought of her foe – a permanent reminder of the lengths she would go to for her country.

She had attempted to find the hunter – Harand – who had supposedly seen her target – Fali – setting her on the trail once again. Unfortunately, there had been a complication. By the time the report came to her notice, the hunter had taken a job and left the city, unobtainable. He had, however, mentioned her companion, Ryheart. She had quite easily ferreted out information on him, and the hunt he was on. He was borderline insane to take such a bounty given his less-than-stellar standing, but debt drove people to do stupid things.

The forest's centre was a large naiad lake, and if Olyra were to set up a base camp to try to root out a monster, it would have been her first choice. A road partially circled the woods, and they'd most likely come upon it, presumably to head towards the Hunter's Guild to hand in their bounty. Presuming they survived the bounty. To that end, Olyra had asked her informants to keep an eye on the roads for the hunter. Now all she had to do was wait.

Act Two
The Supernatural

Chapter Twenty-Seven

Summons

"Loyal subject," the letter Ryheart had received said, "I am writing to you with a summons. I have received reports of a person whose description has piqued my interest. I am told that she has markings upon her eyes and cheek. These symbols bear a significance known to only a few outside of the royal family and match the description given regarding an incident reported by one of my subjects. I very much wish an audience with her."

Ryheart couldn't help but feel a slight tinge of disappointment, along with some relief. So the King wasn't interested in him. He was just his only contact with Fali. He sighed and carried on reading.

"I have been informed by the guild that this person has some degree of association with you. Indeed, they have registered as an additional member of your hunting party. If she is still in your company and matches this description, I beseech thee to convince her to present herself at the royal grounds in Londaya as soon as possible. I have also been informed you are in some trifling debt with the guild, and I understand this may cause some distress to you and impede your ability to fulfil this task. As such, I have ordered the guild to suspend your debt for a month. This will leave you free to carry out this duty. Fulfil it, and I shall wipe said debt in its entirety as a small token of my appreciation."

Reminding himself to breathe, Ryheart did his best to calm himself. He read the passage over again very carefully, making sure he had understood correctly. All his debt, gone. With a snap of the King's fingers. Even better, that would mean the money he earned for the Nemean would be something he could keep. Without crippling debt over his head, he could start making money. He could even leave the guild. Mere days ago, the thought of escape would have been a joy. But this hunt, while dangerous and terrifying and certainly not something he was about to repeat immediately, had given him a glimpse of how hunting could be. How different it was when there was something other than a blocked sewage pipe at risk. He steadied his shaking hands and finished reading.

"I cannot offer any immediate aid beyond this, other than the crest and stamp enclosed. These give you the authority to act in my stead on this matter, and will allow you access to any of my staff's lodgings upon the royal highway without cost. You will also be un-accosted upon your travels. I give you full authority to act in my name upon any matters directly involving this duty. However, I do remind you that to abuse this power for unrelated matters would be to commit treason, as would ignoring this duty. It will also allow you to request a guard escort back to the palace, though I emphasise that only if the person in question, who I am informed is registered as 'Fali' in your hunting documents, wishes so. I reiterate that she is to come entirely of her own volition and not be restrained. I will take any harm befalling her as a personal affront. I thus also ask you to keep her from injury to the best of your ability. If she were to be accosted, it would reflect poorly on our nation's hospitality and reputation. It would be regrettable if your honour as a subject of Brittaya were diminished by any harm befalling her, or an inability to convince her to present herself without coercion.

"If you are no longer in her person or believe the reports erroneous, please inform me as such.

"His Royal Highness,
"King Arendeth Brittaya VI."

Ryheart found he had been keeping his breath held throughout the reading, and he let out a soft blow of air.

Well, that was certainly a miraculous opportunity he couldn't afford to pass up, albeit one fraught with dangers. He wasn't a fan of the word treason being bandied around. Now, he just had to decide how to broach the subject to Fali.

Chapter Twenty-Eight

Partnership

Fali strolled into the camp and waved to Ryheart. Her mind was partially on other things, but she couldn't help but notice that he looked equal parts nervous and excited. She wasn't sure whether that was good or bad, on balance.

"Find what you wanted from the monster?" he asked her by way of greeting.

"Yes, I did," she said, adding with a wry smile, "and a few things I did not want to find."

"Oh?" he asked, confused.

"Someone has tampered with it. That is why it was so large. Who knows what else they have been up to?"

"Oh," he repeated, though in a more concerned tone, "that's not very good, is it?"

"No, it certainly is not," she said, before spotting the sheet of paper in his hand and narrowing her eyes. "That is not more paperwork, is it?"

"No, it isn't. It's a letter," the hunter said, looking at it like it was some precious holy relic. "A letter from the King."

"Oh, that is nice," she said, mildly curious.

"Fali! Aren't we a little blasé? It's a letter from the King! About you!"

"Well, once you have met a King or ten, the novelty wears off a bit," she explained. "What does he want with me?"

Ryheart looked at her like she'd said something morally offensive. "The King, Fali," he repeated stubbornly, "wants a word with you, in person. I don't understand how you can be so calm about that!"

"Well, all I am really interested in is that he does not violate the Fae treaties and keeps their borders intact. If he does choose to ignore said boundaries, he will not be the King for very long; I can tell you that."

"Fali!" he exclaimed in outrage. "That's basically treason!"

"He is not my King, is he?" she said with a slight grin. "Anyway, come along then. What does he want?"

He breathed out like he was calming himself, then looked at her, his green eyes serious.

"Look, I promised I'd be upfront with you and not just treat you like a tool. The King sent a letter saying that he will pay off my debt if I bring you to him. Not just the outstanding part, mind. All of it. I'd be a free man. So, please, please come with me to talk to him. I would truly appreciate it."

She pursed her lips. "I cannot come with you," she said apologetically.

"Can't? Why? You said you'd come back with me anyway! It's barely a half-hour walk from the guild to the royal estate. It's right in the centre of Londaya."

"I know, but the business with this monster is pressing. There is a guide I wish to speak to not too far from here. But it is in the exact opposite direction to Londaya."

"Fali. This is really, really important to me."

"This is more important," she replied automatically.

"Oh, so my life's irrelevant again?"

"No, no," she said with a sigh. She had perhaps said that more carelessly than she might have. "I appreciate your position. I do. How about, since we are both turning over a new leaf with regards to respecting one another, we compromise?"

"In what manner?" he asked dubiously.

"Well, I gather from the fact there is not an armed escort of guards to march me back to him, this is an invitation and not an arrest. Did he give you any specific time frame for delivering me into his company?"

"Well, not exactly," he frowned, "but he said he would suspend my debt for a month."

"Ah. Grand. Then how about you come with me on my little visit," she held up her hand as he was about to object, "we send him a letter before we leave saying you are indeed in my company and will deliver me to him within the said month, as soon as you possibly can. Then, as soon as we are done with my business, I promise you, I will come with you to see the King."

"We can make it back? Within the month?"

"Absolutely. With time to spare, even. If we are quick, we will be back by Sundalisday."

"I suppose that could work," he said, rubbing his brow.

"Well, frankly, it is that or nothing. Not unless you fancy attempting to knock me out to carry me back."

"Alright, deal," he said, holding out his hand.

"You are not bleeding, are you?" she asked, eyes narrowed. "I hate to belabour a point, but I would rather not have a repeat of the last time we formally made a deal."

He laughed at that. "No, just a good old-fashioned human handshake."

She took his hand and laughed. "Very well, then. It is a deal."

"It's not like I had a ton of choice, mind."

"At least you had a choice. You are not magically dragged along behind me."

"I guess. So where are we going?"

"Solisala Hill," she said, taking out a map and stretching it out for him to see, pointing at the spot in question. "Not too far away."

He frowned. "Err, not too far as the harpy flies, sure. But that involves going north-east, right through the Crooked Woods past the barrier. We don't want to go through that. It's an unclaimed territory. It'll be teeming with monsters. Even Fae aren't willing to live there."

"But to get to the royal highway or travel around the outer limit, it is going to take us too long to get there and then back to Londaya. Not unless you have a horse."

"No money for one. Not until we've been back to Londaya."

"If we cut straight through the Crooked Woods, we can be there in about three days. Then we will have enough time to make it back by road, even on foot. We just don't have the time to do both ways."

"Yeah, but the Crooked Woods aren't exactly a pleasant place for a stroll, are they? Even for hunters." He paused, then dryly added, "Especially not bad ones."

"So, we cut through but keep towards the edge of the woods. The strongest monsters are inevitably drawn towards the heart of their place of power, where the corruption is most intense. We can keep out of the way of anything tremendously strong. Besides, if we do come across something, I can deal with it."

"Well, I want it on record that I'm not too keen on this."

"Look, if you would rather, you can stay here with the naiads. I am sure they will happily have you. Once I am done, I will come back and pick you up."

He looked like he was contemplating for a moment. "Look, it's not that I don't trust you. But I've been charged by my King with escorting you and keeping you safe. I think at this point it's treason to leave you. It definitely is if you're harmed. I'll come. I can't exactly say I'm going to be useful, but I'll help in what way I can."

"Oh, do not worry," Fali said with a smile. "I will look after you."

"Oh yeah?" he asked, clearly dubious.

"Of course. A queen must look after their subjects, after all."

"I'm your subject?" he asked, eyebrow raised.

"Why, Ryheart," she said, hand on her chest, "were you not aware you were in my service already?"

Chapter Twenty-Nine

Blood

After Fali had said goodbye to all the naiads – literally all of them – the pair packed up and set off towards the nearest node that would allow them to pass safely through the barrier and out of the forest. The idea of entering unclaimed territory was distinctly preying on Ryheart's mind, so he started a conversation to distract himself.

"So, who is this friend of yours?" he asked as they picked their way through the trees.

"Oh, you know. He is an old acquaintance," Fali replied. He couldn't help but feel she was somewhat evasive with such a vague reply.

"Okay? Fae, human?" he pressed.

"Well, neither. He is, well, technically – technically, mind – sort of a monster."

"A monster?" he exclaimed, incredulous. "You might have said something before we set off!"

"Only technically, Ryheart," she said in a mollifying tone.

"How the hell can he only technically be a monster? Either it eats people, or it doesn't!"

"Well, do not take it personally, dear-heart, but your species does have a tendency towards stabbing and mounting on a wall first, asking questions later. By your textbooks, he is a monster. I would not classify him as such. He just looks monstrous."

"Alright. What is it then?"

"Are you sure you want to know?"

"I think I probably better, yes."

"Well, and you have some very undeserved negative connotations to the word, Ryheart, so do not panic, but the most accurate human description would be a dragon."

He stopped dead in his tracks. "A dragon," he repeated, dumbstruck. He couldn't help but briefly think back to Harand warning him about magical beings causing trouble even when they were trying to help, but he pushed it down. The idea of Harand's paranoia affecting his mind made him feel sick, especially when he was just re-evaluating his attitude towards Fae.

"Yes. A grand dragon," she informed him.

"I don't even know what that is, but it sounds bad."

"Oh, not at all," she said calmly. "He is actually a very nice chap, once you get past all the teeth and scales."

"That's a lot of things to 'get past', Fali," he said flatly.

"Well, I am sure you will manage," she said with a winsome flash of her teeth. "You are a very amiable young man."

"Well, I hope you're right because if we did have to fight a dragon, I'd be absolutely bloody bobbins," he said with a nervous laugh.

"You have more talent than you realise, I think," she said, giving him a warm look that brought a slight flush to his cheeks. "Taking down the Nemean, much less an enhanced one, was very impressive."

"I did feel like I was finally doing something right when I was fighting. Like I belonged. Especially when I delivered the winning stroke, I felt a surge of power."

She stared at him unblinking, and her eyes took on a green swirl of colour, her sudden avid attention making him feel uncomfortable for a different reason. "When you say a surge of power, are we talking metaphorically?"

"Kind of. I don't know. I charged him with a spear, and I just felt, sort of, an explosion of power erupt from me. Like adrenaline, but crazy strong."

She stared at him again, her head cocked this time. "I suppose I did grant you my blood," she murmured to herself.

"What?" he asked. "With the oath? We broke that, right?"

"We broke the oath itself, yes. But you do still have a drop of my magic within you."

"Right, and...?"

"A long time ago, there was an order of knights. The Realm-sworn."

Ryheart frowned. He had no idea where this wild tangent was going, but that name stirred a dim recollection.

"My mother told me a fairy tale about those," he said, memories coming unbidden, the sudden intrusion of a moment he had forgotten bittersweet. "They were human, but they held the power of magic, stolen from the monsters they slew."

She looked at him in mild surprise. "The magic part's right. They did not steal it, though. I gave it to them."

"What?" he asked, stunned. "Weren't they around before the cataclysm? Back when only the supernatural monsters existed?"

"Oh, yes."

"But that was millennia ago, wasn't it?"

"I suppose it was, yes."

He just stared at her.

"What?" she asked mildly after he didn't respond. "I mentioned I was quite old, did I not?"

"There's old, and there's old. That's ancient!"

She narrowed her eyes at him. "It is rude to call a lady ancient, Ryheart," she said primly.

He couldn't help but laugh at that, despite the mind-boggling nature of what she was saying. "How about archaic?" he said with a grin.

"You are on thin ground, Ryheart," she said in a flinty voice, though her lips had a slight curve to them that suggested pantomime.

"Alright. So, what do magical knights have to do with this?"

"Well, as I said. I gave them their abilities."

A sudden spark of intuition hit him. "And did that involve blood in some capacity?"

"I blessed them with the magic of my lifeblood, yes. My blessing gave them a connection to me that invigorated their spirit. It gave them better stamina and strength, kept them free of disease."

"And I have that blessing?" he asked, a thousand questions in his head.

"No. You do not have my blessing; I cannot accidentally give that. You do have my blood inside you, though. That carries its own power."

"What, so I'm magic now or something?"

"Not exactly magic, no. Humans just do not have the capacity for it, at least not naturally. With training, though, my knights could use the spark of my magic within them to ignite their life force and manifest their own unique abilities. It is possible you managed to perform a very crude burst of this instinctively."

"Am I going to get arrested for being unregistered magic the moment I go back home?"

"No, no. It was scarcely a drop. I cannot even sense it. Even if you were using your aura, it is distinctly human. My blood only awakens it. Besides, I would not worry about it. Without my blessing to keep the spark inside you, it will inevitably fade. I daresay it had already burnt out from when you first used it. If you used it at all."

"Oh," he said, and he couldn't help but feel slightly disappointed. Though, uncanny abilities were probably an extra complication he didn't need in his life.

"Come along then, Ryheart," she said, signalling for them to start walking again. "We do have a schedule to keep, after all."

Chapter Thirty

Crooked

The pair walked through the little bubble in the barrier at the node on its outskirts. Their first step into the dangers of unclaimed territory. They had camped under its protective glow and were starting fresh, though Ryheart's sleep had been somewhat marred by the trial ahead of them.

Even barely inside them, he could feel that these woods were nothing like the comparatively pleasant ones they had travelled previously. The trees here were gnarled and twisted, and the branches reached out graspingly towards them. The sun was trying its best to reach them, but it was sickly pale through trees that jealously blocked the light from each other, desperate to grasp whatever they could for themselves.

Fali walked slightly ahead of him, calm but clearly focused and bubbling with intensity. Her head regularly swept the area, her eyes a wary yellow. She scarcely paid attention when Ryheart tried to talk to her, seemingly listening to some far-off noise he couldn't hear himself.

While wary, her alertness carried an air of commanding control to it, and he couldn't help but feel somewhat calmed by her presence. Nevertheless, he was still on edge, jumping at each slight movement, making out faces and figures in the gnarled trees. It took him some time to put a finger on what felt so off, and then he realised it wasn't what he could hear that was strange, but what he couldn't. There was no birdsong. There was the low moan of the wind, the occasional snapped branch under his foot – nothing else.

"Alright, listen," Fali murmured, "given we are somewhat skirting the edge of the forest, we shouldn't meet anything too powerful, but the weaker things can sometimes be the most deceptive. If you see something you do not understand, tell me. Do not stray from my path; do not so much as pick up a twig without my say so. I know you humans have that pesky curiosity burning so brightly in your hearts, but this is not the place for it. If cats cannot get away from curiosity unscathed here, humans certainly cannot."

"Look but don't touch, got it," he said with forced joviality, his voice unconsciously hushed from the oppressive sense of danger.

"Looking is not always a good idea, either."

"Can I talk?" he asked in a hushed voice as they picked their way through the dense growth. "The silence is going to weigh on me a touch."

"Yes, but quietly. I need to keep my ears open, as well as my familiars."

Ryheart sometimes forgot about her lop-eared familiar, which wasn't helped by the fact he couldn't always see it. He felt a new appreciation for the little creature as it occasionally darted into view ahead of them, a streak of grey helping guide their path.

"He's a handy little chap, isn't he?" Ryheart commented.

"I rather like having him around, yes," she said with a small but warm smile, before her gaze returned to the path ahead. "If I tell you to hush, forgive my manners. There will be a good reason."

"Alright, will do," he confirmed, lowering his tone to scarcely a whisper, though she didn't seem to have trouble hearing him.

"I gather you do not know much about supernatural creatures?" she asked, her voice a low murmur, though not as quiet as his.

"Not really, no. I only have a mundane hunting licence. I don't exactly hunt spooky ghosts or anything."

"Ah," she replied simply, her tone neutral.

"I beat the Nemean, though, right? And that was ludicrously strong. That should stand me in good stead, right?"

"To an extent. Strength is not the only supernatural concern, though."

As they walked further, they came alongside a clearing, a large patch of flowers within. They were dazzlingly bright, each petal exquisite. They were an explosion of colour amid the forest's oppressive gloom.

"Damn, they're pretty," he said, feeling a strong desire to get a closer look.

"Do not look at them too long, and do not breathe in too deeply," Fali said in a quiet but firm tone, "and absolutely do not touch them."

"I won't. They're awfully pretty, though," Ryheart said, feeling a strange compulsion to frolic through them.

"Awful is the right word," she said softly without elaboration, her eyes focused elsewhere.

As they walked by, a sickly repulsive smell wafted over the heady scent of the flowers, and he gagged a little. Risking a glance back while they were still close, he picked out tiny fragments of bone within the plants' bedding.

"Are there dead animals in there?" he asked, disgusted.

"Yes," his flame-haired guide murmured. "The pollen paralyses, and then the flowers break you down for fertiliser. It takes days, and you will be awake for it and in agony until something vital dissolves."

"I thought you said things in the outskirts weren't too dangerous!" he exclaimed softly, tearing his eyes away.

"No, I said things were not powerful. They are extremely dangerous. They just rely on deceit. These flowers have fed upon corrupted soil and become aberrations themselves. I detest them. If I had time, I would raze them from existence, but I would have to tear up every root individually to stop them from growing back within a moon. Its pollen would attract all sorts of creatures here to try to protect the colony too. They are positively vile."

As she spoke, she lifted her foot over a vine that lay on the floor. There was a brief glow as a pattern of magical lines briefly shimmered over her boots, and a sharp blade materialised from the heel. She slammed it down on the vine, and there was a screech that rang in the air, and then the growth slithered back into the woods, snake-like. He eyed the blade as it vanished, then glanced at the empty scabbard she had belted on her waist. If some sort of magic could produce an edge from her heel, who knew what she could create from the sheath.

They carried on cautiously, intermittently stopping or changing their path as she pointed out or skirted around some unknown danger. Occasionally she picked up a rock and hurled it into the trees, producing a panicked slithering and twitch of branches from something creeping towards them.

The occasional wolf-like howl rang out, though its cry was shrill, almost like a flute. Gradually the noise got more frequent, and, Ryheart thought, nearer.

"Flrrgsmsh!" Fali cursed, then sighed in an almost resigned fashion.

"What's wrong?" he asked, worried.

"There is a pack of snaggle-hounds following us. I was hoping we could skirt around, but they have picked our scent up, and they will not lose it."

"Alright," he asked, steeling himself, "what's the play?"

"They are spirits possessing dead wood warped into creatures. They are not too much of a problem in and of themselves, but they are noisy buggers, and they will attract all sorts of unwanted attention. Exorcising them individually would take forever, but I have sent my familiar to find their totem tree. If I burn it, they will all be forced out. To that end, I need to leave you here while I chase them away. I cannot herd them and keep you safe."

His heart virtually stopped at that. "Fali, I'm way out of my depth. If you leave me alone, I'll be dead before you're out of sight."

"I am not just abandoning you, Ryheart," she snapped irritably. She clicked her fingers, and a bright spark of magic stood at her fingertip. In about five minutes, she traced a circle on the ground and filled it with intricate symbols. It was like her campsite spell, though much smaller in scale.

"Alright, step inside," she commanded.

He did so gingerly, the circle just about wide enough for him to stand in. Once he did, Fali placed her palm to its edge, and a shimmering blue sphere enclosed him, much brighter than the prior one.

"It is much stronger than the large one I do," she informed him, "and it can take quite a lot of punishment. If I feel anything attack it, I'll immediately come back. The snaggle-hounds cannot stray too far from their stump, so it must be nearby. At most, I should be about an hour. Generally, other creatures would not enter a snaggle's territory, but if somethings caught your scent, it is feasible they might risk it. I shall not be long."

He nodded nervously, and with that, she turned and ran forward, arms over her head, making a strange braying call. He caught a glimpse of a grotesquely twisted creature of bark charging at her. Without slowing her pace, she slapped it in its jowls with a burning hand. It yelped in alarm and ran into the trees, accompanied by a chorus of angry howls as the pack fled. Fali followed them, and he was left alone in the pale glow, only the shimmer of blue separating him from all the monsters of the forest.

Chapter Thirty-One

Guide

Ryheart sat in his protective bubble, with barely enough space to move. Fali hadn't exactly made it for comfort. He peered through the shimmer of the shield, nervously keeping an eye out. He trusted Fali. At least, he thought he did. But being left in the middle of a hostile forest where he had virtually zero chance of defending himself wasn't the most pleasant experience.

He snapped his head around as he heard a branch break, eyes straining to see what it might be. There was the faintest flicker of movement, but whether it was the wind or something alive, he couldn't say. Eyes fixed on the spot; he saw the shrubbery moving. That was definitely something living.

Should he call out to them? He didn't think he'd be likely to scare it off unless it was just an animal. But if it were an animal, it would do no harm. If it weren't, shouting would probably just attract its attention.

The movement stopped, and the forest stood still. Heart ringing in his ears and breath caught, he stood frozen to the spot, but the signs of life didn't come back. He was about to relax when there was a sudden burst of movement, and Fali erupted from the bushes.

"Gods, Fali!" he exclaimed, relieved and angry at once. "What were you doing arsing about in the bushes! You nearly gave me a heart attack!"

"I thought I saw something in there, so I was investigating," Fali said, eyes her neutral blue. "Couldn't find anything, though."

Ryheart frowned. There had been something there; he was sure of it. At least, he had been sure of it. Maybe his nerves had been playing him more than he thought.

"Did you get rid of the hounds?" he asked. He didn't have any solid track of time, but he didn't think it had been quite an hour.

"I chased them away, yes."

"Didn't you say you needed to burn them out, or they'd just come back?"

"Yes, yes," she said dismissively, "that's what I meant. Come along, let's get going."

He sighed and stood up, picking his bag back up, having used it as an impromptu seat. "Where's the rabbit?" he asked.

"Oh, our guide. He's off finding a path. I know where he is, don't worry."

He followed as she led the way, her previous caution seemingly evaporated. She looked downright careless, in fact.

"You are keeping an eye out?" he asked, her seeming contented state having the opposite effect on his own feeling of safety.

"Oh, nothing else sentient will come into this territory. They wouldn't dare."

"Because you chased the hounds out?"

"That's right. I'm keeping watch still, though, don't worry your pretty little head about it," she said, patting him like he was a child.

Her pace quickened, and she was almost skipping over the fallen detritus on the forest floor. Despite her short legs, Ryheart found himself virtually jogging to keep pace with her.

He frowned as they went. The trees seemed to be getting denser, the light paler.

"Are we going deeper?" he asked, slowing his pace a little. They were supposed to be sticking to the edge of the forest, not cutting right through it.

"Well, we wasted time with those hounds, didn't we? Got to make it up."

"That was barely half an hour!" he exclaimed. "Not worth risking our bloody lives over! I mean, any more than we already are doing?"

"Well, we've committed now," she said with a shrug. "You can either come with me or stay here by yourself. Your choice!"

"Oi! Fali!" he shouted as she took off into the forest, even faster. He cursed angrily. What the hell was her problem? They'd just been starting to bond as friends, too.

He didn't like this. He scowled at her as she disappeared into the trees. Swearing again, he set off after her at a jog. What other choice did he have? One way or another, he was utterly dependent on her right now.

Fali watched as the last stump in the snaggle-hounds' territory burned away, the hounds themselves collapsing as their connection to the physical world turned to ash. It had taken a little longer than she had anticipated to chase them to their yard. They had left the limits of their usual hunting grounds for the rare chance to rend human flesh, and had ventured into something else's territory. That was risky business, even for a monster. They tended to be just as protective of their territory against other creatures as they were to humans. Snaggle-hounds were practically – and literally, in fact – brainless, and the primary instinct to hunt had likely driven them beyond caution.

She made sure the stump was irrevocably aflame and then turned back, padding silently through the forest. The last thing she wanted was to attract anything else's attention. The glamour from Ryheart kept her magical presence suppressed, and she kept even the human aura she now gave off to a flicker. The shield she had made would keep Ryheart's presence masked, only the faintest magical glimmer of the protection present to only the most astute eyes.

That, of course, didn't stop anything from simply chancing across Ryheart, or being attracted by the snaggle-hounds' yapping before she chased them away. She hadn't felt any form of pressure against the shield, though, so they seemed to have avoided undue attention.

She felt the tell-tale pulse ahead that her familiar was signalling her with some concern, and she shortly came upon the place she had left the hunter.

She swore. She didn't bother disguising it in troll. Partially because of the severity of her alarm. Partially because there was no one there to hear it. Her shield stood holding solemn vigil over nothing but the leaves and the air.

Briefly, she felt confused, then annoyed, then settled on determined purpose. The bloody hunter had left. A downside of suppressing her aura for camouflage was that it had also dulled her ability to sense others. She hadn't felt him leave, or anything else nearby.

She'd thought his sense of self-preservation, or at the very least his fear, would keep him from doing anything foolish. Examining the ground, she saw two sets of footprints leading away from the shield and swore again. Focusing, she could feel the faintest presence of something foul and magical in the air. The fading malodorous aura lingered unpleasantly.

Making the situation even worse, she could feel the live presence of neither hunter nor creature. She swore once more and dropped all her magical restraints, letting her awareness pour out, scouting the surrounding area. Caution to the wind, she took off along the trail of footprints, her familiar loping ahead of her. Whoever Ryheart had left with, she doubted they were as pleasant company as she.

Chapter Thirty-Two

Imposter

Ryheart didn't know how long they had been jogging, but he did know he was bloody fed up with it. Fali, for her part, had stayed just far enough ahead of him that he hadn't lost her. However, he also didn't have any sort of chance to stop her.

At first, he had felt terrified about their barrelling through the forest with abandon, but for whatever reason, nothing threatening had come near them despite their lack of caution. That, combined with his growing exhaustion and focus on keeping up with his evasive guide, had given him little time to focus on his unease. He just had to hope Fali knew what she was doing, because he was in her realm of experience now, and, well, he certainly didn't.

Finally, they came to a wide clearing, and Fali waited ahead of him. With relief, he stopped, taking deep breaths.

"Gods wept, I'm knackered," he complained. "It's a good job we didn't run into anything, because I'd be too tired to do anything about it."

Fali smiled at that in a manner he found decidedly unnerving. "Well, we can rest in here," she said, pointing to a burrow dug into the ground, a wide maw open in the earth.

"Err, I'd rather not get in a monster hole, thanks."

"Oh, don't worry," she said calmly, "other monsters won't come in. They wouldn't dare."

"Other monsters?" he exclaimed sharply.

"Oh, a slip of the tongue." She waved it off flippantly. "I just mean while I'm here."

"You hate being referred to as a monster," he said, taking a step back. "You've been acting odd, too."

"You're just grumpy from exhaustion."

A small detail clicked in his mind. "Where's your bag? You had your pack with you when you left." Now they'd stopped, and she was in question, other minor discrepancies jumped to the forefront of his mind. "Your eyes haven't changed once since you came back, either."

Fali looked at him for a moment, then she blinked and suddenly said eyes were green. It was almost, he thought, as if she had just realised they were supposed to change.

He felt a dreadful feeling in his stomach. Fali's eyes didn't even change like that. The colours swirled together like an artist mixing paint. Slowly, he drew his sword, holding it like a ward in front of him.

"Oh, and I nearly got you into my burrow," she sighed like she was mildly disappointed. She cricked her neck as she spoke, and it lolled sickeningly, resting on her shoulder. "Ah, well, near enough, I suppose. I did wonder how long it would take you."

A wave of revulsion hit Ryheart as her head bobbed as she spoke, then her head distended with the cracking of bones resetting. Her neck extended, and rows of needle-like teeth split her face into a hideous grin.

"Your little fairy friend was far too complicated to copy perfectly based on your flaky memories. Fortunately, I managed to get you all the way here anyway."

He watched, skin tingling and rooted to the spot as her limbs stretched into pale spider-like legs, and her elongated spine bent over to bring her to a low crawl. It was pale and hairless now, its skin grey and coated in a sickly mucus. It's back arched above the ground, suspended ten feet in the air by half a dozen pincer-like thin legs. A wide maw grinned hideously at its prey, rimmed with jagged teeth, beady black eyes staring unblinkingly at him.

The vile thing slowly advanced, tongue flicking in the air.

Tearing his eyes away from the hideous spectacle, Ryheart found his legs again. Sword in hand, he turned and fled blindly back into the trees. The thing made the Nemean look like a house cat.

The thing cackled behind him, and he heard its legs snapping at the ground. He ran as fast as he could, branches slapping his face and roots threatening to trip him. He was tired from their travels, though, and he already felt he couldn't run for long. He tried to dislodge his bag from his back as he ran. That, at least, would give him a little less weight. The sword in his hand made it extremely awkward to shake off, but he didn't want to give up his only real weapon either. He stumbled slightly as he pulled one shoulder free, and yelped as something behind knocked him to the floor, his sword clattering away in the fall.

Rolling over awkwardly, one of its crooked legs pinioned him to the floor, pressing into his chest through his armour. He wiggled frantically, but it kept him firmly pinned to the ground, cackling.

"Oh, Ryheart," it cooed in a rasping voice, still faintly carrying the hint of Fali's lyrical tone.

Saliva flecked him, hot and rancid as it spoke, and he winced. If he could just get free of that leg, maybe he could get back to his feet.

Taking a breath, he managed to squirm his arm free from under him. Pulling his dagger, he jammed it into the limb that pinned him.

It shrieked in alarm, and he briefly felt a rush of adrenaline as he felt the weight lifted from him. Before he could even get to his feet, though, the stabbed limb curled around his leg. He yelled in alarm as it lifted him clear off the floor, then swung him wildly through the air, slamming him into the ground. He gasped involuntarily as the air was forced out of his lungs, leaving him desperately winded. Before he could get his breath, it lifted him back up where he hung limply, blood dribbling down his arm as its claws dug in.

"Now now, let's not get too rambunctious," it chided, clearly enjoying its prey's desperation as a thin tongue licked across its jagged teeth. "We wouldn't want to spoil the meat, would we? If you behave yourself, I might even kill you before I eat you."

His mind raced, trying to find a way out of his desperate situation, but he found none. It raised him higher, ready to tenderise him against the ground again when his heart leapt.

Fali burst through the trees in a violent charge from behind them, the creature seemingly so absorbed by its prey that it hadn't noticed her. At least, it looked like Fali. Please, gods, let it actually be Fali this time, he prayed.

He caught a glimpse of the Fae's face, eyes blazing with fury. She leapt through the air, and the creature noticed her presence. It half turned to face her, yanking Ryheart wildly through the air as it did, seemingly to use him as a shield.

Fali cleared him with her leap, but as her feet passed, there was a flash of light, and the bladed heels appeared. Ryheart dropped to the floor with a thud, its stabbing leg severed completely and still stuck in his arm.

The creature shrieked furiously, and Ryheart scrambled to his feet. Recovered from its sudden shock, Ryheart yelled as a burning pain seared his arm. The shifter tore its detached limb free with its mouth, gouging a chunk of flesh from him as it came loose.

"Watch out!" he cried as the creature swung at his saviour, using its severed limb to swipe violently at her. She reacted and rolled back with the blow, but not quite fast enough, clearly caught off guard by its sudden extension of range and sheer violence. She stumbled back as it knocked her off balance, leaving her unable to act momentarily.

Ryheart rushed forward to try to slam the monster off its feet to help her, but it jumped nimbly back and shoved him with another long-reaching leg, sending him tumbling towards his ally. Fali had been in the process of recovering and launching a counter of her own. Now instead, she had to pull back and pirouette out of the way to avoid colliding with him. As she did, the creature stabbed at his unprotected back, and he saw Fali's eyes flash amber. She interposed herself between the two shielding him, and its blow instead hit her full force, sending her careening back. As she fell, the creature dived on top of her, its remaining legs all wrapped around her face. The impact sent Fae and beast tumbling and rolling interlocked together in a flail of limbs. A rapid series of snapping bones crunched as they fell, and Ryheart picked himself up to find himself staring at two Falis. Both stood across from each other, on their feet and staring each other down, eyes a wary yellow.

Chapter Thirty-Three

Doppel

Ryheart briefly considered he might just be seeing double as he stared at the pair, borne out of vain hope rather than any conviction.

"How dare you take my form, you filthy creature!" the left Fali exclaimed, sounding affronted the creature had the impertinence to masquerade as her.

"How dare I? How dare you?" the right exclaimed.

"Are you alright, Ryheart?" the first called. "I would rather not take my eyes off this beast."

"Yeah, fine," he called, looking dubiously between the pair. While before, with the clarity of hindsight, there had been dozens of little details that were ever so slightly wrong, now the couple looked identical even with his most intense scrutiny. At least from afar, the transformation was beyond any hope of distinguishing between them. Even the tone of voice and the subtleties of the way she held herself were perfectly matched. Two familiars sat between their masters, staring at each other and flickering out of existence.

"I'm going to come closer and get a better look," he said, picking his sword up where it had fallen.

"Do not!" the first to speak exclaimed in alarm.

"Ha, see that! Clearly, she is the monster," the other replied immediately.

"No, I just do not want you killing him when he comes close enough for you to snap his neck. He is a bloody foolish child who does not know any better! Listen to me, Ryheart, stay away. If you come closer, you are dead."

"Your bag!" Ryheart exclaimed, a sudden idea popping into his head only to be immediately disappointed. Neither of them wore it now.

"She cut it off while we were tumbling, dear-heart," one of them explained, nodding towards the fallen bag.

He made his way over to it warily, keeping an eye on them both as he did so.

"If you are the real me, why do you not just attack me since you know I am a monster?" the right Fali asked.

"Because that silly idiot will get involved, and you will have plenty of chance to break him in two before I can dispose of you. I am somewhat fond of him, so I would rather avoid that if possible," her counterpoint explained huffily. "Why are you not?"

"The same answer," the right replied somewhat irreverently.

Ryheart stooped over and fished his book out from the pack, having somewhat foolishly redistributed it into her share of the gear, not having expected to be separated from her.

He managed to find it rooting around blindly, stepping back with pack and book in hand once he retrieved it.

He opened the book to a random page and spoke as he studied the two. "Dolati, I need help. How do I identify between a monster and someone it's copied?"

"That depends on what kind of creature it is, dear," the book replied calmly. "There are a few that copy the form of others."

"There's lots of snapping of bones and stuff when it changes," Ryheart informed the tome. "It sounds biological. I think it was also watching me for a while too. It turned into Fali before it saw her, but it was imperfect. It was after it touched her that it became perfect."

"Ah. That would be a doppelganger then," Dolati decided. "They copy via a psychic intrusion. If it was copying based on your second-hand memories, that would lead to it being incomplete in its transformation. Direct contact would allow it to copy someone far more convincingly. How long has it been with her?"

"I don't know. Can't be more than a few minutes, though."

"Good. The bond they have gets stronger over time, so they should still have some knowledge it does not possess. It is likely still relying on the surface level."

"Oh, no, no, no," the left one protested.

"Getting worried there, shifter?" the right replied coyly.

"No, I just refuse to go through some farce where he attempts to 'ask something only I would know'. For starters, we have only known each other for a few days. All he has is surface knowledge!"

"That's a pretty flimsy excuse," Ryheart said, beginning to suspect the left Fali of being the imposter.

"Oh, bugger you both!" the suspected shifter replied, stamping her foot tempestuously.

"How can you not tell the difference between us?" the right demanded. "Look at her; she is like a petulant child. When I stamp my foot, it looks imperial."

"How do I kill it?" he asked his paper guide.

"Intensely hot fire will destroy them, and something vorpally sharp will damage them in a manner that they cannot recover from without taking on another body. If you pierce its stomach, you will disable its ability to transform until it can remove the intrusion."

"Vorpally sharp?" he asked.

"Magically and physically sharp, like my boots," the left Fali supplied. "Being maimed by that would damage you, me, or any other creature that exists too, though, so let us not."

"Guess it's fire, then," he said decisively, taking out his flint and steel. "You mentioned that the barrier at the lake had fire in it, and you survived that, so the real one of you should be okay."

"Please," the left one spoke again with a roll of her eyes, "she said intensely hot, Ryheart. Your little tinderbox is hardly going to do the trick."

Chapter Thirty-Four

Fairy

Ryheart eyed the pair before him. He had identified what the monster was. He had even determined how to kill them. Unfortunately, what he didn't know was which one to kill. The longer he took, the better it would become at copying his Fae friend, too.

"If it helps," the right one supplied eagerly, "doppels smell faintly reminiscent of blackberries."

"Is that right?" Ryheart asked the book, an eyebrow raised. "Do doppelgangers smell like blackberries?"

"Well, yes," the book said, "if you have a sense of smell on par with a canine. You will have trouble with your limited senses."

"Bugger. Well?" Ryheart asked the left one. "Would a shifter try to help me identify it?"

"It is not helping you, you silly child! It gave you some advice you could not possibly take advantage of to make itself sound less culpable. I did not suggest it because it is a waste of breath," she snapped in response. "We could also let it mate with you and see whether its eggs hatch in your belly. That is not a particularly helpful suggestion, though, is it?"

Ryheart grimaced at the less than pleasant image. "Well, all that's left is the stabbing thing," he said.

"Oh, I would survive something so mundane, do not worry,"

the right one said piously. "It would hurt, of course, but we must make sacrifices."

"Well?" he asked the other.

"Do not be ridiculous," she snapped. "No, it will not kill me. It will leave you completely open to her killing you, though, especially if I am busy faffing about dislodging a weapon from my gut. Even if you do not manage to pierce me, it will still give her plenty of opportunities to murder you. The only reason you are still alive is thus far you have been sensible enough to keep your distance."

"Well, I don't have any other option, 'Fali'."

"Listen to me, Ryheart," she replied, staring into his eyes, a mixture of a wary yellow and an aggravated crimson, "she is far faster now she has my form. You will be dead before you can react. Especially if you are focused on stabbing me with that ineffectual butter-knife."

He sighed and steeled himself, stepping forward, sword raised.

"Such a shame we do not have a source of fire, is it not?" the right one said pleasantly. "That would save us all this bother."

The left one's eyes lit up at that and narrowed slightly. "Wait! I can prove she is the shifter," she proclaimed.

"How?"

"If she lets me approach and I touch her, I can broadcast her thoughts. It will leave me completely defenceless once I start the spell, but at least you will have a chance if you know who to stab."

"Sound alright?" he asked the counterpart.

"Why, of course," she said. "Sounds like the best situation to me."

Ryheart nodded his head. He was pretty sure the left one was the monster and didn't know what game it was playing, but he was relieved to have a chance to avoid accidentally stabbing his partner.

The offending Fali sauntered across, arms raised above her head, making a clear point she wasn't threatening the other, then very slowly reached up and laid her hand on the other's cheek.

"There is one little thing before I start my spell," she said almost nervously, another thing at odds with the real Fali's ineffable confidence.

"Yeah? What's that?" the other asked, sounding utterly sure of herself.

"You know how we are both Fairy Queens and do not have any source of fire?"

"Yeah?"

"You should have taken the time to dig a little deeper, you know," the first said, almost lovingly stroking her cheek, a smile on her face.

"Ryheart," the right said exasperatedly, "she clearly cannot truly do magic, so she is wasting time. Come put her out of her misery."

"Oh, that is not it at all," the left said calmly. "It is just, when you were trying to convince Ryheart that I am not a fairy?" Her tone became a resolute whisper, and her eyes shone with fiery heat. "You were absolutely right. I am not a fairy."

There was a sudden surge as if a power building inside her hand was suddenly let loose, and a roar of flame burst from the palm. The right Fali shrieked with alarm and tried to tug herself away, but some invisible but inescapable force kept her fixed by her cheek.

Ryheart winced. Even from a distance, he felt the heat as an inferno engulfed the pair. The captured Fali cried and warped, making horrible cracking noise as it panicked and desperately tried to escape. No matter what it attempted, it stayed fixed to the other. She stretched and twisted into horrible misshapen forms to no avail as the fire bellowed, until she reduced to ash with a deathly scream.

The other Fali bathed in the flame a moment, then stepped forth from it, her face still stony. The fire abruptly died, leaving only ash and flickering embers. Hair glossy and unaffected, naked save the soot-caked boots on her feet, she was otherwise untouched by the flame. Her scabbard had survived the heat too, having fallen to the ground as the belt that had held it burnt.

"Are you okay?" Ryheart asked after a moment, stunned.

Before answering, she bent down and retrieved the scabbard, brushing off a few flecks of dirt and soot. "No, I am not alright, as it happens," she said irritably. "I liked that dress."

He snorted and couldn't help but laugh at the absurdity. "But you're okay, yeah?"

"Oh, yes, I suppose so. Hand me my bag, would you? It is only fun being naked by choice."

He retrieved it for her and kept his eyes averted as he handed it over. "It is a good job the silly thing was only semi-competent and did not manage to delve too deep into my memory, is it not? It had copied the illusion of my magic without actually understanding what it was copying. Fortunately, it had not realised I could create fire. Otherwise, it would never have let me get close enough to it to hold it in place and give me time to concentrate a strong enough blaze. If I would have attacked it from far away, I do not know that I could have stopped it from getting to you first."

"Oh, gods," he said, looking at his sword, guiltily, "I'm sorry about the whole stabbing thing."

"Oh, that is fine. Call it a learning experience," the Fae said dismissively. "You were only doing what you thought best. It was not best as it happens; in fact, it was patently unwise. But it is the thought that counts, I suppose."

"What, err, what's the plan?" he asked, looking around nervously. They were right in the heart of the malevolent forest now.

"Well, we are so deep in now, we might as well carry on in a straight line to the edge of the forest. Then we can get onto a proper road and take a tiny detour to chat to my scaly friend. After that, we get right back onto the road in the other direction and beeline to Londaya, so you can introduce me to your King and get your reward."

"Sounds good. I'm sorry I left the shield."

"Well, I said not to leave until I came back, and I did come back as far as you knew, so I cannot blame you."

"Are we going to set off now?"

Fali studied the bit of sky visible through the trees, then shook her head. "It is getting towards late afternoon, and we do not want to be travelling at night. We would be best served resting here and then starting early tomorrow. As distasteful as squatting in a monster's abode is, we are better off staying here, where we know it is comparatively safe."

"Actually in its burrow?" Ryheart exclaimed in alarm.

"Just at the entrance. No other creatures will come to a doppelganger's lair, so it is about the best place we could be. I will set up spell-work to mask our presence, and its stench will stay lingering for weeks."

They walked the short way back to the den, and now the adrenaline of danger had worn off his entire body felt sore.

Fali set up a little barrier within the entrance to keep their presence hidden, and he felt immeasurably grateful for its protection.

The earthy walls of the burrow gave way to dark stone and were decidedly unpleasant. Fali briefly disappeared into the dark of its far recesses, returning after a short time. Whatever was back there, she didn't light anything beyond the immediate entrance up. Ryheart was most certainly not about to nosy at what a doppel's inner nest looked like. Just the entrance was uninviting enough.

They only spoke occasionally in low tones, the surroundings lending a gloomy vibe. Ryheart got into his bedroll early, but despite the relative safety, Fali didn't even take her half an hour. Ryheart watched her standing in the entrance, a silent sentinel guarding against the monsters beyond, till he finally drifted to a fitful sleep.

Chapter Thirty-Five

Departure

Ryheart woke with a start to find Fali stood in the exact same position she had been in when he had gone to sleep.

"Morning, Ryheart," she greeted him in a low tone as he roused himself, without so much as turning her head towards him.

"Morning. Any bother?"

"None at all. Clearly, the things here know to give this place a wide berth."

"Yeah, I can see why," he said dryly, rubbing his still-sore neck.

"Well, there is some extra benefit, too. I have a way to mask your scent, which will keep most things from finding you unless they can sense your spirit magically. And if they can, they will hopefully think a doppel is about and stay away."

"Oh, good."

"There is a teensy catch," she informed him.

"What's that?"

"Well, it involves smearing this over yourself," she said, holding a small pouch out and extending it to him. "I got it from the back of the cave."

"...What is it?" he asked hesitantly, eying the gloopy substance suspiciously.

"Doppelganger goo. It is what their skin is like while they are not taking any form. It helps keep them mutable."

He quickly retracted the hand he had been reaching out. "'Doppelganger goo'," he repeated.

"Well, doppelganger exuviae technically, since it is from their skin moulting. But, well, look at it. Goo is a less misleading term."

"And I have to rub it on myself?"

"Well, that depends," she said with a light shrug. "How many monsters do you want trying to eat you today? If you are fine with the number being higher than zero, then by all means, do not."

"Alright, alright," he said tetchily. Sometimes she was flippant to the point of rudeness.

He dipped his hand into the substance. It was cold and runny but clung to his skin in a way that made his hair stand on edge. He lifted a bit towards his nose to smell.

"I would not," she advised sagely. "You would be better off just putting it on without thinking about it. You can only make it less pleasant for yourself."

He sighed and slathered it across his arms and cheeks. It was thoroughly unpleasant.

"Alright, done," he said, holding the rest of it out to her. She took it and tied it back into its little pouch.

"Wait, are you not going to use it too?" he asked.

"I do not need it," she said with a wave of the hand. "I do not have a scent anything will recognise."

"Oh, just me then. Great," he said sarcastically.

"Ah, the woes of being a smelly human," she said with a theatrical sigh and a grin.

The pair started back out through the doppelganger's territory. Fali's caution wasn't entirely gone, but she seemed less leery with Ryheart slathered in its 'goo' to the point she was mildly chatty with him as they walked.

"There are barely any tracks at all here, other than its own," she informed him, occasionally pointing out one of its more apparent marks to him. "It has a fair territory, which works to our advantage now that it is dead."

"Well, I'm glad nearly getting eaten came with added benefits," he said with a small grin.

"It is rather nice when things work out, is it not?" Fali agreed sunnily.

They carried on walking for several hours, his guide reluctant to stop until they were out of the foreboding territory. While chatty at first, the nearer they got to the edge of the doppelganger's turf, the quieter and more alert she became. He spotted her grey familiar darting back more frequently, and their route subtly changed whenever it did.

He followed along obediently, more and more on edge. Fali stopped in her tracks and softly put a hand on his chest to halt him. She tilted her head as if she was listening to something, and then let out a long, warbling howl that seemed to hang in the air. She stood deadly still for a moment and then gestured for him to follow again.

"What was that about?" he whispered in a low voice.

"There was a gnargle nearby," she replied. "They are a corrupted type of fairy, far less pleasant company than the garden variety. Fortunately, it knows to stay away from doppelgangers."

"That was the cry you did?"

"Yes, it is what they sound like when they are not mimicking someone."

"So, are these gnargles powerful?"

"Awkward, more than powerful. They play tricks on people. Unfortunately, their definition of 'trick' is somewhat expansive."

"Expansive? How so?"

"Well, one example of a trick would be to lure you into a cave with a bear in it. Then, they wake it up, so it kills you."

"Oh, I see what you mean. That's a pretty loose definition, isn't it?"

"Yes. I am not their biggest fan," Fali said, crinkling her nose in distaste.

"You sound like you're talking from personal experience, there," he pointed out.

"Yes, I am," she said without elaboration.

They carried on until the trees started to thin and crossed a stream of running water, a natural barrier that kept the monsters mostly penned in from that end of the forest.

A short ways past, eventually, they broke from the trees and into an open field. The sunlight was joyous to see despite its sudden illumination, and Ryheart couldn't help but feel a swell of joy at being out of the gloom.

"We're out, right? That's it?"

"Well, we are not quite in the Crown land yet, but very few things would leave their place of power or cross natural running water. So we can relax somewhat. We will get to a small road that is patrolled a short way from here."

"That's a relief!" he said, unable to keep a slight skip from his step after the oppressive gloom of the forest. "So?"

"So, what?" Fali asked him, a slight frown on her brow.

"So, it sounded like one of those gnargle things did something to you. What was it?"

She stared at him for a moment, then sighed. "Their King turned me into a goat," she said flatly.

Ryheart couldn't help but snort in laughter. "They what?"

She gave him a withering look. "You heard me. They transformed me into a goat with their Fae-dust. It was extraordinarily inconvenient. Magic is awkward with hooves."

He stared at her for a moment, then, unable to keep his mirth in anymore, laughed uproariously as they made their way back into civilisation.

Chapter Thirty-Six

Road-Stop

After a pleasant walk through an open field dotted with meadow flowers, the unlikely pair eventually came to a stone road that stretched ahead and behind them, one of the King's highways that crisscrossed civilisation. The patchwork nature of the land, split as it was between humans, monsters and Fae, meant the network of roads was patchy or often non-existent. However, a sizeable primary roadway ran the centre of the land, the spine of Brittaya. Smaller but still well maintained and patrolled roads branched from it, such as the one they now found themselves upon. In the case of Brittaya, all roads lead to the Grand Road.

"Alright, let us stop at the next rest house," Fali declared as the afternoon was making its stately way into the evening. "We can have an actual bath and sleep inside something other than a cave."

Ryheart frowned. The places were well maintained and kept by the royal guard but tended to be a tad on the pricey side, given there was usually little other option for miles beyond sleeping on the ground.

"No chance," he protested. "They overcharge up the arse, and if you've forgotten, we haven't made a single bronze beggar since we started."

"You have your silly little crest from the King, do you not?" she said with an airy wave of her hand. "It allows you to board at any of the King's guest lodgings, no? The King owned the roads last time I checked, and unless something has changed, I presume the guard posts along them too?"

"I guess," he said a little nervously. He wasn't entirely sure whether that was the use the King had intended or not.

"Besides which," she said sunnily, "you are working for the King currently. If it does not allow free lodging here, we will just charge it as an expense when we see him."

"Fali!" he said, scandalised. "He's potentially waving my not-insubstantial debt, and I've only had the thing for a day. I don't want to add abuse of the King's trust to my list of problems."

"I am kidding, dear-heart, I am kidding," she reassured him with a small laugh. "If the place is not considered part of His Majesty's offered lodging, we will just use the well for freshwater and find somewhere nearby to sleep."

After a short distance, they came upon the rest stop, a small cluster of buildings on either side of the road and enclosed by a small circular wall. Two guards stood stationed outside the gate. The one who stepped forward as they approached had immaculate armour and a sword at his belt.

"Evening sir, madam. Are we wishing to stop the night, or just passing through?"

"For the night, if we may? I believe the King's hospitality should extend here, should it not?" she asked.

"It does indeed, ma'am. The private guest quarters are small but well kept. May I see your badge of office?"

Ryheart was fishing the crest he had received from his inner pocket to show them when the second guard piped up, his armour slightly rusted and uniform creased. "No point checking that, look at 'em," he said in a sneering tone, looking them up and down. "What would the King want with someone like them?

"Excuse me?" Fali asked mildly, though a slight edge underlaid her otherwise casual tone.

"Yous are some sort of Fae-kin, and he looks like he hasn't washed for a month. What'd the King possibly be doing with her? You trying to scrounge some free lodgings? You can pay for the inn, or you can find a nice bit of ground somewhere like everyone else."

Ryheart gritted his teeth. Not only did the casual disregard for basic politeness set him on edge – though that certainly did – but he had a fair degree of respect for the military guard given their similar job to hunters. Seeing one so poorly representing himself wounded his pride in his countrymen. He also felt a slight twinge of shame that perhaps his own attitude towards the Fae hadn't been entirely opposite to theirs till recently, even if never so pronounced.

Fali still seemed perfectly calm on the surface, but after their short but intense time together, he could see the subtle danger signs. The slight tightening of the mouth, the flinty grey speckling her eyes, forewarning that under her mild demeanour, she was simmering.

Before she reacted, he drew himself up to his full, not insubstantial height, and pulled the royal crest from his pocket.

"Sir," he said in the most authoritative manner he could muster, adlibbing as he went, "do you know who you're addressing? This is Lady Fali, visiting dignitary of the Fae. She has been personally requested to keep the company of His Majesty. I am to escort her as his envoy, and to see she sees neither harm nor foul." As he spoke, he brandished the crest like a weapon at the offending soldier. He hadn't been expecting to throw his weight around, nor knew if strictly it was what the temporary badge of office allowed, but the man had really got on his nerves.

"Now," he continued, "when she returns from her current journey to personally speak to the King, do you think he would like to hear that she had been extended the unmatched courtesy that gives our kingdom its reputation? Or do you think he would like to hear we are a bunch of ill-mannered oafs? Because if you think the latter, I'll be sure to mention you personally when we see him next."

He had perhaps given a little more pageantry than intended, but he had warmed to the role as he went. The guard's face was ashen as he had studied the seal, and his voice was somewhat shaky.

"I'm sorry, sir. I wasn't aware of who I was speaking to. We must ensure only those authorised use the King's personal guest quarters."

"It's not the checking that's at fault," Ryheart snapped. "It's how you did so. More importantly, I'm not the one you need to apologise to."

He stepped aside slightly to allow Fali free reign. While her height was distinctly less imposing than his, she walked with stately grace, her head raised airily in an imperial manner. She laid an affectionate hand briefly on Ryheart's shoulder, then addressed the soldier almost like he was an afterthought.

"Well?" she said after a long silence, fixing him with a cold stare, her voice haughty and self-important in a way it usually wasn't.

"I'm sorry, ma'am."

"My name is Lady Lightflower, and I shall be addressed as such."

"Lady Lightflower."

"I expect to be spoken to in full sentences, not in broken Anglasa. Are you a representative of your King, or some wild beast?"

"My apologies, Lady Lightflower."

"Better," she intoned with a flick of her hair. "I require a separate room for myself and my escort. You will prepare them for me."

"Well, I'm a guard, not a servant. That's not really—"

"After you have done so," she interrupted, "I expect a hot bath drawn for myself. Would you also like one drawing, Ryheart?"

"No, thank you, ma'am," he said, fighting to keep a straight face.

"Very good. I also want a basket of fresh fruit bringing to my quarters. That will be all," she demanded, shooing the guard away dismissively.

"Again, that, well, that's not really—"

"Just get it done," the more polite soldier suggested lightly. "You've dug enough of a grave for yourself already."

The assaulted guard stared at them for a moment as if debating whether to protest, then somewhat sullenly bowed and slinked away.

"Apologies for that, my lady," the remaining soldier offered. "I hope you don't judge us all too harshly. We don't see much supervision out here aside from inspections. It's made the lad a touch brash, to say the least."

"Oh, that is quite alright," Fali said in a kindlier tone, though keeping her lofty bearing.

"Would you like me to arrange an escort to your rooms?" the guard asked. "We don't see much trouble out here, but I really shouldn't leave the gate unattended. Otherwise, I would take you myself."

"I am sure we will manage to find our way if you just point it out," she assured him genially.

"Forgive me asking," he asked, sounding slightly hesitant, "but are you really a noble? I don't doubt your right to be here; it's just that, well, to speak frankly, the few dignitaries I have seen travel through tended to have a carriage and an entourage three miles long. Not that you don't look the part yourself, of course, my lady, but you are travelling awfully light. There are criminals even out here who'd take advantage of lone travellers."

"That is a fair observation," she granted, "but yes, I am indeed a visiting dignitary. Between you and me, Queen, rather than a lady. I just prefer to travel with somewhat fewer hangers-on than you humans."

The guard seemed surprised but kept any doubts he might have had to himself. "Your Highness," he said with a militarily precise bow.

"Do you like your post here?" she asked curiously.

"I can't complain, Your Highness. It's peaceful for the most part, though it would be nice to be posted nearer to family. Not that I'm complaining, mind," he added quickly. "I'll do my duty wherever it takes me."

"What is your name, Lieutenant?" she asked, clearly noting his insignia.

"Humbason, Your Highness."

"I will be sure to mention your exemplary behaviour the next time I am speaking with your King, then."

"Thank you, Your Highness. That would be a great honour."

"Grand. Come along then, Ryheart. Thanks for your time, Captain."

"Ah, Lieutenant, Your Highness," he corrected lightly. "As you said before."

She looked back at him as they walked past. "We will see," she said with a knowing grin.

They walked through into the complex towards the building he had pointed out, and she leant over to Ryheart. "Well played," she murmured, "What on earth brought that on?"

"I don't know. He just got my hackles up," Ryheart said, adding, "Besides, it is my duty to look after your honour, after all."

"Why, Ryheart," Fali said with a warm smile, linking her arm with his, "we are making you into a gentleman."

Chapter Thirty-Seven

Research

Olyra Holloway had waited, patiently, for word of the celestial Fae to arrive at her desk. Finally, it had come. Her decision to ask informants to monitor way-stops along the Weir Wood adjacent roads had paid off. She had received word that the party had stayed at one north of Londaya. For some reason, they were travelling away from the city where they would have to hand in their bounty. They were, however, on foot. If Olyra went by horse, switching every waystation for a new fresh steed, she should be able to catch up with him and see whatever this magical being was. Maybe it wasn't the same creature that had broken her nose, but she had to be sure. She packed her gear and took off towards the nearest stables.

Ryheart relaxed in his room, along the hall from Fali's.
  He felt slightly strange and couldn't quite put his finger on why. Then, he realised. He was used to spending much of his life solo, but this was the first significant bit of time since he had met his flighty travelling companion that he had to himself. At least, the first bit of time where he wasn't in immediate mortal peril. He smiled wryly. The tiny whirlwind had barely been in his life for a week, yet she had become a seemingly permanent fixture of it. And he still didn't know what she was.

He fished the speaking tome out of his bag and then leant back on the bed casually. Damn, it was nice to lay on something that wasn't rocks or grass for a change.

Flicking the book open to a random page, he addressed it, still feeling a little sheepish about talking to a book.

"Hey, err, Dolati."

"Hello, Ryheart," the book intoned in its rich voice. He was slightly surprised it recognised him immediately, despite previously having said that it couldn't see.

"Can you sense my life essence with magic?" he questioned on impulse.

"No, dear. I am, as previously mentioned, a book."

"Then how did you recognise me?"

"I remembered your voice."

"Oh," he said, feeling simultaneously both a bit silly and a bit disappointed that it was something so mundane.

"What do we wish to study today?" it asked him, graciously ignoring his blunder.

"Well, I wondered if we could speak a bit more about my mysterious friend. The one I mentioned earlier."

"Ah. Our red-haired Janaeus Doela. Do we have any new information on her?"

"Yeah. She's strong. Like, ludicrously strong. She does have fire magic, like the fire sprites you showed me. But she also fixed a magical shield that was huge, forest-wide. The naiads called her a goddess, too. And the King's interested in her. She also mentioned hiding her magic signature, so it didn't attract attention."

"Hmm. Does she have any defining physical features beyond the red hair?"

"Well. It's not a feature exactly," he mused, "but she has a rabbit with her. She called it her familiar. It's hard to see, sometimes. Like it isn't quite entirely here."

"And does she have, by any chance," the book questioned in a contemplative tone, "markings by her eyes?"

"She does, yes. I thought they were just tattoos, but yeah. Green triangles sit by her eyes."

"You should have led with that," the book murmured, "and a sigil somewhere upon her person?"

"I don't know if it's a 'sigil' or whatever, but she has a blue marking on her cheek. I've recently noticed that it glows when she does magic."

"And you are not hostile to her?"

"No, she's my friend," he said firmly.

He jumped slightly as the book started flipping pages of its own accord in a whirl of paper, then landed on a single entry.

'Realm-dancer', it read.

"Don't be daft," he scoffed automatically. Realm-dancers were the stuff of children's stories, benevolent spiritual beings who escorted the dead to the afterlife on behalf of some benevolent god. Made up to make people feel better about dying in a cruel world.

"I am never daft," the book protested indignantly, sounding affronted. "The criteria you just mentioned fits a realm-dancer. It only fits a realm-dancer. Or at least an excellent imitation of one. I am incapable of errors in logic. The only way I could have misinterpreted the knowledge stored within me is if you have misinformed me."

"No way. Of all the monsters and ghouls or whatever, no one's so much as seen a realm-dancer. Even dragons leave bones," he protested. "Besides which, of all the ways I might describe her temperament, peaceful isn't very high on the list."

"I'm not aware of the social climate of the era, dear, nor am I capable of learning it. I am the recorded output of my author's knowledge of this subject, created to document all creatures that live in, or visit, the garden. What you described matches only one entry within me." There was a brief pause, then the book added, "If you do wish to learn more about the beliefs and politics of creatures of the garden, please refer to one of my sister volumes.

They will be able to document the historical actions of the garden's sentient races and their cultural development."

Ryheart couldn't help but laugh. "I'm sorry, did you just advertise to me?"

"I have no idea what you mean, dear," the book protested mildly. "I was simply proffering alternate avenues of learning. I can even recommend some works by other authors if you prefer. Though I can hardly guarantee they will be as accurate as I."

He laughed again, smiling. "Alright, alright. Let's say I believe 'realm-dancers' exist. Fali doesn't even have wings like the one in here," he said, pointing at the illustrated figure on the page, winged and holding a shield and spear. "She said 'a bird ate them', but I'm pretty sure that was bollocks."

"Ryheart, dear," the book replied in a tone that sounded like it would have been accompanied by an eye roll if the book had eyes to roll, "she is one of the most magically gifted beings in existence. Her very essence is pure creation, pure magic. They are capable of using any element or kind of spell, of directly shaping reality itself. Realm-dancers exist within the physical and spiritual realms simultaneously. Their primary tasks are to guard the barriers between the realms of reality, all that lies within them and to escort souls between them. Hence the title realm-dancer. They are the children and servants of the Twin-Divinities, standing even above the gods of the garden."

"Okay, and the wings?" he repeated weakly, trying to process the implications.

"A glamour would be a mere parlour trick for even a lower caste of realm-dancer. You said yourself she has performed all manner of feats. Has not one of them at least matched something as simple as a minor alteration of sight?"

He contemplated the mildly spectacular things he had witnessed her do. "One or two, yes," he murmured. "Alright, well, you've given me some things to think about. Goodnight, Dolati."

"You are very welcome, dear," the book said, gently closing itself with a muffled thud of paper.

Chapter Thirty-Eight

Intel

Olyra climbed from her horse, mind alert despite the rapid travel to catch up with her potential target. She had arrived at the rest stop her informant reported Ryheart and his accomplice had stopped in too late to catch them. She had ridden non-stop to the next station along the way but hadn't come across them. She wasn't yet at a loss, though.

There was a relatively large outpost not too far away, and given its proximity to Londaya, it was well equipped.

Olyra commandeered their communications room after some minor bullying via pulling rank, and sat before the mirror that stood in closed doors.

Scrying mirrors were few and far between, given their heavy magic use and the fact that few Fae were skilled enough to create them, or were willing to stay in civilisation long enough to do so. Though they could be prefilled with magic and activated by magicless humans, their power drained so quickly that there were simply better things for the Fae they did have employed to be doing. Most of which were in Londaya. Consequently, the mirrors were strictly for royal or military use and, even then, restricted.

She hated them because the Fae who created them insisted that it was essential to the spell that made them function, that they were rhymed at to work. Olyra couldn't help but feel like that was just some private Fae joke, and she felt positively ridiculous doing so. She paused a moment as she thought of a sufficient rhyme.

"Mirror on the wall, let me communicate with the naiad matriarch's hall."

There was a moment of flickering, and then a naiad appeared in front of a mirror, old and stately. The water of her hair had a silvery tinge to it, and it trickled slowly like leaky plumbing.

"How can we assist you, ma'am?" the naiad asked politely.

"Have you managed to get a hold of anyone from the lake at the Weir Wood yet?" Olyra questioned crisply. The naiads could all communicate with each other via pools of water. The catch was that the water had to come from the same source on both ends. They also claimed there was no way to enchant the water to hold any power to be activated without their own brand of magic. Only naiads could use it, and both ends needed to have the water on their person ready.

Olyra had contacted the central pool of naiads, who represented the naiads within the country as a whole. Their hierarchy was so loose that they were really nothing more than a figurehead convenient for the government to communicate with easily. Consequently, their lake within the palace grounds was officially considered the capital city – or capital lake – of the naiads, and they had their own mirror for official communications.

"Yes, ma'am. Apologies we couldn't contact them immediately, as it does take a considerable amount of power to flow to them through the current of magic, especially with the shield around them. We have them ready to speak now, if you wish?"

Olyra nodded curtly. The naiads were considered the lowest threat within the Fae allied to the crown, and while that was one less problem for her to worry about, Olyra held them in low regard. As far as she was concerned, the only reason their immutable pacifist nature was sustainable was that other less idyllic races, humans included, babysat them and kept them free of conflict. If humans hadn't been there to create hunters to push back the monsters, she didn't expect they would have lasted all too long.

The naiad curtsied and picked a decanter of water from a shelf behind her, which contained a row of bottles. Presumably, there was water from the source of each lake they had within the country, or at least the surrounding area. Olyra meticulously noted that there were thirteen of them and stored the bit of information away. The matriarch poured the water into a basin, and the glassy head and shoulders of a naiad appeared.

"Ma'am." She addressed her as the previous one had, bowing her head in place of their traditional curtsy given her lack of body.

"I believe you had two visitors to your lake a few days ago. A hunter and a Fae. Is that correct?"

"Three visitors, ma'am," the naiad corrected politely.

If naiads were good for one thing, it was straightforward questioning. They were virtually incapable of lying, as transparent as the water they were made from.

"Three? Who?"

"Two of your own, and one of the beings from before the world."

Olyra frowned. She hated flowery speech. "In plain Anglasa?"

"Two humans and a being I suppose you would call a Fae."

"And what would you call them?"

"We consider her more concept than species, ma'am. I don't know what you would call her," she said apologetically. "Goddess is the nearest honorific we have, though that's not entirely accurate. We consider her an honorary member of our pantheon."

Olyra scoffed. Naiads considered basically every god any species had ever dreamed up as a member of their pantheon. They probably had more gods than people.

"Alright. Names, who are they?" Olyra demanded, forgoing pointless arguments about what constituted a goddess to them.

"Ryheart and Harand are the humans, both hunters. The other is Fali."

That answered who the mystery person was. Harand was the hunter who had first reported the creature to the OPMC.

Evidently, he had also followed them. He wasn't the one she was curious about, however.

"The 'other one'. What's she look like? Red – literally red – hair? A blue glyph on her cheek and green markings by her eyes?"

"That's a fair description, yes," the naiad confirmed, and Olyra felt a thrill of excitement. Her suspicions were seemingly validated.

"Where was she going afterwards?" she asked keenly.

"I couldn't say," the naiad apologised.

"Does anyone there know?" Olyra demanded. The lead couldn't go cold. She needed some idea where they might be heading.

"Well…" the naiad said, seemingly hesitant.

"If you have any information, you better give it to me."

"Perhaps Harand might know them. I believe he's the friend of the other human."

That didn't square with the report she had received, but he was worth a shot if she could get a hold of him.

"And where did he go?"

"Oh, he's still here," the naiad said. "He broke his ribs and nicked a lung, and he has a concussion. He's unfit to travel, so we've been treating him with our healing waters. He's been in and out of consciousness, but he might have spoken with them."

"I need to speak with him immediately."

"He's sleeping right now, and he needs his rest," she protested. "We couldn't wake him."

"I said immediately," Olyra snapped. "I might remind you that in accordance with the treaty of the Seelie court and the King of Brittaya, you are to comply with any demands of the King's officials for any matters that do not break the other terms of said treaty. Failure to do so is a violation of the agreement."

If the naiad had any fear of threats, it wasn't remotely reflected in her expression, but she did nevertheless bow her head.

"If you demand it, ma'am. One moment," she said before disappearing from the basin in a ripple of water, appearing after a short wait.

"He's with me, ma'am. I can't make him appear, but I'll relay his words to you."

"There's absolutely no way to make him visible?" Olyra asked. She thought not, but she would much rather have seen him so she could judge his intent from his expression. At the very least, hear his voice.

"I can't pull him through the current of the living waters with me, I'm afraid," the naiad informed her.

"Alright, fine," she said. She trusted the naiad would relay his messages faithfully, given their complete lack of subterfuge. However, the naiad had no way to verify how true those words were, and Olyra was left blind like this. Still, she would have to work with the naiad relaying messages like they were playing a game of siren's whispers.

"Alright. Harand Devington-Smithe, this is Olyra Holloway of the OPMC. I'm following up an investigation into a wanted person, and I believe your report filing to the Bureau of Registrations is relevant. Do you have any idea where the Fae calling herself Fali, or if not, where the hunter known as Ryheart, is travelling to?"

To the naiad's credit, she repeated the message verbatim, and then after a brief pause as she listened to the hunter's message, responded, complete with an accent, "Yeah, I heard 'em talking. I don't think they realised how much sound travels in this clearing, or that I was awake. They said they're travelling to Solisala Hill."

"Did they say why?"

"The Fae-kin, or whatever she is, said she was going to wake up a 'guide' to speak to it. Whatever this guide is, she was willing to travel through the unclaimed territory to get to it. Ryheart is... look, he's not a bad kid, but he is an idiot. And Fae, even if she does think she's doing no harm, they're dangerous even when they aren't trying to be. Whatever she's waking up, it can't be good."

Olyra ran a quick calculation in her mind. That wasn't too far from here, and she had the advantage of horseback.

"Mirror on the wall, I'd like you now to end this call," she said directly to the mirror, without wasting another word on the naiad or hunter. Standing on ceremony was for politicians.

She turned and strode out of the room. With haste, she might just catch them before it was too late. She did, after all, have orders to kill the creature. If she was indeed still alive, those orders were still in play. It was time to remedy that.

Chapter Thirty-Nine

Traveller

The hunting duo had set off early in the morning after their stay. Before they left, Fali went out of her way to find the disrespectful soldier from the day before and demanded he made her breakfast. Fali had previously displayed a complete lack of interest in food, if not an outright aversion, so he could only presume she did so solely for the pleasure of annoying him.

"So, what's the plan then, boss?" he asked as they set off along the road.

"We go say hello to this dragon," she said with a casual shrug. It was like she was suggesting something no more out of the ordinary than going down the market for some vegetables.

They carried on in silence for a while as he contemplated the idea of having a casual chat with what was generally considered the most dangerous of monsters, when a random question popped into his head unbidden.

"Isn't it strange it hasn't rained at all?" he asked. "I know it's summer, but I'd have at least expected a bit of drizzle. We are in Brittaya, after all. I don't think I've ever been on a hunt outside where I haven't at least got sodden at some point."

"Oh, it has rained," she informed him matter-of-factly. "I just asked the clouds if they could wait until we passed, and they kindly complied. They were only going to be light showers anyway, so they did not mind too much."

He gawked at her, then narrowed his eyes. She had to be winding him up this time. He thought he was getting better at discerning which of her outrageous claims were genuine and which were nonsense.

"You're having me on again," he accused her bluntly.

"Why, Ryheart," she exclaimed, a perfect picture of innocence, "what a thing to accuse me of!"

He was going to argue further when Fali turned around abruptly. Following her gaze, he saw her familiar bounding towards them in a flicker, grey ears bouncing wildly. She cocked her head in response, her attention elsewhere.

"What's the matter?" he asked. With his growing insight into his tempestuous friend's moods, he thought she looked decidedly unpleased for just a moment before her calm expression returned.

"Someone is coming along the road behind us rather fast," she informed him, "unless by an incredible coincidence, I presume to try to find us."

"What? Why? I mean, there's plenty of people travelling this road. Why would they have anything to do with us?"

"I met her before," Fali explained, before murmuring. "It was less than amicable."

Before he could quiz her further, she took hold of his sleeve and pulled him off the road and towards the boundary hedge before a field. He yelped in alarm as she scooped him up over her shoulder like he weighed no more than a child. She leapt clear over the hedge into a crowded field of wheat that was nearly as tall as he was.

"What the Friggana are you doing?" he asked in a hushed tone as she set him down.

"Friggana has no involvement in this," she reassured him, seemingly missing his point.

"I meant, what are we doing jumping into someone's field?"

"I told you, I would rather not interact with the person on the road. We are just taking a slight detour, is all."

"Uh-huh. Great," he muttered, wiping some dirt off his armour. "Who the hell is this person that they're so important that even you hide from her?"

"She is hardly important," Fali sniffed disdainfully, "just a nuisance. She is some agent from one of your little government agencies."

"Which one?" Ryheart asked, dreading the answer. There weren't really any government staff he wanted sniffing around near him, given his current company. He wouldn't even want a librarian after him.

"The 'Operations for the Prevention of Magical Crime', I think she said."

Ryheart's blood froze. "The…" he started loudly, before getting a handle on himself and lowering his voice to a whisper. "The OPMC? You know they're the people who investigate and, if rumours are to be believed, murder people for doing magic stuff they shouldn't be doing, right? Like, say, harbouring magical creatures, or, I don't know, just off the top of my head, going to wake up a freaking dragon?"

"I had pieced that together, yes," Fali murmured.

"Oh, bloody congrats for you! Why didn't you tell me?" he exclaimed as they set off again.

"Well, she thought I was dead," Fali said defensively. "I thought that was the end of it."

"Oh, gods, gods, gods," he panicked. "This is the last thing I need."

"Be calm, Ryheart. If it comes to it, we will just show her your letter. She can hardly murder me when the King personally wants to speak to me, can she?"

"Well, why are we hiding at all then? It doesn't exactly scream innocence, does it?"

"Because I would rather not have to deal with her exacerbating things while I am trying to have a nice conversation with a dragon. Not least because if he did become hostile, I am not sure I could stop him without my wings."

"What? You're going to wake something up you can't even cope with?"

"Not 'could not'. Just not confidently," she corrected.

"That's hardly the issue!"

"Well, I am not going to fight him anyway."

"If they're so strong, how did the knights wipe them all out? Or most of them, I suppose, given you apparently know one."

"Well, he is not exactly a normal dragon. He is a bit more impressive than the average one."

"More impressive? How?"

"Well, there are two – although technically speaking, only one – types of dragon: drakes and true dragons. Drakes are similar in the way crocodiles are to alligators. They are not true dragons, but I suppose when a giant scaled beast is flying at you breathing fire, the distinction's not too prominent in your mind. Drakes, though, are mundane, while true dragons are magical. Drakes, the ones you tended to fight, are considerably less formidable – relatively speaking, of course – but are far more aggressive and bestial. They were not exactly cuddly, to begin with, then the corruption took all their minds."

"...And I gather this isn't a drake we're going to see?"

"No. True dragons are split into elders and ancients. They are intelligent, and in many cases, were kind. About half the elders fell to the corruption and sadly were intelligent enough to be aware. Many of them had to kill their soulmates to save them the madness. Very few remain, and the ones that did were generally mixed up with the fallen ones when you went on your grand hunts."

"And is that what we're going to see?"

"No, the latter, an ancient. One of the grand dragons. Near-elemental forces of nature. I am positive it will have felt the corruption."

"Great," he said with a sigh, Harand's warning briefly flashing through his mind before he dismissed it and gave a wry laugh. "So we have an unstoppable dragon and a magic hunter after us. I'm not sure which I'd less rather meet."

"Oh, Ryheart," Fali said with a warm smile, "you are more scared of her than I am, and she has not even tried to shoot you."

"Shoot you?" he exclaimed. "She tried to shoot you?"

"Yes," Fali replied glibly, "but she missed."

Chapter Forty

Blizzard

Ryheart followed Fali as they made their way along roughly parallel to the main road, keeping a brisk pace as they made their way towards Solisala Hill on their more circuitous route. Fali had assured him the agent who maybe wanted to kill her – and, quite possibly, him – had passed by them along the main road. Nevertheless, his guide was keeping away from the major roadways and sticking to smaller tracks instead.

"So how come this dragon isn't public knowledge?" he asked. "I know we're kind of out of the way, but Solisala Hill is a man-made landmark, and it's not that far out from civilisation. Wouldn't we know about a big fuck-off dragon flying around a big hill?"

Fali sniffed at his swearing but refrained from comment, though she seemed amused by something he had said.

"Man-made?" she queried inquisitively.

"Yeah, it's a ritual site made by our ancestors."

"You humans say anything old that you do not understand was 'for ritual purposes'," she said with a teasing grin.

"Well, alright, what is it then?" he asked a touch grumpily.

"You will find out when we get there," she said with a knowing smile that if anything was even more infuriating. "It is getting cold up ahead, by the way," she said after a moment, the smile replaced by a frown. "You might want to put on a coat. Perhaps gloves, too. Humans have such delicate little pinkies."

Somewhat irrationally, he found the suggestion he needed a coat in summer mildly offended his sensibilities.

"Didn't even pack one." He shrugged. "Coats are for winter, Fali."

"Well, it is a good job that I packed one for you then, is it not?" she said matter-of-factly.

He stared at her for a moment angrily, then sighed. "You need to learn to pack more efficiently," he intoned pointedly.

"Why, do you have a vendetta against warm clothing or something?"

"I do in the middle of bloody summer, yeah!" he exclaimed. "I'm not a baby, Fali!"

"Alright, alright," she replied soothingly. "It was only a suggestion."

They carried on, and within five minutes, there was a distinct cool to the air, which he ignored. Within ten, there was a definite chill.

He remained resolute out of pure stubbornness until his breath started to steam in the air and a particularly bracing gust of wind swept over him.

"Alright, fine," he surrendered. "Is it in my bag or yours?"

"Mine," she supplied, helpfully retrieving it for him in a pleasant manner that was even more annoying than if she had gloated. "There is snow up ahead, so it is probably a good shout."

"Yeah, you win," he said, taking the gloves she offered as well. "Don't you want any?" he asked her, given she still wore nothing but her dress and scabbard belt.

"No. Unlike you, I actually do not feel the cold," she said with a grin. There was the gloating.

"It is bloody cold," he grumbled. "Unusually cold."

"Unnaturally cold, actually," Fali corrected thoughtfully.

"What does that mean?"

"Nothing good," she said frankly, quickening her pace ever so slightly. "I cannot sense anything here, magic or life essence.

The blizzard's permeated with magic, and it is completely blocking the feel of anything else. I think it is the dragon, though."

"What is?" he said with a frown.

"The cold."

"What? Aren't they all fire and that?"

"Regular ones, yes. This is an ancient, though. Specifically, the bringer of ice. A large, very powerful elemental."

"...How powerful are we talking?"

"Remember the last ice age?" she said in a low murmur.

"I know of it, yes," he said reluctantly.

"He caused it."

Ryheart couldn't quite find the words, so he just parroted them. "He caused it?"

"Yes, sweeping a blizzard along below his wings."

"Is that what's happening now?" he asked in alarm.

"No. Well, it should not be. This snow here is nothing. It is simply the side effect of his aura radiating as he wakes up. It is not time yet, though."

"Time?"

"Yes. Ice ages are a part of the balance of the world. They reshape the land and cool it. It is far too early, though."

"So, this is being caused by him waking up," Ryheart asked slowly, Harand's warning flashing unbidden to his mind. "And you said we were coming here to talk to him, yes?"

"Yes," she asked, clearly distracted, "why?"

"So you were going to wake it up yourself and bury the country in snow? To get some answers for your crusade?"

"No!"

"Well, I don't know how you can talk to someone without waking them up first, Fali!"

"Spiritually," she said, looking at him directly now, seemingly picking up on his train of thought. "His body would have remained asleep while our spirits connected. I—"

Sentence abruptly dying, she whirled around, and he caught a glimpse of her eyes as they flashed a bright yellow. Before he could even process what was happening, an armour-covered figure tackled her roughly to the ground, a flintlock pistol pressed directly to the Fae's temple.

"I'm not fucking around this time," the new figure declared in an authoritative voice. "If I feel you so much as move a toe, this shot is going in your head. If I see him move, same goes."

"Hello, Olyra," Fali greeted in a ludicrously calm voice. "That would be unwise."

Ryheart watched in disbelief, frozen to the spot.

"Why would that be?" the soldier questioned. "So you can wake up the dragon and destroy the country with it?"

"Because said dragon is right next to us, and as you have evidently heard, he is already starting to wake up. It is perhaps not the best idea to make loud noises nearby him. Particularly not ones infused with magic."

"He can't be that nearby," she scoffed. "There's nothing here but the hill."

"He is the hill."

Even the soldier seemed taken aback by that. "Fuck off. Not even dragons are that big."

"Choose to believe me or not. But I am telling you that if you shoot me, you will wake it up and kill the only thing on this side of reality that could stop it. So, unless you fancy vacating this little island you all live on, I suggest you put the weapon away and let me deal with him."

"Say I believe you. What's your big plan to stop this, then?"

"Well, in broad strokes, I was going to sing to him and ask if he would mind going back to sleep."

"Your plan to stop the magic dragon waking up and destroying Brittaya is jabbering in its ear?" she asked incredulously. "How about I arrest you and then come back here with an army?"

"It will not matter if you came back with three soldiers or three hundred soldiers. You would be like children screaming at the tide to stop coming in."

"You were deemed a magical threat. Waking a dragon would be quite the magical threat. Far as I know, that's exactly why you're here. I have orders from my office to detain or eliminate you. This dragon business isn't helping your case."

The wind howled around them in a blizzard now, seemingly blanketing the hill in a wall of snow.

"I swear to you by the Twin-Divinities: he is near breaking point," Fali informed her. "If I do not reverse this now, even if I manage to stop it, the damage to your weather systems will already have occurred, and you will spend the next hundred years buried in snow."

"How do I know everything you're saying isn't designed to make me let you go?" Olyra asked, her tone measured but less aggressive now.

"Ryheart has orders from the King to bring me unharmed to meet with him. He did not send guards or militia to detain me. He sent an invitation. Do you not think a direct order from the King trumps your own? The King trusts me. You should too."

"Bullshit," Olyra scoffed.

"I do," Ryheart said, finding his voice again, throat suddenly dry. "I can show you. I have a seal and a letter."

Olyra turned to look at him for the slightest, briefest of glances. Even as her eyes left Fali, the Fae sat suddenly upright, crashing her forehead into her assailant and yanking the gun from her hand.

Ryheart froze as his mind raced. All this was all so far beyond his pay grade. He didn't know what was happening. He didn't know how much danger he was in. But one thought consistently rang true in his mind. He trusted Fali. He didn't even fully understand why, but he did. He trusted her.

He sprinted forward as Olyra fell backwards and interposed himself between the soldier and his friend.

"Go sort out the dragon!" he shouted at Fali.

She locked eyes with him for the briefest of moments, flooded with gratitude as apparent as the purple that swirled into them. Then she was gone, vanished into the blizzard. He was left alone to stand against the soldier who wanted to kill her. And now, probably, to kill him.

Chapter Forty-One

Stand-Off

The soldier climbed to her feet and stared at Ryheart, eyes ablaze. Angry scarring lay upon her cheek, her nose misshapen.

She pulled a rifle from the strapping on her back and raised it, a contraption of flint, wood and steel that Ryheart had rarely seen up close. It was aimed directly at him. He suddenly felt less sure about his decision.

"I'm going to follow her now," Olyra informed him in a tone that brooked no argument. "Is that going to a problem?"

"…It depends what you're going to do when you follow her," Ryheart managed to push out through a suddenly dry mouth.

"If the dragon is real, I'm going to shoot it in the head," she said flatly. "If the dragon isn't real, I'm going to shoot her in the head."

"Why? She wasn't lying about the King's order, you know," he bargained, trying to delay her as much as possible. She put her rifle back in its sling, and he felt a brief glimmer of hope, but that was dashed when she cracked her knuckles threateningly instead. She was only holstering the rifle due to the noise it would make, giving him only an ultimatum in response.

"This is your last and only chance. You move out of my way, or I move you out of the way."

He took in a deep breath. Maybe she'd stop shy of killing him if he was lucky.

"The King charged me with protecting her from any harm," he justified half to himself, "and I trust her."

She didn't even bother with a response. She just altered her weight ever so slightly, then charged.

Taken off guard by her speed and ferocity, he just barely managed to block her punch with a clumsy guard, his padded armour partially absorbing the blow. He did, however, stumble backwards, and in the brief moment his balance was off-kilter, she swept his legs out from under him, and he slammed to the ground.

She dashed past him as he fell. She must have thought him at best a nuisance, and clearly, her attention was primarily on her target. If he could take advantage of that, he might at least buy enough time for Fali to do what she needed to do. At least till the soldier's patience ran out.

He grabbed for her as she ran past, managing to hook her ankle. Yanking as hard as he could, he brought her to the ground, face first. They both climbed to their feet, but she was quicker, and she clubbed him in the head with a blow that felt like his brain was shook loose from his skull. He lunged back at her, and she dodged deftly, delivering another jab to his chest. This one he felt even through the armour.

Thank the gods, she didn't seem to be trying to kill him, and he certainly wasn't about to lethally escalate by drawing his sword. But he still wasn't going to last very long like this. His experience was all fighting beasts, wild animals. And he wasn't exactly very good at that. She evidently had experience fighting other people.

He delivered a series of short punches to her chest, but she let them bounce harmlessly off her superior armour, his hand throbbing even through his leather gauntlets. Every time he aimed at her head, the one target he might do damage to, she bobbed clear near-effortlessly.

She jabbed at him again, and he just barely blocked it, his arm numb from the battering. He felt a surge of frustration. He couldn't even distract her for more than a minute when Fali was counting on him? Pathetic. He couldn't earn a wage; he couldn't hunt; he couldn't even be a decent distraction. He wanted to be better. He needed to be better. For himself, and for Fali.

Feeling a surge from deep within, a spark of light shone inside him, as it had when he delivered the critical blow to the Nemean.

He swung at his opponent, power erupting with his anger. Adrenaline burst through him, and his fist nearly shone with a crackle of energy as he aimed for her unprotected face.

Taken off guard by the sudden ferocity and strength, his opponent just managed to redirect the blow to her armoured chest. A shockwave of force burst as the strength built up within exploded on impact. She was hurled through the air before crashing to the ground in a flurry of snow.

For the briefest of moments, Olyra was stunned into inaction as she lay on the ground. She wasn't in the habit of underestimating her opponents. Doubly so, after the tiny red-haired creature had thoroughly outclassed her despite what her small frame inferred about her. But the hunter had seemed borderline inept. His blows had been clumsy, and he was blatantly untrained in unarmed combat. If it weren't for the fact that Olyra didn't wish to do serious harm to a civilian despite her words, this would already be over.

This, though, changed things. That blow had carried some magical force. Magic he shouldn't possess. The reports she had read suggested he was about as plainly human as a human could be. Did he have some illegal artefact in his possession giving him artificial magical power, like the armament band that let her channel borrowed life into her weapon? Whatever it was, he had just moved from nuisance to a legitimate threat. One that was within her purview to arrest or eliminate.

Her ribs ached even through her supreme armour. It was like she'd just been hit with a battering ram, though the metal itself was intact. It almost felt like the blow had transferred through her armour and directly to her. Did it flow through objects and straight to the living? If she hadn't rolled with the strike, that could have done some legitimate damage.

She got to her feet. She needed to end this now before it got out of control. Especially since her primary target could be moments away from waking a catastrophic threat, though Olyra had doubts said dragon was real. She climbed to her feet and tried one last time.

"Alright, I'm not in the habit of repeating requests, but I'm giving you one last chance. I'm not playing with safety mittens on anymore. Cease hostilities, or I'm putting you down, and you won't be getting back up again."

"You still going to try to kill Fali?" her intermediate quarry asked.

"Orders are orders."

Ryheart sighed, seemingly a mix of determination and resignation. "Well, they are for me, too."

She shrugged. "That's your choice. It's a bad one, but it's yours."

Fali raced up the hill as fast as she could. This would have been a damn sight faster if her wings had grown back. Snow was piled to her waist now as she stormed through it. The blizzard blocked both view and feel of the pair she had left below. She very much hoped she had judged accurately that despite her clear drive, Olyra's animosity towards her wasn't reflected upon Ryheart, at least to the extent she might kill one of her own.

She wouldn't have risked it, but the blizzard was worryingly intense now, and without being able to feel anything other than the dragon's overwhelming presence, she wasn't sure if he was hours or seconds away from waking. So, once again, she had to leave it in Ryheart's hands to pull through. Maybe, just maybe, he'd even be able to persuade her to stand down. If there was anything humans excelled at compared to other creatures, it was arguing. Ryheart did have a certain charm, even in his cluelessness.

Heaven, he had pulled through against the Nemean despite the seeming impossibility of that situation. She just had to trust that his strange combination of mild talent and exceptional luck would carry him through.

Chapter Forty-Two

Melody

Alert for the real danger Ryheart posed this time, Olyra stepped forward in a defensive stance, guard up and compact like a boxer. He started to lunge again, but this time her trained senses picked up a slight distortion in the air as he did, indicating his mysterious talent was in play. She darted out of the way and then deftly followed up with an elbow to the side of his head. He staggered back, then lashed out with a flurry of desperate punches before she could capitalise. He either had limited mastery over his power, or it was extremely taxing to use, because only one attack had the hum of magic. She nimbly dodged that one, then let the others clatter off her armour, focusing only on protecting her head and waiting for the crackle that indicated danger.

His forehead glistened with sweat, clearly overexerting himself. Waiting for her moment, Olyra waited until he made one last desperate powered attack, overextending as she moved out of its course. She grabbed his wrist as he stepped forward and yanked it, taking him off balance, his arm twisting awkwardly. She brought her other arm down elbow first, and he yelped in pain as she nearly cracked the bone. Before he could recover, she removed her first hand from his wrist and smashed his jaw, snapping his head back and dropping him to the floor, limp. She took a second to check his pulse, then raced up to the hill: secondary target down; primary remaining.

Pushing all extraneous thoughts away, Fali sat down upon the crest of the hill and closed her eyes with a resolute breath.

"Keep an eye out for me, will you, dearest?" she requested of her long-eared familiar, asking more for the familiarity of comfort than for need. With that, she shunted her consciousness from her body.

Drifting above her motionless physical form like a leaf on the wind, she let out an intangible breath and closed her eyes. Then, she began to sing. The soft cadence of her voice built in waves until it encircled the entire hill in a cacophony of ethereal noise, a choir all by herself.

A bright shimmering enveloped the hill, and then the vast, monumental head of a dragon raised from the earth before her, intangible as she.

The prehistoric creature replied to her song in kind, its voice an earthy baritone that countered and harmonised her higher tones. The colossal being had icy-blue scales thick as walls. As it focused one eye upon her, that alone positively dwarfed the red-haired figure before it.

"Greetings. Are you well, Queen of Realms?" he asked in his throbbing song.

"Well, Lord of Ice, I thank you for your kind concern," she replied, matching his ancient style of song and putting on the most majestic singing voice she could muster as she carried her notes in counterpoint. The song allowed their souls to intertwine and give their meaning in a manner that transcended the need for speech, the words more formality than a necessity.

"How do you fare?" she questioned.

"Troubled, my lady, in truth. I do not enjoy waking and having to perform my duty. I presume you are here to see my task done?"

"My eyes would rather see you sleep peacefully once more, until the appointed time for your task. You are not scheduled to bury the world in ice for ages thrice yet to come. I would not question your ability for all the world, good dragon, for surely you are paramount at your task, but have you perhaps mistaken your time to awake?"

The dragon snorted derisively, causing a great howl of wind even in his incorporeal form. "I awake not with the passage of moons but with a specific purpose. As my last age of ice was to stop the advent of the empty-ones that spread the mortal plain and threatened to overwhelm it, I awake now to prevent it once more. A great source of the void has begun to grow in this land. It is great enough, even to wake me from my slumber. I intend to bury the land in ice now. Doing so will freeze it in its infancy before it can spread and result in catastrophe from which the return is dire."

"Ah," Fali said with a frown, troubled enough with both news and his plan that she lost her formal tone momentarily. It appeared that the same thing that had awoken him had pulled her from her own 'hibernation' in a similar manner. "That would prove somewhat inconvenient for the peoples living here. There are rather a lot of them, human and Fae alike."

"My task is preserving the world itself, Light Mother, as, ultimately, is yours," he chided softly. "I know you are fond of the mortals that nest here, but my duty is my paramount concern. I care not for the mere inconvenience of mortals when reality itself is threatened. The mortals here will migrate or be frozen, and in time, the green shall return, and the creatures shall prosper."

Fali hesitated for a moment. "And were I to order you to stay your wings?"

"I have nought but respect for you, my Queen. But while on the celestial scale, I am beneath you, my purpose here was given to me by a higher power. Indeed, the same one that governs even your duty. I would gladly bow to you in any other matter, but in this, I stay unbent. In this, I have equal standing to you if our purposes were to collide, both derived from the same source as they are."

Fali sighed and felt a brief flash of irritation at not having a solid foot to stamp to vent her anger, though that was probably for the better. She was reluctant to push any confrontation, especially as she wasn't sure she could come out of one favourably, at least wingless here in the mundane, cut off from her place of power.

"Your purpose indeed comes from the same source as mine, and I cannot fault you for the dedication in its direction," she acquiesced diplomatically. "However, as you say, I have my purpose, and it involves protecting all life, even the little ones. In this case, I believe both our tasks have the same solution, as my presence was pulled here by the same thing that awoke you from your rest. Indeed, I came to ask you for better direction to its source, connected to the land as you are. Given we are at an impasse, and neither can give up our duty, perhaps we could strike a compromise that satisfies both convictions?"

"I shall listen, as long as you do not ask me to renege on my solemn vows."

"My purpose here, ultimately, is the purification of the land and the restoration of flow between realms, as you know. And while your efforts can freeze this new threat in place and stymy its progress, it can only do that – halt it. At best, you would retard its growth. It is in my power to not just halt but cure this wound, and perhaps eventually even restore the garden itself. The fact you have not fully awakened suggests this source of corruption is yet in its infancy. If you allow me, I shall personally see it stamped out. In this way, your duty is fulfilled through me, and in turn, I can ensure a more delicate hand. Thus, my duty is upheld to protect the life that grows here, and your duty to see no new corruption grows is also. While the spirit of the land was given to your care, that was in our absence. As I am now present, while you cannot abandon your duty, surely at least a small reprieve to allow my hand to remedy the situation is warranted? You, after all, are only to carry your task out if the situation is dire and beyond other measures. Can you truly determine the situation unavoidable if you have not allowed other avenues their course?"

"Your softness for the mortals might be your end one day, Light Mother," the dragon warned.

"Perhaps. I would rather they be my end than I theirs, though."

There was an extended pause as the dragon contemplated, and Fali found herself holding her intangible breath, then, finally, the dragon spoke. "Your words carry weight to them. I do not entirely agree this is the best course of action, however, I acquiesce you have the right to attempt to pre-emptively stop the void further encroaching into our world, where I could only halt it after the fact. However, know that if you cannot perform the task before it transgresses, you, nor any other, will be able to stay my claw again."

Fali felt a wave of relief as her nerves stopped trying to escape her.

"You are wise and kind, and I swear to you the most solemn vow that I shall uphold this duty or die in its pursuit. I am grateful for your courteous cooperation, and one shall not forget your willingness to aid my task." Fali paused and let some formality fall away with an impish grin. "I believe the current custom is to shake hands upon making a deal, but I am not sure your claws and my tiny little hands are quite suited to it."

The dragon chuckled, a bellowing echo that rolled across their private realm like thunder. Then, a glaring alarm from her familiar rang in the back of her mind that the body she had left behind was in imminent danger. She whipped herself back, and a mighty crack rang around her as the world under her feet shook itself apart.

Chapter Forty-Three

Dragon

Olyra steamed through the snow as fast as she could, virtually wading through a drift. The wind stung bitterly on her face. She pushed the hunter from her mind. She bore him no real ill will, but a choice between striking him or performing her duty? Not a question. She had orders to apprehend or kill the celestial creature. With its re-emergence in the world of the living, that duty was back in play. She was a clear and imminent threat until catalogued or destroyed.

The snow made every step an effort, but the wind seemed to be calming now. The storm, too, seemed to be obscuring her vision less.

Olyra crested the hill, and there Fali was. Her target. The one she had killed once already. She sat motionless, seemingly at peace. She might even have been meditating, bizarrely.

Briefly, Olyra skimmed over her options. The spheres she had used previously would be rendered ineffective by the wind, even with it dying down. She had been told alive was preferable – not essential – but all her deadliest tools were also her noisiest ones, and keeping noise to a minimum was tantamount if the creatures' wild stories about dragons proved accurate. Consequently, she left her firearms holstered and instead pulled out her capture grenade. The thing would explode iron filings and iron ribbons that would magnetise part mechanically and part magically, tightening around and constricting the foe. Several creatures had a weakness to pure iron, so with luck, this might render her entirely incapable of escape.

Softly inhaling, she weighed the grenade in her hand and then launched it at the motionless Fae. Between heartbeats, she watched it hurtle forward on target.

The Fae's head suddenly snapped up, alert, and before either of them could react, Olyra was thrown violently off her feet. She tumbled to the powdered ground, shaking with such violence that even with her training, she couldn't find her feet as she fell. Bearing low and bracing herself, her thoughts churned with the earth as it seemingly tore itself apart. She could almost feel her brain shaking inside her skull until, finally, the movement stopped.

Waiting a moment to confirm there was no aftershock, she lifted her head.

Her heart nearly stopped.

She shook with a deep, primal fear that she couldn't contain despite all her experience and training.

She could barely even comprehend the magnitude of the creature before her. Even had she believed Fali's words entirely, they couldn't have prepared her for the sheer scale of it. The dragon's magnificent head blotted out the sky, and she couldn't imagine how much remained underground. An avalanche of snow stormed down its neck as it raised its great form, a whole field of grass and flowers settled upon it. The uncovered parts had scales that shone blue against the white snow, and its emerald eye alone took up almost her entire vision as it lowered.

For a brief, terrifying moment, its black slit of a pupil glanced at Olyra, and she felt she might die from sheer alarm. Then with a great blink of its scaly lid, it unfocused from her, and its gaze wandered away as if she were no more significant than a blade of grass.

A figure caught her attention, and she saw Fali stood on her feet. On her, the creature's attention now lay. It opened its cavernous mouth and let out a deep sound, each note prolonged and pronounced. The minuscule figure before it lifted her head and joined its song, her voice much higher and more vibrant but somehow just as loud as the dragons. She reached her hand out, palm forward, and the creature pressed its snout against it, the palm dwarfed even by the single scale it touched.

There was a bright spark of incandescent light. Olyra instinctively screwed her eyes shut, and then she was thrown to the ground as its great bulk shifted once again. After another terrible eternity of shaking, finally, the noise quieted, and the world was still once more. As she lifted her head tentatively, if she hadn't just seen it, she wouldn't have even known the dragon had been there. The snow started to run off in rivers down the hill. Olyra found herself bracing to avoid being swept away. Within minutes, there was no snow at all. Indeed, there was no trace of what had transpired aside from the dampness of the grass. The hill was seamlessly covered, and she had lost track of exactly where its head had raised.

The air seemed unnaturally quiet after the discord, and with some surprise, Olyra found herself drenched with sweat despite the cold, her heart still trying its hardest to beat its way out of her ribs.

She looked over at Fali, eyes wide, trying to snap herself into something resembling a composed state as the Fae regarded her for a moment.

"So," the creature said to her, in a manner that was extremely casual given the monumental scale of what had just occurred, "do you believe me now?"

Act Three

The Unnatural

Chapter Forty-Four

Interview

Shocked and subdued by what she had just witnessed, Olyra fell into step beside the creature, putting her mission aside for the moment given the circumstances. Whatever her intel said of the target – of her – she did appear to have just saved a lot of people from the monstrosity they had just witnessed.

"So, is it gone for good?" Olyra asked in a hushed voice.

"Yes. At least, until long after your time. That is unless anyone comes and threatens him," the warrior said with a direct look at Olyra. "No one is going to have any reason to do that, are they?"

Olyra shuddered at the idea of a military investigation waking the monstrous beast. It might be best to leave that information out of whatever report she might make.

"I don't think anyone needs to know," she replied softly.

"Good girl. We shall make a sensible lady out of you yet."

"What was that singing? I have no idea what language it was, but I sort of… intuited some of the meaning. Parts of it, at least."

"The Old-Tongue. The oldest tongue, as it happens. A rather formal version of it, but it has its charms."

"You were talking to it?" Olyra exclaimed in disbelief.

"Oh, yes. He is rather polite. Rather a one-track mind, but pleasant company nonetheless."

Somewhat blindsided by current events, Olyra suddenly remembered the state she had left Ryheart in.

"Fali. Ryheart was somewhat insistent that I didn't follow you, and, well, I had to stop him."

"Luckily for you, I can sense he is alive now the storm is gone," the creature said with an unblinking gaze and matter-of-fact tone that made Olyra's blood run cold, "otherwise you would not be breathing right now."

They got to the bottom of the hill, and Fali walked over to Ryheart, still sprawled out on the ground. She briefly rested her palm on the arm Olyra had twisted, and her hand glowed softly for a moment.

"Consider it fortuitous that this was only a slight fracture and not broken," she said over her shoulder to Olyra. "Now then. What are we going to do with you?" she said, straightening up and gesturing to the soldier.

"Do with me?" Olyra asked, eyes narrowing and hand moving ever so slightly towards her holster. "In what regard?"

"Oh, put that away," Fali said disgustedly. Turning her back, she walked over to a fallen tree near the hill, showing a complete lack of wariness towards her opponent. "You will not need it. Besides which, it would not do you much good anyway."

Olyra watched in bemusement as the petite creature sat daintily upon the log, and gestured for the warrior to join her. "Now, please, take a seat."

"For what purpose?" Olyra questioned.

"For heaven's sake, Olyra," the creature snapped with a stomp of her foot, "because I want to chat with you. You can join me voluntarily, or you can gain a concussion. Choose."

Olyra weighed her options, then sat beside her.

"Now," Fali addressed her, "you have shown you have ways of following us, and I would rather not waste time covering my tracks. I have already demonstrated I am opposed to killing you – opposed, mind, not unwilling. So, I shall convince you I am not the threat you believe I am."

Olyra considered her for a moment. Without a weakness to exploit, she had little chance of beating the creature. After what she had just witnessed, she wasn't entirely sure she should be taking her out anyway.

"Alright. Let's talk, no tricks," Olyra said, holding out a hand. Fali eyed the appendage a moment as if strangely weary of the gesture, then reached out and shook it. Olyra was surprised by how soft and gentle her skin was. For all observation to the contrary, it felt like they had never seen exertion in their life.

"Now," Fali said, "why specifically are you trying to capture or kill me?"

"You're an otherworldly creature that appeared from the ether outside the capital city, with magic so vast you were detectable before you even appeared. It's our responsibility to restrain and catalogue unknown entities to safeguard the land. You declined capture, so capture became kill. Simply, you're too much of an unknown to allow to exist unimpeded. You could be a monster. You could even be an empty-one."

At the mention of empty-ones, the creature's eyes shone with angry fire. "Ridiculous," her impromptu interrogator scoffed, "if I were an aberration of the void, you would be dead. Everyone in your little city would be dead. You do not even believe that yourself. You have seen my wings. You have sensed my true presence, even as spiritually unattuned as humans are. You know what I am, deep down. You are just too stubborn to accept it."

"You did make a beeline for the biggest threat I've ever seen and wake it up."

Fali narrowed her eyes slightly at that. "Come now, Olyra. You are more perceptive than that. I put it back to sleep, as you are well aware. Now, your authority ultimately comes from the King, does it not?"

"We operate autonomously for the most part, but yes."

"Well, I was not lying about his wanting to see me," Fali said, pulling an opened envelope from her bag, handing it across to her.

Olyra studied the document in detail. It did appear genuine, and the seal legitimate.

"Now," Fali continued, "if the King himself wishes me unharmed, the only recourse you have is to leave me alone."

"Can I test you aren't corrupted by the void?"

"By all means." The creature waved invitingly.

"I have some blessed water." Olyra reached for her pouch and pulled out a small metal flask. "Pour some on your hand."

"I can do one better than that," Fali affirmed. Taking the flask, she tipped her head back, pouring the water on her face and in her mouth liberally before gargling and swallowing it in an overly exaggerated fashion. "There, I haven't so much as fizzled."

"Okay. Can I ask why you're here?"

"In simplified terms, there is some bad magic happening. I intend to fix it with good magic. I am here to save human life, not threaten it. As soon as I do so, I will present myself to the King. Satisfied?"

"Somewhat. I have one last question."

"Ask away."

"Can I come with you?"

Fali looked genuinely surprised, and her eyes took an amber hue. "Come with us?"

"Yes."

"Are you actually asking my permission for you to spy on me, Olyra?"

"Yes. I mean, kind of. I suspect you're telling the truth. But suspicion isn't enough to get me to stand down, and certainly not my superiors. If I travel with you, I can fulfil my duty to ensure you don't get up to mischief, and report back your good behaviour. If you send me away, they'll send someone else, at least until the King explicitly tells them to stop. I can see you safely back to him, and then you're in a higher authority's hands anyway."

Fali clasped her hands and exhaled deeply. "Well, that is not entirely my decision. Wait here, and I will speak with Ryheart. But to make one thing clear. You can snoop on me all you like, but if you harm Ryheart or anyone else under my protection again," she said in a flat voice, "no force on earth will stay my hand. Now, wait here, and we will see."

Chapter Forty-Five

Pledge

Ryheart felt a gentle tingle upon his forehead. Opening his eyes groggily, he saw Fali knelt before him, eyes a mix of purple he had come to associate with affection, flecked with a grey that seemed to be there when she was apprehensive.

"Did we win?" he asked wryly. "Because I didn't."

"Well, the country's not about to be buried in a hundred years of ice anytime soon, so in that regard, we did."

"Oh, good. I bloody hate snow," he replied. "What happened to Olyra?"

"She is, ah, waiting for us."

"Waiting?" he asked, eyebrow raised. "That seemed a bit beyond her five minutes ago."

"Yes, well. It was rather an eventful five minutes. She wants to come with us."

He laughed at the notion, then stopped when he saw the lack of humour on her face. "And you want her to?" he asked, rubbing his temples.

"Want is a strong word," she replied softly. "'Can see little workable alternative to' is closer to the mark."

"Olyra?"

"Yes."

"The Olyra that knocked me out?"

"Yes."

"And tried to shoot you in the head?"

"That is the one, dear-heart, yes."

"Well, that's a very appealing prospect, for sure," he scoffed.

"We are in a hurry, and I do not have the time to devote to covering our tracks. Regardless, she has proven adept at finding us. If she stays with us, it keeps others away from us. And she can handle herself."

"I bloody know she can handle herself," he half-shouted darkly. "She knocked me on my arsehole!"

"I know, Ryheart. I know. I would have 'knocked her on her arsehole' if she had done anything permanent to you. I am still half-tempted."

"Why don't you then?" He couldn't help feeling slightly betrayed. They might not have exactly started on the friendliest of terms, but he'd grown a genuine attachment to Fali. Hell, he'd been willing to take a gunshot for her in the heat of the moment. And now here she was inviting the one with the gun to their little party.

"Because if I tell her to leave us alone, she will not listen. If I knock her out, she will follow us again. Probably with backup. Like it or not, nothing short of a brutal murder is going to stop her." She looked him full in the eyes now, words coldly blunt. "Would you like me to murder her?"

"No! Of course not, just… gods damn it."

"Well then," she said, her tone gentle again, "the options are she follows us and pops up when it is most inconvenient, or we keep her where we can watch her."

He sighed. "I get the logic. At least it's only for a few days while we hoof it back to the King and get all this finished with, right?"

Worryingly, Fali didn't reply right off. She just looked into his eyes for a long moment, then sighed. "I cannot go back to the King."

He jerked upright at that. "Come again?"

"I cannot. At least, not right away."

"Fali," he said flatly. "You promised."

"I know I did. And I still intend to keep that promise. I just… need to delay it."

"That's what you said before we came here! The dragon was the delay!"

"I know, Ryheart," she said, making no excuses, which made it even harder. "I know your debt, your livelihood, is important. I am not dismissing it as meaningless compared to the big picture like I was before. You have been a patient and loyal friend these past few days, and I intend to see your debt paid. Truly. But this – lives are at stake, Ryheart. I cannot just abandon the duty I have to their lives in pursuit of fulfilling my obligation to yours."

He sighed and rubbed his forehead, answering after a pause. "What do we need to do?"

"We?"

"I've come this far with you. I might as well see it through."

She laid a warm hand on his cheek for a moment, and her eyes shone with gratitude. "The thing that awoke the dragon was a growing disturbance in the fabric of the world to the east. I felt its location through him. I do not know precisely what it is, but it is catastrophic."

"Worse than a giant magical ice dragon?"

"Yes. He only woke up to stop this before it truly happened, before it got too far along to be stopped."

"Wonderful," he said dryly. "I don't do the supernatural, but I guess that hasn't stopped me so far."

"Yes. Well, to that end," Fali said, "perhaps it would be best if we parted company now. You could wait at the nearest waystation with your badge. Once – if – I manage to deal with this problem, I swear I would find you again. No matter what else came up."

"Look, this wouldn't be my first choice if I were solo. But, well… we're a hunting party, aren't we? We help each other out. Besides, if it's as dangerous as you say, this isn't just about me. I can't just go hide in a corner if there are lives at risk."

"Okay. But willingness is not preparedness. You have proven to have a degree of talent with mundane monsters, and luck cannot be underestimated. However, to be blunt, Ryheart, I do not know that you could cope with something unnatural of this magnitude. Olyra demonstrated that, and she is not even supernatural, let alone corrupted."

"Then teach me," he said, uncharacteristic steel to his voice. She looked at him questioningly but didn't speak, so he pushed on while momentum was carrying his words, strangely impassioned.

"For the brief period I've known you, I've travelled further than I've ever been in my life and seen Fae I've only read about. I've fought a monster so far beyond my pay grade it's crazy. Beat it, even. A chance to get out of debt, not partially but completely, has been given to me. While I was in and out of consciousness down there, I saw a creature I thought didn't even exist, and heard you singing the most beautiful song I've ever heard." He took a breath and then summed up the courage to look into her beautiful shining eyes. "Above all that, for the first time in my entire life, I've actually felt like I'm worth a damn. We saved those naiads. I did that. I saved their lives. You've given me a sense of purpose I never knew was possible. I owe you my company, at the very least. If I'm not of use to you, train me, so I am. If I can't help with your task, I can at least keep Olyra away from you if she tries to get in your way again."

"That is not a light commitment to make, dearest," she said gently. "I am a queen, you know. The role of master and disciple, let alone of liege and vassal, is a serious one. And I cannot teach you well enough, or fast enough, without a bond that serious. If you take this on, you will not be able to back out. Not without breaking an oath." She fixed him with a stare, then continued, "If you do commit to my service, you will be my first human vassal in generations. In return, I would offer you a drop of my blood to give you a connection to my power, but, well, I have already accidentally done so. However, with my blessing bequeathed upon you, it will not fizzle out. It will burn far brighter inside you, and it will last until your final breath. Through it, you'll be able to commune with magic on a level few humans ever can. My blood will be the spark to ignite the potential buried within your spirit, and we will work together to bring it to its fullest. I will commit myself to honing you into the greatest version of yourself you can be in mind, body and spirit. It will take discipline, commitment, dedication. Beyond that, my connection to you will grant you strength, stamina and vitality above your mortal shell. You will be the first, most honoured disciple of this age." She touched his chin gently. "Stay true to me, and I will give you all the blessing my grace can bestow. Your name and honour shall be recorded in my heart forever, until the end of my days."

Ryheart's heart hammered in his chest, and then a strange calm came over him. This act felt strangely, profoundly right, on a scale he scarcely comprehended. He only had one slight reservation. "Will I no longer be a subject of my King?" he asked. He was Brittayan, after all, and patriotism virtually ran in his bones.

"Let's call you a dual citizen," she said with a soft smile. "I doubt anything I ask would ever violate your duty to your King, but I won't compel your service if ever it does. You will be free to do whatever honour compels of you."

"Then I accept," he said, in a rare fit of solemnity.

"Kneel then, Ryheart," she instructed, "of no family name?"

"Not important enough to have one."

"That will not do," she murmured, contemplating momentarily. "Ryheart Lightblessed. I think that fits for my vessel in the garden, does it not?"

"Ryheart Lightblessed," he said, trying the name out loud. He doubted it would have any legality behind it, but the gesture was strangely touching. "Thank you."

"Grand. Then kneel, Ryheart Lightblessed."

He did so somewhat awkwardly, not accustomed to the ceremony. As he did, Fali reached her hand above her empty scabbard, and a gleaming hilt appeared there. She raised a sword aloft, the blade silver metal that gleamed in the air, the guard a winged flower. He briefly caught a glimpse of an arcane pattern etched on the blade as she lowered it to rest flat upon his brow. The faint glimmer of power the drop of blood within had given him suddenly burst with strength and a renewed vigour that warmed his heart.

"Now then, Disciple Ryheart, Squire of the Realm-sworn Knights, first of your time. Rise. I told you a moment ago offhand that willingness was not preparedness. Now, we are going to prepare you to win, and win by preparation. First, though, let us go welcome our new little friend, and we will be on our way."

Chapter Forty-Six

Trio

The group set off, the atmosphere made somewhat awkward by their new less-than-ideal addition. Olyra's demeanour was probably politely referred to as domineering, Ryheart thought, and their pace was a rigid march set by her. She didn't so much as ask; she just set off and expected they would follow.

"I know we're in a hurry, but can't we slow down a bit?" Ryheart asked after some time at their substantial pace. "We have a long journey ahead of us, you know."

"All the more reason to keep pace, wouldn't you say? We want to make some progress before dark," Olyra said dismissively without so much as turning her head. "Once we get to the next stop along the way, we can get horses there and get to this little soiree of Fali's. Then we can deliver you both safely to the King. If we keep a decent pace, we can be in the saddle by midday tomorrow. Surely a hunter can manage a little light march, or do they let anyone in nowadays?"

Ryheart decided against further comment, but he did aim an impolite finger at her back. After a long jaunt, they finally reached a point Olyra was pleased with and set up camp. Fali busied herself cooking while Olyra and Ryheart set up their tents. Ryheart's shabby and somewhat ramshackle tent looked a tad impotent compared to Olyra's sturdy canvas, but the soldier didn't comment. Ryheart observed Olyra, noting that she, in turn, was almost always watching Fali. Her scrutiny seemed particularly keen as Fali set their little cooking pot simmering with only a touch.

"That isn't porridge, is it?" Ryheart asked, eying the pot distrustfully.

"It is," Fali confirmed lightly. "Why?"

"I hate porridge. Bloody awful," he said, wrinkling his nose in distaste.

"Well, surprisingly, the way-stop did not have very much food you can buy with a budget of no money, so we are running a bit low. So, it is that or an empty stomach," their cook said with a sniff. "Your choice."

"Porridge it is, then."

"I rather thought it might be," Fali said with a mischievous grin.

"Better than rations," Olyra chimed in.

"Yes. Speaking of, you are going to have to buy said rations for all of us," Fali informed her primly. "Ryheart has less money than a goblin, and I haven't bought anything since a slab of meat for a bunch of turnips was the common exchange rate."

"I can budget that," Olyra obliged. "I suppose I'm hiring the horses as well, then?"

"Well, if you are offering, it would be rude of us to refuse, would it not, Ryheart?" she said with a grin.

"Absolutely. And we certainly don't want to be rude."

Olyra sighed and made a little note in her ledger but didn't object.

"I presume you would not be against taking the first watch?" Fali suggested lightly. "I know we are in civilisation, but cutthroats can be just as much a nuisance as monsters."

Ryheart noticed that despite her apparent worry, she had elected not to create one of her shields while they were under watch.

"Doesn't bother me," Olyra said with a shrug. "Even when I'm by myself, I wake up every hour to check my surroundings."

"That is a very nervous life, friend," the Fae pointed out lightly.

"Nervous is better than dead," Olyra replied with a shrug.

"Well, at least one of you looks after security," Fali said with a glance at Ryheart.

"So, where exactly are we going?" Olyra asked.

"Yeah, I wouldn't mind knowing either," Ryheart chimed in.

Their guide had told them the general situation, that they were out to find and pre-empt some force of corruption, but not precisely what that entailed.

"That direction," Fali said laconically, pointing at the horizon.

"Don't want to tell me about our destination?" Olyra asked shrewdly.

"No. I just do not know," Fali admitted candidly. "The dragon knew something is causing corruption to seep from the void and into this realm in a way that breaks the seal upon such things. Now he has pointed it out to me, I have a lock on it, but I could not tell you precisely. I estimate around a week's travel if we go by horse. Fortunately, the terrain did not seem too foreboding on the map."

"Marve-fuckin'-llous," Olyra muttered. "I love having no intel to work with."

"Hopefully, I can narrow it down more as we get nearer. Something's stopping me getting a definitive fix on it for now."

"Let's hope," Olyra agreed.

"Well, I think we are going to go to sleep now. Long day," Fali said after the human pair had eaten. "Watch the camp, will you?"

"What, in that little thing?" Olyra asked, with a dubious glance at their tent.

"Why, yes. I am only petite, dear," Fali said. "I will come to relieve you after a bit."

"Don't let the bed-imps bite," Olyra said sardonically.

Ryheart frowned, puzzled, and followed Fali to the tent. For starters, Fali barely slept, and the tent was far too small for two people to berth comfortably.

They climbed in and even sat up; they scarcely had room to fit.

"This is, err, cosy," Ryheart murmured.

"Indeed, it is. Do you trust me?" Fali asked, somewhat obliquely.

"Err. I did till you asked, why?"

"Close your eyes. We are going to need a little more room than this."

Ryheart stared at her in puzzlement, but she didn't offer any further explanation. He sighed and did so.

He briefly felt her soft fingers on his forehead, then a tingle.

"Alright, open them now, dear-heart," Fali commanded Ryheart softly.

When he did, he nearly jumped out of his skin. No longer were they in the little tent. Instead, they stood in a large, seemingly endless field, sky bright and cheery. Hundreds of small, circular, ornamental gardens surrounded them, each contained within a low idyllic fence. As he looked around, bewildered, he saw some of them looked like traditional Brittayan country gardens, uniform and immaculate with stone walls around them. Others had a distinctly foreign feel, with bamboo fences, rock gardens, pools and the like.

Far off in the distance, he could make out patches of garden that were wildly overgrown, the sky black and stormy over them with the occasional flash of lightning.

"Where in the name of the gods are we?" he asked in disbelief.

"My memories," she said simply, "or a visualisation of them at least. I can bring you here now we are linked. We needed more room, and this is the easiest way to keep Olyra out of the loop whilst I begin your training."

"What if she tries to shoot you?"

"My familiar is keeping an eye on her."

"So, what are the gardens?" he asked, thoughts jumbled.

"Each one is a different recollection."

"Your memories are beautiful," he said in awe.

"Why, thank you," she said with a warm smile and purple eyes that made his stomach churn.

"What are those storm clouds?" he asked, pointing at a particularly violent display.

"The bad ones," she dismissed without elaboration. Ryheart got the distinct sense pushing wouldn't get him any more than that. Without a word, she leant over the fence of the nearest garden and waved him over. Joining her, he watched, enthralled, as two miniature figures of Fali and Olyra appeared in the centre, locked in a violent battle.

"Not that this isn't fascinating, but why are we here?" he asked, eyes still on the tiny display.

"We are here to look at your memories, if we may. You know, I have not seen you in action the entire time we have been together. We were separated during your fight with the Nemean, and with Olyra. The nearest I have seen is you nearly getting eaten by a doppelganger."

Ryheart blushed slightly at that but pushed forward.

"So you want to watch me fight?" he asked, understanding where she was leading.

"Exactly. I want to know exactly how Olyra beat you, and what you need to avoid that happening again if it comes to it."

"She was just better," he admitted candidly. "I'm used to fighting dumb monsters, not people. I don't exactly have a handle on this power you gave me, either."

"Well, let us see specifically how she exploited that. We can increase your general skill, no problem. Frankly, we can only improve in that regard. But I do not want just to teach you how to fight; I want to teach you how to fight her. How to fight a barghest. How to fight a kelpie. And when previous experience fails you, how to figure that out even while you fight."

"Alright. I'm in. What do I have to do?"

"Oh, I just need to focus this on you." As she spoke, she tapped his head once more, and the world around them melted away like watercolours scrubbed from a canvas.

Chapter Forty-Seven

Memorandum

A long white hallway sketched itself around the pair; wooden doors stretched in front of them, a small, bounty-like description upon each.

"Oh, Ryheart," Fali said in an almost disappointed tone, "this is a very drab way to keep your memories."

"I didn't exactly choose it," he said defensively.

"Ah, that is alright. Men nearly always store their things in such bland, unimaginative ways. I can hardly blame you for your sex, can I?"

"Gee, thanks," he said dryly. "So where do we go?"

"You tell me?" she said with a shrug. "These are your memories. I have not the slightest idea what is behind those doors. Try to focus on your fight with Olyra, and you should feel where it is."

"Alright," he said dubiously, concentrating on the soldier. He thought about her strong musculature, her ebony skin and her blunt manner. The immediate, almost casual violence locked behind her methodical, assessing eyes.

He felt a pull and stopped a few doors down. He couldn't say why it was that door. He just knew.

"I think this one?"

Fali shrugged and gestured for him to try. He opened it tentatively and poked his head inside, just to be sure nothing embarrassing lurked there. Inside was a square space, filled with the landscape he had battled Olyra in. The pair of them, him and her, stood motionless, actors waiting for a cue.

It felt bizarre to be staring at a full-size, fully fleshed-out version of himself.

"Well, it is not the prettiest way to keep your memories, but the clarity is excellent," Fali said admiringly.

"Err, yeah, thanks. How do I...?" he started to ask, then, again, sort of just knew the answer. He waved his hand, and the figures began their little battle. Their little, one-sided battle. He couldn't help but feel a bit embarrassed watching it. Olyra had dominated the fight quite spectacularly. Aside from his one surprise use of his new power, he hadn't landed a single solid blow on her. He had only kept up because of the warrior's surprising restraint towards doing him significant harm. Even he could see that there were several times she could have lethally escalated if she had wished.

Fali tutted once but was otherwise silent.

Eventually, Olyra knocked him out, and the figures abruptly disappeared.

"Well, your martial prowess is lacking," Fali noted bluntly, "but I am impressed you managed to draw power out of my blood without my patronage, or conscious knowledge of how to do so."

"Thanks. It just sort of exploded, when I thought about, well..." Ryheart thought of his feeling towards Fali and towards his impotence at the time, then trailed off, "about the situation I was in."

"Strong feelings towards one's patron and their goals helps," Fali informed him. He wasn't quite sure whether that was a general point or if she had intuited his thoughts. "Whilst her armour gave her an advantage, if you could have made effective use of your 'talent', let's call it, you would have had an even playing field. Perhaps the upper hand, even."

"Every time I tried, she dodged it."

"Yes. Let us see if we cannot remedy that in the week," she agreed. "Now, is there anything else you wish to see before we leave?"

As comfortable as he had become with his friendship with Fali, he didn't think it overly prudent to go poking around random memories with her present. Particularly since he had seen her naked.

"Not at the moment."

"Fair enough," she said, and as she tapped his head again, everything washed away around them until they stood in a small field, stark white purity surrounding them. The place carried the smell of the flowers that always pervaded from Fali.

"So where are we now?" he asked.

"We are drifting," she said, "nowhere in particular."

"Who are we going to watch fighting this time, then?" he asked, confused.

"Me and you. And we will not just be watching."

"We're going to fight?" he asked, the prospect making him feel uncomfortable for a variety of reasons.

"Well, I can hardly teach you to fight without doing so, can I?" she said with a small smile, stretching daintily as if preparing for a picnic. "Now, I believe I have a handle on Olyra's capabilities. I am going to constrain myself to roughly her speed and reactions. Try to knock me off my feet. Like you did with her."

"You, err, you don't have armour like she did," he pointed out.

"Trust me, dear-heart, that will not be an issue," she said with a worryingly confident smile. "For starters, do not forget your power derives from me. Secondly, well, you would have to hit me for that to be a relevant problem. Now, come."

Feeling a little awkward about attacking an unarmoured friend, even in practice, he nevertheless complied.

She dodged the first few of his punches, then stopped even bothering. She just let them glance off at a slight angle. Even through his padded gloves, his hand smarted at the blow. She wasn't wearing armour, but he felt like he was punching a stone wall.

Not entertaining his basic abilities as any threat, he focused on the power within him. Since their strange ceremony, he had been palpably aware of it sleeping within him. Now at his summoning, it burst awake with a rush of power scarcely recognisable. If before he had felt a trickle, this was like a torrent. He couldn't help grinning with exhilaration as the power and adrenaline coursed through him.

With a shout, he launched a thundering blow at her. This punch, she didn't ignore. She didn't get hit by it either, however. She deftly sidestepped the strike, then, unlike Olyra, stood and calmly waited for him to try again.

Grunting with consternation, he rushed her again, and once more, she nimbly leaned aside. He didn't let up this time, caught in the sheer power raging in him. He launched a flurry at her, mixing in powered blows, but again, she dodged each one.

Frustrated, he tried to call on even more of the power, trying to overwhelm her with sheer force and speed of blow. He tried another jab, and this time she didn't even wait for him to throw it. He had scarcely even begun to move his arm when she slapped the offending limb back down.

"Ryheart," she snapped, "stop flexing your muscles and flex your brain. I am easily dodging every attempt you make. How?"

"You're too fast," he grunted, breathing heavily from the exertion. Pulling upon this power was proving tremendously draining.

"No," she dismissed, clearly irritated, "it is not speed. I am reacting before you even throw a punch. How?"

"You know when I'm going to attack with the talent," he said, with sudden realisation.

"Exactly. I can feel the crackle in the air, smell the ozone emanating. Heck, your hand is practically glowing. I do not need to be fast; I know what you are attempting almost before you do."

"You're reacting to the talent, not the punch itself."

"Exactly. Olyra has plenty of experience fighting magical creatures. I am sure she knows the tell-tale signs magic is about to erupt. While your power is not strictly magic, it is similar enough. Now, we know the issue. How can we avoid it? Fighting is not just about outclassing someone. It is about observation and adaption. Capitalising on what your opponent is, or is not, doing. You need to be able to work out why your attack is not working, or we might as well call this a day before we even start."

He frowned. He'd never had to worry about fighting something sentient before, not seriously. This was different from fighting dumb beasts. Evidently, the use of talent was the issue, but how could he fix it? He had no clue if it was even possible to disguise those tell-tale signs she had mentioned; they were just a by-product he had no control over.

If he couldn't disguise them, though, what? He could, perhaps, minimise the time they were present. He had been letting the power course through him the entire time he had been throwing punches.

Trying his best to restrain himself, he delivered a punch, only opening the floodgates after he started swinging.

She dodged, but much later this time, and with far less safety room between her and his fist.

"Excellent," she said in an approving voice. "The bulk of the force comes from the transference of power when you connect, not from the punch itself, so there is no need to let it out until you connect. You are still too early, though. Again!"

He swung again, a fraction later with the talent, and a fraction closer.

"Again!" she repeated. He followed up his first punch with another immediately, and she had to step back to avoid it this time. "Good, good. Keep coming!"

He was not only new to the power itself but new to rapidly summoning it, and the process was exceptionally taxing. He could palpably feel his reserves emptying with each swing.

Mixing regular punches with the powered ones, he launched a last-ditch flurry. As she couldn't confidently predict which blows were feints and which might be about to spark with power, she had to dodge every one of them, keeping her off balance and on the defensive.

He directed a rapid jab at her midsection, then, as she stepped sideways, swung at her with his other fist. Leaving it as late as he could manage, he flared up all the power he could summon. The blow hit her, and there was a sudden spark of light. The energy flowed from his fist to her in an explosion, flinging her clean of her feet. With a graceful roll, she sprang back up.

"Yes!" he cried triumphantly, panting with exertion. "Err, are you alright?"

"Grand," she said with a smile he thought contained a degree of pride. "You got there eventually."

"Give me a minute, and we can go again."

"No. You have adapted a remarkable amount in a short time. You need to internalise what you have learned and let it sink from conscious thought into muscle memory. Get a step closer to doing it without the need for active thought."

"Aww, come on, I can go again! Just let me catch my breath."

"No," she repeated, firmer this time. "While I admire the enthusiasm, if you keep going while you are fatigued, you will get sloppier and internalise bad form. Frankly, part of the reason you are an interesting disciple is you have so little experience you are practically a blank slate for me to work on. You have not picked up any bad habits you need to break. The last thing we need is to sully that foundation. We work hard, then rest. My presence will speed up your development now we have a bond, but the higher development will also tire you faster."

"Alright, alright," he acquiesced. "I did well, though, right?"

"Yes, yes," she said with a small laugh, "very well."

"I did hit you," he said with a grin, joining her laughter.

"Yes, you did," she said warmly, mischievous grin returning. "Tomorrow, I'm going to hit back, though."

She walked back over to him, addressing him once their laughter subsided. "One last thing before we finish. Now your heart is bonded to mine, we can use that to communicate with one another wordlessly. It is not talking so much as projecting a concept to the other. It takes time to learn to do so over long distances and for you to project yourself, but we should just about be able to get you able to recognise a few basic signals while we are close."

"Even if we can only do it while we're close enough to talk normally, that has all kinds of uses," Ryheart pondered. "Would have come in handy while we were dealing with the doppelganger."

"Exactly," Fali said with a smile, "and we can use it to gossip about Olyra."

Chapter Forty-Eight

Ride

The trio reached the way-stop at almost precisely midday, and Ryheart begrudgingly had to admit that Olyra's forced march was at least highly accurate in timekeeping, though not out loud.

Olyra dutifully rented three horses for them, along with a fourth to carry their bags, so they could rotate and give each horse somewhat of a break with the lighter load, allowing them to travel further without stopping.

Ryheart had only a little experience riding, provided in his brief guild training, but their pace allowed him to adjust. Both Fali and Olyra seemed to prefer a steady but long day, with an early stop but an even earlier start, rather than a mad sprint that would inevitably tire them out.

He was enjoying being off his feet and not carrying his pack, though after some time, he – specifically, his rear end – began to chafe somewhat with the constant bounce. Olyra sat tall-backed and proud upon her horse like she was in a parade; Fali sat sideways with her legs dangling as if she were on a swing.

"Is that not unwise?" Olyra had asked her, but Fali was naturally nonchalant.

"Oh, the horse and I have an understanding," she had answered. "He will not throw me off." Ryheart wasn't entirely sure how literal she was being.

"How's the rabbit keep up?" Olyra asked her, glancing back at the sometimes-present creature.

"I thought we finished playing at interrogation?" Fali pointed out lightly, in what Ryheart recognised to be her sometimes wry sense of humour.

"It was just a question," Olyra said defensively with a shrug. "Don't answer if you don't want."

Sighing softly, the Fae answered, "He does not have to keep up because he is not really here. Or at least, not entirely here. He can hop between realms to cover the distance."

"Is that like the, err, trick you showed me?" Ryheart asked, not wanting to let slip about their night-time soirees.

"Yes, somewhat. He is not entirely present, at least not in the plains of reality humans can see."

"Is that like your wings?" Olyra queried. "They were the same. Visible one minute and gone the next. Even when I knew they were there."

Fali seemed surprised by her intuition. "Yes, nearly exactly similar. They are my anchor to my realm, so they are not entirely here. Consequently, they do not always show. Fae with keener eyes than yours can see them more reliably."

"See your wings?" Ryheart asked. "I seem to remember you saying a bird ate them."

"Err, yes," Fali said, blushing ever so slightly. Ryheart couldn't help but grin at having gained a point on her in some small capacity. "That was a teeny bit of a fib."

"Why, Fali," he said, mimicking her inflexion and putting his hand on his chest as she sometimes did, "what a thing a do. Are you suggesting you haven't always been truthful with me?"

He stared at her eyes wide, and then they both burst into a laugh. They had come a long way with each other in the past days together.

"So, what did happen to them?" he asked after their mirth subsided.

"I, ah, thought it convenient to hide them for a time," Fali said with a not overly subtle glance towards Olyra that suggested she was the culprit.

"Fair enough," he said, picking up on the fact she was attempting to keep civility between the group.

"So this magic disturbance we're riding to," Olyra asked, "any idea at all what's causing it?"

"Some, possibly," Fali admitted. "I would rather not speculate."

"It's good to be prepared for what's ahead."

"Yes, it is. I would rather we not start to convince ourselves of an outcome before we have a clear picture, though. Avoid falling into the trap of making the evidence fit the theory, rather than the theory fit the evidence. Besides, I am sure you have something to deal with nearly all manner of Fae in those pockets, do you not?"

"Why only nearly? What do you think I can't deal with?"

"Why, me, of course," Fali said in a mild tone. "Surely you have determined that by now?"

Even the stoic Olyra couldn't help a small laugh at the sheer gall.

They carried on well past the point Ryheart was feeling raw, then stopped again and made camp slightly off the road. Now they had the horses, they stuck to more circuitous but safer routes, rather than cutting through wild country. Once they stopped for the eve again, Olyra sat meticulously cleaning her equipment and armour.

Ryheart watched, her almost mechanical efficiency near hypnotic. She occasionally glanced over at him, her finger tapping faster every time.

"Alright, give that to me," she demanded, pointing her finger at his battered armour. "I can't stand seeing it in such a state any longer. It's more likely to give you an infection than protect you."

They spent the next couple of hours re-padding and strapping the leather armour, filing rust from the bits of metal. Ryheart begrudgingly had to admit that while Olyra was blunt to the point of being abrasive, there was a certain charm in her directness. By the time they had finished, his armour, while still not the finest quality, looked better than it had even when he first bought it.

Once again, Fali and Ryheart retired early to their little tent. He found calling on the thrilling new power he had at a moment's notice a touch easier to do now, and it tired him that bit less. Despite their nightly sessions, he also seemed to get a whole night's sleep. He wasn't sure time was passing correctly while they were in the strange dreamscape Fali took them to. He did become exhausted like what he was doing was real, though.

As well as teaching him to harness his new talent, she started to get him used to recognising simple mental suggestions. The idea he should 'wait', 'run' or 'fight' would flash in his mind and somehow just intrinsically felt like Fali in a way he couldn't entirely explain.

He also found if he concentrated, he could feel a gentle presence radiating from her and, even with his eyes closed, could tell the vague direction she was in while she was nearby.

Lastly, she began to teach him a series of martial stances. Eventually, he got curious enough about it to ask her directly.

"What is this martial art we're learning?" he asked.

"Why, I do not really know," she replied after a pause. "I never bothered to name it."

Chapter Forty-Nine

Suffala

As the group travelled, the roads they were on gradually got smaller and less well maintained, winding along natural paths rather than cutting through. On the fourth day of their travels, they came to a small village called Suffala comfortably nestled within a valley, a smattering of buildings with little in the way of town planning.

Along the east of the village ran farmland, bursting with a vibrant array of crops, aside from a sickly looking patch of wilt.

"That is unusual," Fali pointed out with a nod.

"How so?" Ryheart asked.

"Well, is it not customary to leave part of your land fallow so the soil enriches? They have every inch planted; they will drain it dry."

"Is that what's causing the ill-looking patch?"

"Perhaps. It is a bit localised. We should have a poke around here, anyway."

"Why?" Olyra asked, frowning. "Why are we wasting time here?"

"Because I am having trouble keeping a hold of the trail," Fali admitted. "It should be getting easier as we get closer. Instead, it is more difficult. We can ask if the locals have any idea about anything strange. I am a tad outdated, but I presume the local pub's still as good a place as any? I am happy to bow to your greater experience, regardless."

Olyra gave a thin smile. "The best place for gossip is still with a drink in your hand. Or in the gossiper's hands, anyway."

"Grand. We can probably stable the horses and get a room, too."

They found the place to be a small but rosy tavern, old wooden tables and stools scattered throughout. The patrons appeared to be entirely locals, and the new strange arrivals brought a few glances.

"Do you have rooms?" Fali asked the matronly patron at the bar.

"Wouldn't be much of an inn if we didn't."

"Marvellous. I suppose these two need to eat, too. Any food on?"

"We have stew and bread, only a day old. D'you want three bowls?"

"Just two, thank you."

Now used to eating while Fali simply observed, Ryheart and Olyra finished their meals quickly. The food was good, though simple.

"We're probably better off circulating individually," Olyra suggested. "People might be less talkative if three people interrogate them."

"Ah, chat, Olyra," Fali corrected lightly.

"A slip of the tongue," Olyra said with one of her sardonic smiles.

"So, what are we asking about?" Ryheart asked.

"If anything strange has occurred nearby," Fali said. "A disturbance this large must have had at least some effect on its surroundings."

They scattered, and Ryheart found himself with three older men. After their initial curiosity, once Olyra had bought them all a round of drinks, the newcomers were suddenly like one of the old crew. Olyra sat murmuring to a young couple, and Fali appeared to have found herself in a drinking competition with a small crowd that was fascinated by her strange appearance.

After talking for some time, the three gradually drifted back to each other.

"Any intel?" Olyra quizzed. "All I got was some cows have gone missing. They're blaming it on monsters, but the guild won't send anyone."

"Promising," Fali said.

"Maybe. Village folk think their lunch going missing is because of a monster, though," Olyra murmured in a low voice.

"It is the farm next to the one with the little crop problem, though," Ryheart said. "Can't hurt to check. Speaking of superstitions, I don't know how relevant this is, but apparently, the local legend around here is a witch steals naughty children, but that's not exactly an uncommon folktale. You find anything, Fali?"

Fali glanced at Olyra briefly before speaking. "Apparently, the crop farm uses some kind of magic."

Olyra's eyes lit up at that. "As in unlicensed magic?"

"I could not say. I presume you have much less of a presence out here?"

"Our sensors are primarily within major cities, yes," Olyra admitted.

"Well, given you have a walking sensor with you, let us find out, shall we?"

They walked to the farm, a cheerful wooden sign declaring it Donovan Farm. A muscular farmer was working in the field, wisps of auburn hair peeking from his straw hat.

Wiping his hands on his rough trousers, he held out a hand. "Good afternoon," he said, a musical lilt to his voice that carried clear from the neighbouring island of Eiruya, "My name is Cian Donovan. Are you after my services?"

Olyra stepped ahead of the group and shook his hand firmly. "That we are. We're hunter-scouts, out to appraise if the place needs a bounty hunter dispatching. You wouldn't happen to know about anything of the sort, would you?"

"Ah," he said, slightly deflated, "so you won't be wanting any produce?"

"Well, actually, we're anticipating being in the area a while, so we're looking to buy at least a few days' worth."

The farmer's interest immediately perked up again. Olyra and the young man haggled for near ten minutes, despite her having paid face value for everything else they had bought. In the end, they settled on a price that was, if anything, generous. The farmer seemed thrilled by the price, and her willingness to play the game even more so. They spat and shook hands on the deal.

"Excellent. If it's good, we'll be wanting as much as three horses can carry for the way back."

"It's the best this side of the Selkie Ocean, I promise y'that."

"Oh? How do you know that for sure?"

"Well," he said, lowering his voice conspiratorially, "y'wont go spreading this around, will you? We get on with Fae a bit better around here nowadays, but them city folk have some queer aversion to anything magical."

"Yes, I've heard," Olyra said mildly. "I won't tell a soul."

"Well, there's a group of them dryads that live to the east past the tributaries. We have a little trade with them. Every couple of months, they fetch us a big wagonload of soil. I don't think it's magical, really, but it's the most fertile soil you've ever laid eyes on."

"How in Brittaya did you get them to do that? They couldn't care less about money."

"Ah. My old granda' lived near a grove, back home. He found out they're absolutely mad for sugar. He used to feed them sweets, and they'd bless his garden. Now we send them a wagon full of baked goods, and they bring us back the same one with soil in it."

"That is genius," Fali murmured. "I have bribed them with sugar to get them to do things for me before, but I would have never thought of upscaling it. You humans."

"You aren't after setting yourself up as competition, are ye?" the farmer jested.

"Ah, no. We are a tad nomadic for that. How come the soil in that patch there is so poor?" Fali asked, subtly taking control of the conversation from Olyra. "Those crops seem less than healthy."

"Haven't the foggiest," he said with a frown. "Last planting, we had a few of the old crates left. That corner, we broke out the new delivery for. Buggered the entire crop there. Need to have a word next time I see them."

"Mind if I take a look?" Fali asked.

"What's a hunter-scout know about soil? Ye getting notions?"

"Not a lot," she admitted, "but dryad blessings and magic, I know."

"Can't hurt." The farmer shrugged, leading them to a storage shed, booting the door open. "In them crates there. There's a bit left in the open one."

The crates were bulky oblongs stacked upon other containers, and Fali had to stand on tiptoes to reach inside. She sniffed the clod of soil she extracted, touched it to her tongue, then spat it violently back out. She remained calm, but Ryheart noticed the flecks of grey clouding her eyes that suggested she was ill at ease.

"Can I open the other crates?" she asked, the humour gone from her voice.

"Knock yourself out."

Fali proceeded to walk down the line, opening each crate and sniffing the loam. If the humour was gone before, now she was positively deadpan, and there were embers of blood-red in her eyes he hadn't witnessed before.

"I recommend in the strongest terms you do not use another ounce of this soil on your farm."

"Why?" Cian questioned.

"Because it is not dryad loam. It is desecrated grave dirt."

"Grave dirt? Why would the buggerin' woodies send me that?"

"They did not. I believe, if you were to trace the route into the forest, you would find your wagon dumped off the path, with your gifts still in it. Further along, you would likely find your soil dumped."

"Someone swapped the dirt?" the farmer said, puzzled.

"Yes."

"Wouldn't the woodies notice?"

Their red-haired guide paused a moment, then locked eyes with him. "You said you were going to speak to the dryads next time they came. They do the actual wagon run?"

"We gave them the horse and cart, but yes. They know the forest much better."

"Last you spoke to them, did they seem off?"

"Well…" the farmer mused, "I didn't think anything of it, but dryads have a peculiar way of speaking. Not an accent, but different slang. Lots of talk about trees and fertility. This time she was very formal. Almost archaic. Less chatty. Why, was something wrong with her?"

"I think 'her', was not her."

"But she looked identical! All gangly and twiggy."

"We ran into a shapeshifter that you'd be amazed by," Ryheart chimed in. "Is that what you're thinking, Fali?"

"Along similar lines."

"What about the actual dryad then?" Olyra asked. "Why'd they not turn up?"

Fali didn't answer for a long moment, and then she sighed sadly. "I believe she is dead."

"Dead?" the farmer exclaimed, suddenly very pale. "Why?"

"Eight vampires and whoever imitated her is a lot for one dryad to deal with. Especially taken by surprise away from their grove and sisters."

"Vampires," Ryheart said with a shiver. "Why eight?"

"The crates," Olyra pre-empted with a snap of her fingers. "Eight crates of grave dirt, eight vampires."

"Exactly. All that running water to the east would make it generally impossible for them to find their way here, even by night. With someone to cart them across packed in deathbed soil, though, they could move freely."

"Why would anyone do that?" Ryheart asked, flabbergasted.

"That, I do not know. Vampires are not the most social creatures, even within their nests. The suggestion they are cooperating with something is deeply troubling."

"There is a black market for monsters," Olyra suggested. "Underground fighting, rare materials for illegal rituals. Selling to the highest bidder."

"Yes, but why here, if so? No offence to Cian here, but this village is too small and remote to make any money from that. And whoever drove the cart is a shifter or has a glamour."

"Why come here at all?"

"I do not know," Fali admitted candidly, "but I do not think they came specifically to this village. To be frank, if they were still here, there would be more than just crops spoiled. I believe they left as soon as night fell. The business with the cart was just to remain undetected. How long ago did they deliver?"

"Near a month ago," the farmer supplied.

"Elkesozzpath," Fali spat vehemently. "That is too long for a solid trail. When did the cows start going missing from the neighbouring field?"

"Around the same time, come to think of it. Old Daris has gone to try to convince one of them outposts to come to investigate, but they said he was talking bollocks, so he's went along to the capital."

"Alright. Well, given no one has gone missing since then, I think they are staying away. However, I would stay indoors at night."

"I'll tell folk hunters have advised them to. Folk usually do what hunters tell 'em. Should we hang garlic?"

"It would not hurt. It is not a ward, mind, but vampires have good noses, and it smells horrendous. What I would do is lock all your doors and cover all your windows. If there are any first-generation vampires, they could compel you to let them in. Thank you for the help, Cian. Hopefully, we will see you again after we resolve this."

With that, she bowed her head and then they walked away.

Chapter Fifty

Indifference

"That was very smooth back there," Fali complimented Olyra as they left the farm.

"What was?" Ryheart queried.

"The food. We did not need it; we have the provisions Olyra bought on the way here. People tend to be more forthcoming with information once they have made a profit from you, though."

"Especially if they anticipate making more down the line," Olyra added.

"Oh. That's a bit clinical, isn't it?" Ryheart mused.

"Yes. Effective, though," Olyra said with a tight smile. "What's the plan?"

"We go back to the inn for the night," Fali decided, "pick this back up at first light. I do not intend to go looking for vampires in the dark if we can help it."

They bedded for the night in clean but pokey rooms, Ryheart sleeping fitfully. For the first time since they had started their training ritual, Fali didn't teach him anything further. She simply suggested via a mental nudge 'sleep'.

After an uneventful night, they trudged into the pasture Cian had mentioned, cows eying them lazily.

"Sniffed anything out?" Olyra asked after Fali had led them around the field.

"I am not a dog, Olyra," she said primly, "but, yes. Vampires have walked this dirt. I believe they have simply carried cows away. That is why no one has taken this seriously. Monsters usually kill, eat or drain on the spot. They do not usually clean up after themselves. I believe whatever brought them here has convinced them to be secretive."

"So where now?" Ryheart asked.

"Let us find out," Fali said, sitting down in the soil, then looking up at Olyra. "You are not going to try to shoot me this time, are you?"

"I'll restrain myself," she replied dryly.

"Grand. That tends to hamper concentration somewhat. I am having trouble tracking their 'scent' the same way I'm having trouble finding the disturbance. Now then…" she said, closing her eyes and trailing off.

"How long will it take?" Ryheart asked after a minute of awkward silence.

The Fae simply held her hand up in response.

"Ah. Quaint," Fali murmured after another interminable minute.

"Quaint?"

"There is magic ahead trying to make me uninterested in paying attention to it. It is rather powerful, but extraordinary clumsy. No finesse. It is like a sledgehammer beating on your brain saying, 'There is nothing noteworthy over here, do not bother looking.'"

"Vampires aren't my speciality, but I haven't heard of them doing that sort of thing," Olyra mused.

"No, their magic is all internal. This is a bona fide spell."

"What Fae are responsible?" Olyra demanded.

"I am not sure they are. This feels distinctly human, which explains the clumsiness. You have no instinct for it."

"So, someone did this with an artefact or something?" Ryheart asked.

"Humans can use magical trinkets other races have made," Fali informed, "like Olyra's little band that lets her channel stored magic into her weapon, but this is too strong for that. You cannot actively use magic; you do not have it your blood."

"So how can it be human then?"

"There are rare ways humans can have magical affinity forced into their system for an extreme price. It is extraordinarily dangerous."

"What, they're that powerful?"

"Quite the opposite. Invariably they are quite weak, at least on a cosmic scale. It is the lack of restrictions and knowledge of limits that is dangerous. There are certain things possible with magic that can have catastrophic consequences if botched. Some spells can have a dire effect even performed correctly. Humans, however, seem to find curiosity stronger than sense."

"Like what?" Ryheart asked, suppressing a shiver.

"Mucking about with the weather, for starters."

"Didn't you call a wind when we engaged?" Olyra asked dubiously.

"You also asked the clouds not to rain," Ryheart added, "assuming you weren't taking the piss."

"Yes, but I know what I am doing, and I tidied up after myself. Humans all too often find out what they need to know, not what they should know. If I had just left the wind to carry on its business, you could have had a hurricane inside your little city."

"I hadn't thought about magic having natural reactions," Olyra admitted.

"That is exactly the issue. You never do. You just make your little half-constructed spells and then forget them, and you never remember to clean up after yourself. Do not even get me started on when you try to muck about with time."

"Time?" Olyra asked, wide-eyed.

"Divinities, it is the first thing any enchanted with a modicum of real power and a bargain book of spell-work thinks they can handle. It is far too complicated and power-consuming for nearly anyone to pull off, thank heavens. Now and then, though, they get lucky and manage something. Perhaps they freeze time or slow it down briefly. It makes an absolute wreck of reality in the area. The pocket of time is stopped and restarted, fine. But then that little bubble's out of sync with the rest of creation. Left unchecked, it can destabilise the barriers between realms. Let alone actually travelling through time, tearing all sorts of holes as you go."

"Can you do that?" Ryheart asked, astonished.

"What, make a mess of things?"

"No, travel through time!"

"Oh. Yes, at times."

"What do you mean, 'at times'?"

"Well. I know how, and possess the capacity. I cannot act upon it except to fix a break someone else has made, though."

"What are you, to be charged with fixing time?" Ryheart asked in a small voice.

Fali fixed him with a long stare, then gently laid a hand on his. "I think you know, deep down. I think in your heart, you always have. Your mind just will not quite let itself catch up yet. Soon, though. Soon."

"You said magic humans aren't powerful," Olyra interjected, "but you also said this human spell is powerful. How's that work?"

"I do not know." Fali frowned. "It is far beyond the ken of even an enchanted human's power. A human might well be ambitious enough to think they could control vampires and make this spell. But to actually do so? No. Not without a patron. This field of obfuscation is unmistakably human, though. I would stake my crown upon it."

"Your crown?" Olyra asked.

"Yes, did I not mention that I was a queen, dear-heart?" Fali asked with a hint of her usual mischief. Ryheart couldn't help feeling a slight surge of jealousy at her calling someone he still viewed at best as a wary ally by such a term of endearment.

"So if you can't stay interested enough in the place, how are we going to get there?"

"Well, I can push through that, but stopping the effect will also stop me from sensing its centre. Unfortunately, the magic in the area will disrupt my familiar, so we cannot rely upon him. Instead, we are going to narrow that down by avian means."

"Avian means?"

"Yes. I cannot really say it more directly than that," Fali said with a light shrug as if her meaning were self-evident. Her stubbornness towards explanations drove Ryheart up the wall, but he couldn't help but chuckle.

"You know," Olyra said to him, "she might just be the most infuriating person I've ever met."

"Yes," he agreed, "I think the most annoying part is how she manages to make it charming."

"It's bloody adorable. I hate that it's adorable."

"Now then, stand very still for me, you two," Fali commanded.

"Why? It's not dangerous, is it?" Olyra asked, eyes narrowed.

"Oh, of course not," Fali dismissed. "I would hardly be about to risk harming Ryheart, would I? I like him."

"And me?"

"You, I am still working on," she said, eliciting a small laugh from the stoic soldier. "Now, stand very still, please."

Despite her slight suspicion, Olyra stood militarily still. Fali let out a small series of chirps, and then after a few minutes in which she refused to answer questions, a tawny sparrow swooped down and nestled on top of Olyra's head.

Fali proceeded to whistle back and forth intermittently for several minutes while Olyra looked decidedly uncomfortable, and then finally, the bird flew away.

"Did it have to use my head?" Olyra asked pointedly.

"Why, where else would it land?"

"Your head?"

"Oh, no, that wouldn't do! Body language is crucial for birds."

"What about his head, then?" she said, pointing at Ryheart.

"He is a bit taller than you," Fali said in a sweetly reasonable tone. "I would have had to stand on my tiptoes to speak to it."

"Alright, fine," Olyra said with a sigh. "What did you learn?"

"Well, he has the loveliest nest in the forest."

"What did it say that was useful?" she clarified in an exasperated voice.

"Well, there is a reason bird-brained is an expression. The advantage is they are too dense to be bamboozled by such spells. There is a small building in the centre of these woods, and the trees are exceptionally sick around it. That is where we are headed. Now, one last thing before we go. I am becoming more convinced that there is some exceptionally dark magic involved here, beyond even vampires. If you want to turn back, this might be the last chance you have."

"I promised I'd follow you," Ryheart said after a moment. "I'll be where you need me."

"All I care about is protecting the country from magical threats," Olyra said. "Regardless of what you think of me, I mean it."

"Very well." Fali addressed them both, "Come along then."

Chapter Fifty-One

Obfuscation

As they travelled, the forest took on a sickly, pale tone. The Crooked Woods had been twisted and cruel. Here the trees were just ill, tired and barely clinging to life.

At first, as they walked, Ryheart felt disinterested, as if carrying on was some tedious chore. As they continued, his disinterest turned to unease, and then outright revulsion. He found himself dragging his feet and sweating from the effort. As he felt he could no longer cope, Fali called them to stop. Even Olyra's implacable expression showed relief, and she turned her back from the direction they were travelling. Ryheart had to fight the impulse not to run back to the village.

"Alright, we are hardly making progress anymore, and this is only going to get worse. Take my hands," Fali commanded, holding a palm out to each of them.

"Why?" Olyra asked hesitantly.

"Because it is getting to the point that it is hard for even me to ignore this passively. I will shield our minds from the effect, and it is much easier with direct contact. It means I will not be able to sense the corruption anymore, but that's what the bird's directions were for."

Ryheart took her hand, feeling a little embarrassed, and so did Olyra. He was surprised how his skin tingled as he touched her glowing hand, but with relief, he immediately felt the oppressive force pushing on his mind fade away.

"Honestly, you Brittayans have so many hang-ups about physical contact," Fali tutted. "You are like children."

"You Brittayans?" he asked as they set off again.

"Yes, you and Olyra, dear-heart. Who else?"

Ryheart couldn't help but feel like a child being led around by the hand, especially with her gentle scolding.

"I don't know. I just assumed you were one?" he said, feeling awkward. "You don't have an accent, and you kind of look sort of inherently Brittayan."

"Ah, that. I am not of any nationality. Remember, I am a creature of magic. Not like other Fae, who are still born here. I am not just a creature with magic; I am magic. I am not flesh and blood the way you are."

"Is that why you bleed crazy colours?" Olyra asked. Ryheart determined not to ask when she had seen said blood.

"Yes. My magic reacts with ambient magic in the atmosphere and dissipates."

"So, did you, err, choose to look Brittayan?" Ryheart asked further.

"No. When you met me, you met me in Brittaya. I have no accent, at least that you could hear. So, given you are Brittayan yourself, you presumed I was and saw me as such. If you had met me in a different country speaking their language, you would likely have visualised me with more, ah, foreign persuasion."

"So, what, I imagined you?"

"Not exactly, no. I am always this height and build naturally formed. My eyes, hair, everything important remains. I am just not 'white', or anything else, for that matter."

"So what colour is your skin?"

"Magic-coloured. My presence radiating always gives whatever you perceive a golden tinge, but aside from that, human eyes cannot process the colour; hence you fill the gaps in." She paused and looked across to him. "Is my colour really so important, dear-heart?"

"No, no," he said firmly, "not at all. It's just weird I don't see the real you, I guess."

"You see who I am," she said, squeezing his hand lightly. "That is the real me."

"I did wonder about that," Olyra mused.

"About what?"

"Well, you, err, changed colours."

"Oh?"

"It's a bit… silly," Olyra said hesitantly. Uncharacteristically, Ryheart thought she looked almost embarrassed.

"How so?" Fali prompted lightly.

"Well, you came from the stars when you materialised, seemingly, and your code phrase was 'The celestial disturbance'. Anyway, when I first saw you, you were sort of, well, green."

Fali was silent for a moment, then burst out in a peal of laughter.

"Oh, my. I am sorry, Olyra. That is a new one."

"If we can't see magic," Olyra said, firmly changing the subject, "why can we see spells?"

"You do not see the magic itself, just the effect it leaves. Similar to how you do not see light, you just see what it reflects off. Earlier I was trying to sense the corruption we are after, but this spell has put a blanket over it. While we were outside it, I could at least 'see' the blanket. Now we are in it; I cannot feel anything at all other than the effect of the spell trying to push us away. Now that I am shielding us from it, I cannot even feel that."

They carried on at the rough trajectory they had been following, and the forest got even more depressing, if anything. Ryheart found he missed the reassuring – if flighty – presence of Fali's grey familiar bounding ahead of them, signalling they were heading the right way. Without him, he felt strangely directionless.

Their chaperone's gentle touch kept his mind clear, however.

They walked for some time, and Fali's pace quickened subtly, then blatantly, until she was almost pulling them along. As the sunlight started to fade, they suddenly broke into a glade of healthy green trees, life and vibrancy that lifted Ryheart's spirits.

"Have we ended up on the other side of the spell?" he asked. "I presumed it would be worst at the centre."

Fali was clearly puzzled too and, for the first time, seemed lost for an explanation. "I would have sworn we had gone the right way, but I cannot feel a trace of the obfuscation anymore, and the place is not suffering from corruption. Possibly there was a redirection spell mixed in, and I did not notice it turn us around."

She let out a small barrage of troll curses, then let both their hands go. Ryheart felt no urgency to leave the place anymore, whatever was happening.

Chapter Fifty-Two

Cottage

They carried on for a short way led by a thoroughly disgruntled Fali and, to their surprise, came across a small cottage, a young lady sweeping her doorstep.

She looked up as they approached and waved welcomingly.

"Weapons out?" Olyra murmured.

"Let us not assault an innocent lady unless it comes to it," Fali cautioned. "Do be on guard, though."

"'Ello, my darlings," the lady said with a gentle smile. "I don't get many visitors around these parts. Why, you must be over thirty miles from Suffala."

Fali swore under her breath at the mention of distance but replied in a sunny tone, nonetheless. "Hello there, friend. We are not intruding, are we?"

"Oh, no. It's a blessing to have visitors. I welcome a bit of occasional company, though not enough to live with it. It's getting late, though, and even peaceful woods can be dangerous. Sup with me, and you can rest the night."

"That is very gracious of you," Fali said with a polite bow of her head.

Their host led them into the building, the remaining sunlight casting a warm glow into the tiny kitchen they were in.

"Whereabouts are you all from?" she asked as she busied

herself at a small cook fire, boiling an iron kettle. "I'll make you all a nice brew."

"Londaya," Olyra supplied after a glance at Fali.

"Oh my, I haven't been to the capital for an age. How is it nowadays?"

"Full of people and noise," Fali supplied dryly.

"That's my experience, too. A quiet life and clean air are all I wish."

"Yes, you are rather secluded," Fali commented.

"Oh, there's a village not too far north from here and Suffala to the south. I grow all the food I need, though, so I rarely get out. Now then, here's a nice cuppa," she said sunnily, handing them out. "What were your names again?"

"Fali," the Fae answered, not giving the others pause to answer. "Yourself?"

"Dollanetha, love. Glad to make your acquaintance."

As she turned to place the kettle back on the stove, Ryheart went to take a sip from the cup. Fali, however, delicately sniffed her own and then quietly, wordlessly, pushed his hand back down with a sidelong glance. Olyra caught the exchange and nodded her head slightly.

"I don't know how you brew your tea in the capital nowadays, but the old ways as good as any," Dollanetha said over her shoulder as she bustled about.

"Absolutely," Fali replied with a smile. "We just let it cool a little."

"Ah. Do you mind my asking what you're doing in these parts of the woods?" she asked, coming over. "Those two are hunters judging from their clothes, but you look dressed in your Sundalisday best, off to pray to your patron deity."

"Oh, they are hunters, yes. I am travelling to Lindla. I am a rather delicate girl myself and do not have much knack for travel. Papa has some coin and friends in the guild, so he paid these two to accompany me, Foresh and Lalayi," Fali supplied fictitiously.

"It is not official guild work, but coin is coin. They even gave me a sword! Have you ever held one?"

"I can't say I have, no," Dollanetha said, looking bemused. "Nearest I've come are tools."

"Well," Fali continued airily, "it is quite the heaviest thing I have ever held. I could not possibly carry it, so I just have this empty scabbard. Honestly, that is why I have these two anyway, to protect me. Would you like some gold lions to cover our stay for the night?" she asked.

Ryheart tried to keep his expression neutral. Gold lions hadn't been the currency for near a century. He was sure even with her lack of interest in money, Fali would have picked up on the fact golden crowns were now in use. He had mentioned them enough. Dollanetha didn't notice the slip.

"Oh, no, that's alright. I don't have much use for money myself."

"Ah. How very kind of you," Fali said, lifting the cup and blowing on it daintily before taking a long sip.

"How is it?" Dollanetha asked. "Stand up to your fancy Londaya tea shops?"

"Why, yes, it is delightful. It is so well brewed, I can scarcely taste the poison." Fali spoke in such a calm and pleasant way that it took a moment for her words to sink in. When they did, Ryheart bolted upright in his chair.

"When you make a glamour in future, dear," the Fae continued conversationally, "you should try to include smell and taste, as well as the obvious senses. They are little details and easily overlooked, I know, but the little things can give it away. It was compelling otherwise, though. Layering this glamour underneath the obfuscation was impressive."

"I don't know what you're accusing me of," Dollanetha said stiffly, "but I've been nothing but a gracious host, and you have no right to come spouting wild nonsense just because I'm Fae-blood. A ridiculous persecution like this made me move in the first place!"

"Oh, do give up," Fali said, the warmth replaced with a flat, icy tone. "If you are going to try to murder us, at least have the decency to admit so."

"Oh, well. You can't blame a girl for trying," Dollanetha said, a wicked grin on her face. Within a blink, the room changed.

Ryheart nearly bolted from his seat. The once-pleasant visage of their host was horrific. But as he picked out detail, he saw it too was an illusion, but of the mundane kind. She had a terrifying gaping jaw of teeth tattooed around her real mouth, with incisors filed to points. She had a second pair of glaring eyes, but they too were seemingly inked upon her. Despite the situation, she still seemed calm.

"If you're going to be called a monster just for your blood," their horrific host said by way of explanation, "you might as well embrace it."

"Is that what you think an empty-one looks like?" Fali said, sounding both derisive and appalled. "You look like a child playing dress-up."

"Empty-one?" Dollanetha hissed.

"I can smell the stench of the void all over you. Whatever it promised you, you shall not get it. All you will get is an early grave, and your soul torn asunder."

"You know nothing of my plans," she murmured.

"No. But I would like to. Tell me," Fali commanded simply.

"Why would I?" the witch scoffed.

"Because you gave me your name, and there is a power in that. Doubly so, given you've touched magic. It opens a door through your defences that one talented enough can step through."

"You gave me your name too, creature."

"An approximation." Fali shrugged. "A rough translation. I gave fake names for these two. You, however, were silly enough to give me your true name. I can feel it. Now, I think it would be better if we understood each other before we try to kill one another, do you not?"

255

The witch gritted her teeth, seemingly under a great strain, a vein throbbing in her forehead till she relented. "I lived in Suffala, many moons ago, born to a Fae and a human. The village hated me for it. Anything went wrong, it was my fault. The human in me all but smothered any magic potential I might have had, but my skin carried a slight ember to it. That was enough. Enough for them to blame me when a child went missing. Enough to kill my mother and drive me from the village."

"If you have no magic, how did you do all this?" Ryheart asked. She stared at him defiantly, till Fali repeated the question.

"They chased me to the forest. I fell into a cave. I heard whispers there. They instructed me on how to speak to them. Summon them. How I could build a sanctuary. They touched me and gave me the power my human blood denied me. I'm going to create an enclave for them, here, in the world. Allow them true passage as more than just a shade and a whisper."

"To what end?" Fali asked sadly.

"A sanctuary. For them, and all the Fae-blood that humans only look at with contempt and malice."

"And the dryad you murdered? No place for her in your little sanctuary?" Olyra asked.

"That... the vampires are unruly even under my sway. I couldn't stop them. Her sacrifice will be remembered come utopia."

"A sacrifice she did not choose to make," Fali countered. "I sympathise with your past. Truly. Humans can be brutish and unreasonable. But they are getting there. Slowly."

"They still tell stories about the evil witch Fae who steals children in the village," the witch scoffed. "They're incorrigible."

"Despite my sympathies, I cannot condone your actions. The stink of the void is upon your heart, and empty-ones cannot be allowed to walk this realm in physical form. Furthermore, your powers are a blasphemy."

"And what makes them blasphemy? That you don't like them?"

"Primarily that your soul was ripped in half and filled with the void to give you them. Repent now, and I offer you clemency. You shall not receive another chance."

The witch contemplated her a moment, taking in the markings on the Fae's face. Her own visage paled slightly, but her jaw set.

"Where were you when they murdered my mother, and I was forced to raise myself in these gods-forsaken woods? My master has helped me; all you offer is platitudes. It's far too late to follow any path but this one."

"Very well. One last thing, the vampires. Where do they come into this?"

"They too ultimately derive from my master. They feed into my power so I can finish my work and summon him."

"Ah. Well then, that is about the limit of what your name can compel from you. I suppose you better summon your little vampires, and we can put this sad tale to rest."

"Oh. They prefer their food delivered," the witch said, flashing her sharpened teeth.

She pressed on the table, and Ryheart's stomach suddenly rushed to his mouth as he felt himself falling, stone whizzing all around him. The drop was short but violent. Before he could scarcely react, he landed with a bone-shaking stop, breaking the chair under him in two and smashing to the ground. A narrow ray of light illuminated them from above, and then, with a grating of stone, fell shut, leaving him in complete darkness.

Chapter Fifty-Three

Hunter

Ryheart climbed out of the splintered wood he had fallen in, wincing. Fortunately, his armour and the chair had broken his fall somewhat. He was, however, in absolute darkness, and his heartbeat echoed in his ears. He frantically groped through his bag for his flint. Finding it, he set some old cloth aflame and peered into the gloom.

Searching a little less desperately, he was now infinitely more grateful for Fali's obsessive packing. He retrieved a small tub of fungus that she'd informed him would last as fuel for hours, and placed it within his lantern. The strange substance gave the fire a sickly green colour, painting the tunnel before him in eerie shades. He briefly begrudged that, musing his current predicament would be less spooky if only his light were a lovely pastel shade.

While it made him visible, he figured vampires would have little trouble seeing him anyway, so he might as well be able to see them too. He pulled a stake Fali had fashioned for him from his belt, the heft reassuring. Bracing himself, he began to eke along the passage.

His one faint hope was that Fali had said vampires lay dormant in the day and were sluggish until the night lay upon the land. Whether that counted underground or not, he didn't know, but he clung to the comforting notion regardless.

Hand tracing along the wall to his left as he went, he nearly fell as the stone gave way to a small opening. Peering through, he found a small circular room inside. A musty smell wafted from the entrance, and his heart froze as he held the lantern up and saw a coffin within. A closed coffin.

Not wishing to leave anything to come up behind him, he crept into the room and softly laid his hand on the edge of the coffin, stake raised.

Bracing his nerves, he flung the lid aside and thrust his stake down with a yell. He caught the grotesque parody of humanity within, its face gaunt and bloodless.

Stake an inch from its heart, with preternatural speed, its eyes snapped open, and its claw-like hand grabbed his wrist, clammy and cold as death. Straining against it, he couldn't overpower it. It glared at him with inhuman hatred, eyes ravenous. Springing forward, he put his knee upon it, putting all his body weight into his thrust. Even pinned, it held him back. Worse, it was overpowering him.

With a yell of desperation, he let go with one hand. Summoning his talent, he slammed his fist down upon the stake. The power rippled through the wood and into the creature, and it shrieked as its body spasmed. For a second, its power left it, and he drove the stake deep. It gave a blood-curdling scream, and its features softened. Then it turned to dust, and he tumbled into the coffin as all resistance suddenly disappeared.

Panting, he gave himself a second to gather himself. Maybe, just maybe, if the others were asleep, he would be okay. Unfortunately, he doubted even the dead – or at least, not precisely alive – would have slept through that howl.

He left the room and made his way deeper, edging his way along. His heart hammered so loud it was like a marching band following him, proclaiming him a free buffet for any hungry vampires.

Before him, he saw a faint light, and his heart started to thump harder. He could barely restrain himself from running pell-mell towards it.

It was fortunate he didn't because only a thin ledge protruded from the tunnel, opening to a vast circular chasm descending far below to the unknown, torches burning in embrasures around it. A staircase was carved into the edge, circling down to oblivion. Whatever was down there, the entire vast hollow seemed to focus upon it, on that one point of supreme darkness. Even the torches seemed merely there to feed the dark, to make it even starker by contrast. Looking down within it triggered a deep, primordial fear within him greater than even his current predicament, and a deep shiver shook him cold.

He saw cave entrances like the one he had come out of dotting the walkway that circled the chasm. The best bet, he thought, was that Olyra and Fali had both ended up within their own tunnels.

Unfortunately, there was a slight obstacle to his plan to unite with them. In fact, there were three. A trio of vampires skulked from tunnels, two to his right and one to his left. He dashed for the nearest cave but was beaten to it. He backed reluctantly into the one he had emerged from. It was narrower there, and he was at least sure of the footing.

With a deep breath, he pushed his rising panic away and squared himself, his stake held before him.

At least I'll die a real hunter, he thought grimly to himself as the creatures stalked towards their prey. At least I'm not in a bloody sewer.

Chapter Fifty-Four

Soldier

Olyra dropped down the shaft she had suddenly plunged into. She didn't manage to react before falling, but as she fell, she grabbed her gauntleted hands and feet at the walls, grinding against the rough stone and slowing her. Sparks flew up, and the heat made her flinch as embers flicked against her, but she managed to land on her feet, plunged into complete darkness.

With a calm borne from practice, she contained the impulse to panic and calmly but swiftly removed a small jar from her belt. Opening it let wisps of OPMC-provided fairy dust hover out, and she smeared it on her gauntlets and the barrel of her weapons. A warm golden glow lit them up, giving a steady halo of light while keeping her hands free.

She couldn't determine if the tunnels were artificial or not in the low light but inferred there must be other tunnels running almost parallel, given the others hadn't fallen to the same pit.

She reasoned she might, just, be able to climb back up the shaft above her. She wasn't optimistic about managing to move whatever had sealed the top, however. Wedged in a shaft was also the last place she wished to be if vampires came upon her, so she made a slow, steady march along the tunnel. She held her flintlock pistol in one hand and stake in the other, pouring a small pool of borrowed power into the firearm. While the ammo itself would do nothing, she had been told, theoretically at least, that the artificial magic her armament band allowed her to pump into the weapon might harm them. Vampires weren't her speciality, but she had at least a couple of things within her kit that could deal with them. Moving as low and silent as she could, she made her way slowly along as if she were infiltrating an enemy stronghold.

She reasoned stealth might be pointless given the creatures' unworldly senses, but falling back into manoeuvres was comforting. Even if practically useless, it gave her a sense of control.

Back to the wall to minimise angles of attack, it gave way behind her to a small enclosure. Crouching, she peered in to find a coffin upon a small scattering of dirt.

Scanning the room, she saw nothing other than the coffin. Perhaps her stealth had paid off after all.

She leapt forward and launched the lid from the coffin, ready to strike. Only, the coffin was empty. A deafening shriek made her hair stand on end, and she whirled instinctively, catching a glimpse of a nightmare descending from the ceiling.

It slammed her painfully into the wall. With a cry borne half of determination and half of panic, she wedged herself between the wall and the vampire. Both legs upon its chest, she pushed with all her might.

The creature was forced back momentarily, giving her just enough time to gain her footing. Even as she righted herself, she aimed her flintlock and fired a burst of enhanced power, light streaking at the creature. It dodged nimbly, hopping from wall to floor, and knocked the gun from her grasp, raking claws at her face. She winced as burning pain racked her, then it slammed her to the ground, pinning her.

It lowered its head to her neck, but she felt no breath of the living. She felt no breath at all, its lungs having long since ceased to draw air. All she felt was a deathly chill grip her heart. Desperately she tried to wrench the creature from her, to beat it away, but its undead frame was too strong, grip too tight.

Inching one hand down to her belt desperately, she pulled a grenade from her pouch and enabled it. A similar gambit had worked against the warrior Fae, and she prayed silently to gods she had never really believed in that this would work now.

A flash of pain pierced her as its fangs sank into her neck, and she felt her spirit draining away. She closed her eyes tight, and her grenade exploded in a bright flash of violent light. A sun grenade, her colleagues had dubbed it. No physical force came from it, only a brightly intense light that razed every cranny of the room.

It wasn't true sunlight or even magical, so it couldn't damage the beast. But blessedly, it shrieked and shielded its eyes in panic, releasing its grip upon her neck. It would last only the briefest moment, but a moment was all she needed. She wasn't about to waste it.

Rolling over and jumping to her feet, she grabbed the stake it had knocked away and plunged it into the creature. Her aim rang true, and its face took on a look of blessed relief before it turned to ash.

Panting, Olyra allowed herself a slight reprieve. She took a calming breath, then focused again upon the mission. She had beaten the creature, but it had cost her the best trick she had, and nearly ended with her as food, or worse.

She let out a slow breath, then carried on. Whatever awaited her, she would meet it like a professional.

Chapter Fifty-Five

Queen

Fali felt a surge of alarm as the ground gave way under her. Springing from her chair as it started to fall, she landed upon the table before her. There was a grating of stone as the enchanted rock closed again. She turned to the witch, cursing that she hadn't noticed the trap. It had taken time to pierce the glamour. She had perceived the imminent danger of the poison but failed to see the second trap.

"Are you not going to save your friends?" the witch taunted. "Or have you abandoned your pawns so readily to their fate?"

"I have faith in them," Fali said, pushing them from her mind. "They have more talent than you think. Besides which, your tactics are that of a coward. I am sure you would rather protect your own life than kill them. And, believe me, your life is very much in danger. Your creatures are the best shield you have against me."

"My powers have been amplified beyond mortal ken. Even you cannot—" The witch didn't finish her sentence as a wave of force from Fali's hand pummelled her, wrenching her from where she stood and tossing her to the floor.

"I have no time for your posturing, silly child. Be gone."

It was perhaps a bit ostentatious, but she wanted the witch so panicked she would both recall her vampires away from the humans and equally would lead her to the spell she had created.

The witch herself had only small talent for magic, the vampires that fed it providing all the power that her previous work had displayed. The nuance of her spell-work, too, had been whispered to her by otherworldly instructors. By herself, she was, at best, a nuisance. Her work, however, was dangerous. Destroying that was paramount. Even if she killed the witch, the spell might be close enough to fruition that it could complete itself with a push from the other side. She had to scare the witch into leading her to it. Inevitably she would seek the protection of her master's power. They always did.

The witch pulled a small leather pouch from her dress, a hex-bag. Pulling the cord that sealed it, an ethereal green blaze wreathed the bag. With a screamed curse, she threw it at her foe. Fali watched contemptuously, then flicked her wrist. Wresting control of the unearthly fire away from the witch, she returned it. The flame roared and multiplied, scorching the stone around the surprised target as she threw herself out of the way.

"Who are you?" the witch asked in awe.

"Death," Fali proclaimed, striding forward. The witch climbed to her feet and fled down the passage behind her. Fali gave her some free distance, then sprang after her.

They tore through rooms and down into a cellar, the witch practically flinging herself inside. Within, a tunnel descended further into the earth.

The witch slammed her hand into a rune carved into the wall, and another pit opened, this one deep. Fali rolled her eyes and leapt over it gracefully, sending a crackle of lightning towards the witch to keep the fear of death prominently in her mind. Haste was essential, and she wanted the witch so panicked she would consider no options other than the sanctuary of her master. The spells she flung were big and flashy but lacked real power behind them. Fali wished to keep as much as possible in reserve for what she prayed might be avoided but felt in her bones was inevitable.

In calmer mind, the witch might have discerned they were all bark and no bite, but the loud and cataclysmic-seeming bursts of magic kept her on the brink of terror. She let out a yelp as the hem of her cloak set aflame. They came to a long corridor looping down, a small clearing opening into other passages. Two vampires darted from either side, hissing angrily as the witch turned triumphantly and commanded them with a gesture.

Fali, however, didn't slow down. They were lesser vampires, third or fourth generation and long removed from the power of their original progenitor. These hadn't received their abilities directly from the empty-one who had removed their soul. Only the slightest second-hand slither of manifest void was present in the absence their soul used to fill. They were strong and fast, but practically beasts.

Without breaking step, she jumped to the corridor's wall, pushed off and took their heads with her magically bladed heels, then let burst a flare of sunlight to disintegrate the pair.

What little colour the witch had left in her pale visage drained, and she took off even faster than before.

The narrow passageway came to a dead end, but as Fali's quarry approached it, the stone wall split open with a horrible grinding. Before it, the floor suddenly opened to a vast abyss, and the witch flung herself down it with abandon.

"Protect your charge!" she screamed, and Fali leapt down after her. She had the distinct feeling that the cavern's bottom would be the end of the road one way or the other. A raw power emanated from it, built up and stored similar to the grand reservoir of magic within the Weir Wood.

A shriek rang above her. Twisting, Fali found two more vampires diving down with her. She incinerated one with a burst of light, but the other grappled her as they fell. She managed to get a boot on his chest and pushed him off her, then cleaved him in two with her bladed heel.

She turned back to watch her descent. A sudden green glow emanated from the pit, and she felt a violent flare of magic as an ethereal shield erupted in the chasm between her and the witch.

She braced for impact and smashed into the dome of power with no time to stop her descent. It crackled, and she skidded painfully down it, knocked to the floor in a burst of magic, steaming.

She cursed. She hadn't expected a bloody shield spell to be active so deep within the earth, tied into the summoning spell she needed to stop.

Before she could rise, she was slammed to the floor, a vice-like grip pinning her down. The sire of the nest was upon her, considerably stronger than the others. She fought to raise her head and saw the witch grinning at her, safely behind the shimmering green force that now separated them.

Chapter Fifty-Six

Reunion

Ryheart steeled himself as the three vampires boxed him into the tunnel, when a sudden commotion rang behind them. A voice screamed out, muffled by rock, then two of the vampires turned and ran towards it.

He felt a momentary rush of relief and praised whatever had scared them off, because it certainly wasn't him. There was, however, still one left to deal with.

It dashed forward, and he tried to jab the stake at its heart, but it twisted away from it and tackled him to the ground. Ryheart grunted in pain as they slammed to the floor, its hands wrapped around his neck. His vision began to swim as he desperately tried to eke out a breath, when the creature shrieked and arched back, grip loosened.

Olyra stood behind the creature, a stake buried in its back. The creature's recoil gave him a chance to kick it from him and fill his lungs with a desperate gasp of musty air.

He staggered to his feet, but it beat him to it, swinging its arm and slamming Olyra into the wall with a crunch. He leapt forward as it descended on her, ripping the stake from its back. Enraged, it turned back to him, and Olyra swept it from its legs with a kick.

"Now!" Olyra yelled as it fell to the ground. He drove the stake down into its chest. It howled in pain, then melted away.

"You alright?" he asked, panting for breath, holding out a hand to help Olyra up.

"No major damage," Olyra said, taking his hand, an angry gash upon her brow. "Looks worse than it is," she said as she saw his concern.

"If you say so," he said gratefully. "Thanks for the assist."

"Well, you might not like me, but I wasn't about to leave you to die alone in the dark," she said before the slightest of smiles. "Besides, it was the sensible option. You could have ended up becoming another vampire to deal with."

"Practical as always," he said, but he couldn't help feeling a small degree of camaraderie between them. Fighting for your life together tended to do that, it seemed.

"So, we have a choice, Ryheart. Do we stay here and hope vampires don't kill us, or do we follow Fali down the big hole and hope vampires don't kill us?"

"You saw her?" he asked, new hope and vigour in his voice.

"Just for a second. Those other two vampires followed her. Good job, or we might have been in bother. Look, much as I hate to admit it, we're both way out of our league here. It wouldn't reflect badly on you if you just want to find your way out to run for the hills."

"Gods, I'll be the first to admit I'm out of my depth. I'm not even sure I have a depth. I'm bloody terrified. But as proud as Fali is, she can't do everything by herself. She might need me. She might need us."

"Well, in for a beggar, in for a crown. There's as much chance of running into a vampire trying to find an exit as trying to find her," Olyra replied. "So, at the risk of sounding soppy, let's go help her."

They worked their way back out of the corridor, and Olyra peered out either side of the tunnel. "Clear," she called, waving him forward.

Ryheart felt distinctly sick looking down at the cavern bed, now omitting a sickly green glow. A large dome of shimmering magic sat in the bottom of the pit. It radiated power, and its surface shimmered and flowed like the shield that had protected the naiad's forest. But while that had felt benign and passive, somehow calming to look at, this one made his skin crawl. The rippling of its surface reminded him more of insects swarming a carcass than the natural flow of a river, flaring angrily.

A series of intricate patterns ran through the large sphere. Everything outside of it was swamped in darkness.

He spotted a small carved staircase winding down the edge of the chasm. "I guess that's our way down, then."

Olyra nodded, staring at the spell below. "That does not look good," she observed.

"No. No, it does not," he agreed emphatically. "So, I guess that's where we're headed, then?"

"Yeah. Yeah, that's where we're headed."

He grimaced, then they began their descent.

Chapter Fifty-Seven

Servant

The vampire sire held its victim in a death grip. Its spawn had died. All of them had died. But its new prey would go well towards building the strength to begin a new nest.

The witch screamed at him through the barrier that encircled the summoning ritual of his master. The master who, long ago, had torn out his ultimate progenitor's soul and replaced it with a sliver of the void the world longed to return to. A return to how it had been before the Twin-Divinities had filled it with their unbearable creations.

"Kill her and be done with it!" the witch shrieked at him, and he hissed lowly in reflex. He would have drained her long ago if his master's sigil upon her hadn't compelled him to spare her for a time, while she used the life force they siphoned to power the magic spells she could not finish herself.

They were close to the spell's completion. If the vampire drained his captives' power rather than snapping her soft neck, it might just be enough.

Besides, despite her evident magical power, the prey he had trapped before him was so small and fragile. Her skin was so tender and smooth.

Unable to resist, he sank his teeth into the creature's soft neck, and he felt the intoxicating rush as the void in him temporarily filled with life. It wouldn't last. It would never last. But for a single, blissful moment, he felt what it was to be alive, the warmth in his veins ecstasy. Then the warmth turned to flickering embers. Then to smouldering heat. Then to a raging fire.

Shrieking and convulsing as the blood boiled within him, his skin steamed from the heat.

"Sunlight!" Burning as if the fire of day was upon him, he shrieked in panic at the witch, "Where's the sunlight?"

His prey pushed him aside, and he looked up, bewildered, as the small figure crouched beside him.

A look of intense disgust filled her eyes for a moment, then was replaced by something he hadn't seen since he was human. What was that? Pity? Sympathy?

As he felt his skin blister and boil, she spoke in a soft voice.

"I am the sunlight," she murmured to him.

Then, he felt nothing at all.

Dollanetha watched in disbelief as her last vampire was defeated without so much as a finger lifted.

The spell had taken her so long, so many years of her life. It was so close to completion. With one last push, she might just finish it. Then her place of power would expand from this little cave to the entire forest, and her master would achieve physical form, here in the realm of mortals. She had built the spell so slowly, deep underground to avoid detection. Even with her master's patronage, she hadn't had enough power to fulfil the demands of such a complex summoning circle. Taking the vampires into her thrall had significantly increased the rate she could power the spell but had the unintended side effect of corruption seeping into the surrounding forest, poisoning it. She had thought her glamour and obfuscation spell had hidden it.

Then, the intruders had walked in, seemingly oblivious. In nearly one night, they were ruining a work that had taken her a hundred years. But they wouldn't ruin it. They mustn't! She would make up for her mistake in leading the intruders to her works. She would appease her master for jeopardising their designs. She would fix this. She had to fix this.

Her pursuer, for all her power, hadn't been able to catch her. And Dollanetha was safely within her shield. Here in the scarce remains of an ancient place of dark ritual that had fallen into the very depths of the earth, at her magnum opus, she could perform a communion.

The intruder climbed to her feet and stared at her with those eyes. Those piercing, shining eyes.

"Listen to me, Dollanetha, very carefully," Fali said in a commanding but gentle tone. "If you place any value upon your existence, do not enter the nexus of that spell."

"Like you weren't going to kill me anyway," she spat.

"I was," the being said candidly, "but that would be a blessing compared to what awaits you in that circle."

"I've chosen my path now. It will lead where it leads."

The creature sighed sadly and gestured for her to proceed. "Then go. Walk your path. It is a bad choice, but it is yours to make. See what reward your master gives you for your devotion."

Within the centre of the summoning circle stood an altar, an ancient stone basin Dollanetha had found here, deep in the earth, the focal point of all her work.

She would summon her master, or at least his shade. He would only be able to briefly manifest, but long enough for him to dispatch her foe. Then, they could start again. Carefully this time, till she could summon him permanently. Chanting in the tongue her master had taught her, she invoked his power. As she spoke the harsh, guttural language, she cut her palm with her dagger, the warm blood draining into the stone. A thick black shadow started to rise from it, swirling around her, anchoring itself to her. It wrapped around her chest and her throat almost gently. Then it began to squeeze.

"Master?" she asked, awash with fear, suddenly aware of the ramifications. "I've given you all the power I have, I swear!"

But she hadn't. She hadn't given all she could. Her magic was drained dry, not enough to complete the spell. Her soul, however, what was left of it, remained untapped. She shrieked in agony as the rolling shadow began to burn away her flesh, unable to tolerate the unworldly incursion into the mortal realm. She looked outside the shield in panic. The creature stood, watching. Out of reflex, she reached towards the being for help. But even had she wanted to, the shield, Dollanetha's own shield, that she had toiled over for so long, stood between them. Cutting her off from the only help she might receive. The creature's face was unflinching, but sympathy reflected in her eyes. The tendril reached inside and touched Dollanetha's heart. She let out one last agonised scream, and then it beat its last.

Chapter Fifty-Eight

Calm

Fali sighed sadly as the witch's soul was consumed, its raw essence burning to power the spell as her physical form evaporated. The ending had been inevitable the moment Dollanetha had stepped inside the shield. There was only one reward the demonic offered. The shield shimmered and fell as the witch's link to it abruptly ended.

Fali could see now the spell had been created within a primordial place of worship, deep in the bowels of the earth. The stone floor was smooth, and the remains of broken pillars scattered the ground between the deep grooves of the summoning circle carved into it.

Those lines were now filled with a thick, roiling shadow as the spell completed itself. It had no use for the shield anymore; it only cared for the summoning. Fali could reach it now. But she was powerless to stop it. Even she couldn't stop the power of a soul completing its last rites, even with the empty-one having twisted it maliciously to its use.

Olyra and Ryheart flew down the stairs carved into the side of the chasm and ran to her. Ryheart's face took on a look of undisguised delight as he saw her, and for a second, her own eyes reflected that with a bright violet, before hardening to a flinty grey.

"I almost wish you had not come," she said mournfully. Ryheart looked wounded.

"We're glad you weren't eaten by vampires, too," Olyra said dryly.

"I am glad you are okay. Both of you. But this... I do not have time to argue, or for anything beyond the essentials. I would beseech you by all that is divine, to run. To run as far and as fast as you can. I might even compel you to do so if I could spare the magic. So, I give this one warning. If you enter the circle with me, we win or we die. There will be no escape."

"What happens if we lose?" Ryheart said, sounding unusually determined. Perhaps he had grown even more than she had realised over these days they had spent together.

"At best, the nearest village is slaughtered before it is stopped. Perhaps, if it is smart enough to hide and strike from the shadows, the country. An empty-one is about to be summoned here. Not just as an interloper. It will truly belong here, and nothing will be able to make it leave save its obliteration, even if it retreats from this realm. For us personally, in your case, your souls will be trapped in the void for eternity until consumed. For me, I will be erased as if I never existed."

"I won't abandon my duty," Olyra said.

"And I'm not about to leave you to your fate," Ryheart said, uncommonly fierce.

Fali closed her eyes for just a moment in acceptance. "Then step in," she commanded.

The pair stepped over the threshold of the spell, and Fali placed her hand upon the altar.

"The lines for the shield are still here, tied into the central framework of the summoning. The spell is still not fully powered, so for a time, the empty-one will require the spell-work to stay in place to tie it here before it stabilises. I cannot cleanse the spell-work while its presence infests it, but I can tie my essence to the spell as well and activate the shield. The spell and shield will be intrinsically linked, so the only way to break one will be to break both. We will all be trapped in here until me, or the empty-one, is obliterated."

"Kill it, or we all die. Got it," Ryheart summarised.

"Grand. Now, what am I?"

"What?" Ryheart exclaimed, taken aback by the abrupt question.

"I have not been able to explicitly tell you what I am because my presence is currently unique, and even to mention my kin would draw ritual attention to me. But now, alerting someone to our presence is ideal. You have not quite been able to express it because the world was not ready for it. But in your heart, I think you know. I think you have known, deep down, since you laid eyes upon me."

Fali found she had been staring at Ryheart through her explanation, and she turned her gaze to Olyra, also.

The pair looked at each other and then back to her.

"Realm-dancer," they said in unison.

"Thank you," Fali said with a gentle smile.

She capitalised on the symbolic harmony of the moment. The spell that kept her wings from appearing after they had regrown shattered, and they folded back into existence, anchoring her connection back to her realm. A chorus sang in their ears, and a blazing light shone forth. The connection re-established, she finally let her restrained power loose. It was intensely bright but strangely gentle, bathing her in a pillar of white fire that glimmered with all the colours of existence. After a moment, it died down to a soft glow as she reigned it in, held just below the surface.

"Thank you both. Now then, if you insist on staying, you would be best served hiding until I signal. Hit and run only. It is not just strength and speed you have to worry about. Simply put, the empty-one should not exist in contact with creation. Its very presence is corrosive to reality. Unshielded, you would both be gone at a touch. You have both absorbed some of my grace as it radiated from me, and my current light will shield you – to an extent. Even so, I would give you both a handful of touches at most before it burns through the protection I can give. Olyra, less so, given you have spent less time in my presence. Its mental affliction will also affect you greater. You both insist on staying?"

The pair nodded, resolute despite their clear apprehension. Of all humans, she had picked an excellent couple to accompany her for her task. Though, they'd somewhat been selected for her.

Fali activated the shield, and it flared up, entombing them with the manifesting empty-one. Once again, the area lit up. The shield now a mix of its prior sickly green and a shimmering blue.

"Now then, we win, or we die. Go!" the realm-dancer shouted, and the two took cover behind pillars, ready to face the intruder into their reality.

Fali stood calm and implacable, for a moment at one with the space surrounding her, taking in every curve of stone, every crack and crevice.

The warmth was gone from her eyes now, leaving nothing but a look of steadfast dedication. Her face was blank, and her mind seemingly calm and in perfect clarity. Her eyes locked into a simmering red as she gazed steadily at the monstrosity that formed before her. It towered over her with limbs like tree trunks, each of its long, sinuous fingers ending in razor-edged claws. A great set of horns protruded from its head, and its eyes burned not with fire but with icy, bottomless glimpses into the void it came from. In stark contrast to her shining aura of light, its very being seeming to seethe and roil with shifting shadows as if both the creature and the world it now inhabited could scarcely bear its existence. Inky tendrils crept from it that even now, while both stood motionless, probed and writhed at the limit of the light she was casting. Its wings, too, were a dark reflection of her own, gigantic shadows that seemed to blot out all they touched.

It was a created empty-one, twisted into being from the souls they had captured before realm-dancers could escort them to the next world. It was not an empty-one manifest direct from the void, but that didn't make it less dangerous. What it lacked in intelligence and finesse it made up for in pure, unrelenting strength. Worse, it bore no sigil to identify it. As creatures of the void, they shunned any individuality that tied them to creation, that moved them further from the absolute absence they wished to bring. A name or sigil would have been a brand, a sign of failure. The fact it didn't have one meant either it had never failed or had since redeemed itself.

As the pair of hated opposites eyed one another, neither moved. They didn't give the slightest flex of muscle or twitch of expression. Their auras pushed violently at each other. The incandescent light of creation and the total darkness of absence testing and probing one another, undulating at each other's limit, waiting for the moment they clashed in earnest.

The moment seemed to last seconds, minutes, hours, and then with the slightest, virtually undetectable shifting of weight, Fali burst into action in a blaze of movement.

Snapping her fingers, a burst of lightning shot at the empty-one, who contemptuously swiped the probing attack aside like it was no more than an itch. It released a torrent of darkness that snaked and roiled towards her, a writhing ocean of shadow.

In response, the realm-dancer drew a pattern in the air and streaks of light brought themselves into existence as she traced the design into the fabric of the world. The symbol hung immaterially upon the air before her, and then she placed her palm upon the spell. A streak of white light blasted forwards in a great flare of magical energy, pushing against the seething shadow and shredding all darkness that it touched, piercing the mass and streaking straight at the empty-one itself.

Before her attack even met its target, she was gone, launched into the air, striking forth like a rocket.

With a hideous roar, the aberration pushed the light back with an explosion of power as she dived towards it. It raised its arm to defend itself, and from the sickening nothingness surrounding it, a jagged, great blade formed and extended to meet her defenceless body.

Still in motion, Fali moved a hand to her scabbard and grabbed the empty space, producing a sword of her own. Its metal blade shone with a bright white, and she slammed it down into the empty-one's raised weapon.

The two opposing blades met with a violent clang that sent shockwaves through the small room, reacting in a fountain of sparks of light, shards of darkness. Before the warrior could respond, her opponent's free arm shot out and slammed her hard in the stomach.

Careening away from the impact, she slammed to the floor, rolling with the motion and pivoting back to her feet. She used the momentum to turn back to her foe, engaging it once more.

Chapter Fifty-Nine

Storm

Swords clashed, and bodies flew at such speeds Ryheart could barely keep track. He'd known Fali was holding back when they'd trained together. Indeed, she had told him as much. But the speed and finesse she was displaying now was staggering. The oily void rippled from the empty-one in waves, and even at this distance, hidden behind a collapsed pillar, the feeling of emptiness it instilled in him was making him feel sick to his core. He had to fight with nearly all his willpower simply not to retch.

As the pair fought, their flurries of blades were interwoven effortlessly with kicks, punches and bursts of magic, fighting with body and weapon alike.

Fali came in low with a sweep of her bladed heel and then swung at the creature's unprotected middle as it jumped her kick. Moving its blade down to block, the empty-one elbowed her solidly in the face as she met it, then it swiped her sword out of her hand with its massive bulk.

Staggering back, she leapt just out of reach of another swing. She grabbed her sword from the floor as she rolled and launched herself high over another swing in one movement.

Her bladed feet sliced at its neck, but the light grazes failed to cause any severe damage as its shadowy wings jabbed at her, forcing a retreat.

It was apparent even to his inexperienced eye as Ryheart watched that while Fali had the upper hand in agility and manoeuvrability, the empty-one was physically the stronger by a vast proportion. As well as that, despite its immense bulk, its blows were effortless and overwhelmingly fast in a speed born of pure hate and aggression.

Further, the few blows Fali had managed to land seemed to have had negligible, if any, effect on the creature's seemingly impenetrable hide. Meanwhile, each of its strikes had hit her with a thunderous bang and a toll reaped upon her. Her aura still blazed a brilliant white, but the impenetrable darkness seemed to be encroaching ever further across the chamber.

As Ryheart watched, a wild despairing fear rose in his stomach as voices whispered in his head of the truth he tried desperately to ignore.

Fali was losing. All the terrible things that would happen once she fell ran through his mind wildly, and he found his skin deathly cold and drenched with sweat.

The realm-dancer backed away slightly with a graceful leap, then ran her hand down the flat of her blade. As if obeying some unspoken command, the longsword she had held thinned into a narrow rapier with her gesture, and she changed her stance. Now she stood holding the blade like a fencer, standing side on to the empty-one, arm nearly fully extended.

The length of the blade held at arm's reach gave her a more comparable range to the empty-one, but hers was lighter, defter.

It batted at her blade angrily, but rather than meeting its overwhelming force head-on, she instead lightly dipped her blade under and around its own, slashing at the empty-one's exposed torso and then backing away before it could strike her. Each twitch of her wrist carving a small but deep gash in its leathery flesh.

Her fiery hair streamed around her, and she was like a candle flame as Ryheart watched her, flickering and darting in and out of the shadows, holding back the darkness with her small but fierce light.

A tendril coiled across the floor and wrapped tightly around her leg, and triumphantly the hulking beast roared and swiped to tear her asunder as it constricted her movement.

With supernatural speed, she traced another pattern in the air, and it shone between her and her doom. The spell seemed the same as her previous blast of light, but the thunder of the blade bearing down at her appeared unstoppable. Fali's answering blast wouldn't fire in time to meet it.

In a flash, her arm shot out to the shining glyphs. This time she didn't place her palm on the symbol. Instead, she slammed the length of her arm into it, and it seemed to meld with her arm like an aegis strapped in place.

Smashing the shimmering shield into the side of the empty-one's blade with a noise that shook the stones about them, it collided with a crackle of explosive light, and the sword veered markedly off course. It hadn't been an attack like last time, but a defence!

Even as the creature's blade impacted into the ground with a mighty crash, her sword came up and then sliced down.

As it careened downwards, she ran her other palm along the blade, changing it once again. This time its gleaming metal thickened into a one-sided edge, focused purely on slicing.

A sickening sound and a furious, deafening howl of rage shook the room's foundations as the empty-one's arm severed from its torso. The limb hit the ground with an angry hiss as the very earth itself rejected its existence. A spray of the void the empty-one contained streaked from its stump and blotted out the air around it.

Fali's shield came back up again and detached from her arm to hover in the air as it had before. This time she rested her palm against it as Ryheart had first expected. With the energy absorbed from its violent clash, it blasted both arm and weapon that had moments ago threatened her life into nothingness before the creature could recover.

While by no means out of danger, Ryheart couldn't help but feel a surge of hope at the blow. The empty-one had held the advantage at first, no question, but it had been unable to adapt to her changing tactics. Every impact it had landed early on had been a part of Fali probing its abilities even as they clashed. She had been learning its style and methods, allowing her to now rapidly adapt. Not only that, but the damage it had done to her seemed to be fading. Magic pumped through her veins, reinvigorating and healing her.

Enraged and wounded but still ruthlessly deadly, the empty-one shrieked and smashed its massive forehead into its diminutive opponent as her blast quietened. The blow caught her entirely off guard, unable to adequately react entangled as she was with her offensive spell. Her attack died with a last splutter as she staggered back, the empty-one's physical power still vastly dwarfing hers. Worse, its brutal impact left behind shards of writhing shadow that clawed at her eyes and obstructed her vision.

As she struggled to regain her balance, a heavy blow from its mammoth foot smashed her across the room. With a powerful impact, she hit the wall, her blade skittering again from her hand, this time far from her grasp.

Olyra watched enraptured as the realm-dancer and the empty-one fought, exchanging blows nearly beyond her comprehension.

Her heart pounded in her chest like it was trying its hardest to use up all the beats it had left, and she felt sick to her very core as the shadow swallowed the light in front of them.

She told herself desperately it was the empty-one's proximity causing the terror in her stomach, and she could beat it. She was trained. She was a soldier. Fali had warned her the aura it cast would affect them, but she felt like her mind was on the brink of insanity.

The terror isn't real, she told herself. But even if it wasn't real, it was still there. It still gnawed at her brain even as the analytical part of her mind watched and catalogued the fight. Her desire to help wrestled with her desire to run away and never stop running. But there was nowhere to run, and no way to help.

She felt a blossoming hope burst into her chest as the empty-one's arm severed. Then just as suddenly, that small mercy was violently wrenched from her and dismay flooded over her as the realm-dancer was brutally smashed away.

The realm-dancer, their only hope, was on the ground, weaponless, blind and helpless. Her rational mind told her Fali had said she would signal for help if she needed it, but the terror gnawed even at the professional calm she fought to maintain. What if their one light in the darkness couldn't give them orders anymore? What if she was down for good?

She had a desperate, overwhelming urge to do something, anything, to take back control of the situation. She was an OPMC agent, dammit! If she was going down, she was going down fighting, not cowering in a damp corner!

Shouting in defiance at the shadow, she leapt from the pillar she had used as cover and charged. Letting her armament band flow free, she let forth a volley of powered shots at the distracted empty-one as it bore down on the realm-dancer.

Taken aback by the sudden intruder to the decimation of its prey, the empty-one shrieked as the barrage hit it in the face, one of them striking a sunken eye.

The abhorrent creature turned to face Olyra. Its maw gaped open, and there was a rush of air as it inhaled. It seemed all the warmth was sucked out of the cavern as if it was consuming the very essence of life and deleting it. Its breath finished, and for a moment, the room pitched into impenetrable darkness. Then its mouth snapped open again. The light flared back up, and an all-engulfing blast of shadow raged towards the soldier to annihilate her where she stood.

Chapter Sixty

Choice

The empty-one's blow had caught Fali off guard. It had reacted to her attack and its dismemberment far quicker than she'd anticipated, striking her before her spell finished. Disintegrating the arm so it couldn't quickly reabsorb the power within had been a blow, but it had cost her.

If she had used her lungs to breathe air, it would have been knocked out of her. As it was, she breathed only to recover ambient magic to speed her natural rejuvenation. Said magic, she had now used a moderate amount of, and she breathed heavily to keep her supply as full as possible.

The blow had hurt tremendously, and her head was ringing. The vast empty-one's foot had caught her stomach and face alike. Worse, shards of shadow had lodged into her, eating away at her very being and blinding her.

Rather than stopping herself in the air with her wings, she let the momentum carry her backwards away from her foe, giving her precious distance and time to recover. Her sword was far away, but the empty-one wouldn't be able to hold her sword any more than she could hold its own. Her blade might be out of reach, but the empty-one's was obliterated. It could form another one, but that would take time and resources it wouldn't have the chance to use if she kept up the pressure.

She let a flare of light loose to clear the burning shadow from her form as she flew. As she did, she became suddenly aware of the noise of feet, too delicate and rapid to be the empty-one's, followed by the ringing of shots and a howl of anger.

Crashing to the floor hard, she raised her head to see the soldier charging recklessly at the aberration.

The bloody soldier.

She swore angrily. A moment was all she needed to gather herself, but a moment was longer than the soldier could afford.

The empty-one's mouth opened, and Fali felt her light torn from her and absorbed. Then its maw gaped to blast the annoyance in front of it to oblivion.

With crystal clarity as time seemed to slow to a crawl before her, Fali knew she had a choice.

She could dash for her sword and be upon the empty-one before it could disengage its attack in much the same manner as it had just done to her. The fight would be over, the empty-one slain. All it would cost was one little soul. Olyra would inevitably be razed into oblivion, her soul so tattered that even the afterlife wouldn't be able to salvage her essence.

She knew, knew what she had to do. She knew from her countless aeons' experience; she knew from her training; she knew from her position. Unequivocally, the choice to make – the only choice – was to obliterate the empty-one. Allowing it to exist any longer, not taking this perfect chance, was dangerous and irresponsible. Something she knew better than to do. To let emotion and sentimentality dictate her tactical options was not only unacceptable but it was also beneath her.

Regardless of all this, she knew in her heart, before even thinking, what she would do. There was only one choice she could make, after all.

She swore one last time. Perhaps her fondness for the humans had changed her even more than she had changed them. Activating all the speed-boosting magic she could generate by pouring all her power into the glyphs in her boots, she rolled to her feet and dashed forward. An earlier sentiment echoed in her mind. The choice might be a bad one, but it was hers.

Racing towards the empty-one to save its intended victim from complete annihilation, she constructed a shield as she went. Even with her practised movements, she wouldn't have the time to create fully reinforced protection. Nor would she be able to fully channel her power into it without a loss of the essential haste carrying her forward. The symmetry and lines of energy that held the shield in place were incomplete, and she shouted the command of protection in the Old-Tongue to enforce the patchy spell-work. Doing so verbally was an inefficient and ineffectual way to perform or strengthen a spell. It was something novices of her kind did to make learning easier. She would have been embarrassed in any other situation, but she had no time for any better reinforcement, and certainly no time for embarrassment.

She reached Olyra just as the blast hit.

Flinging the protection up in front of her, she held it desperately against the storm enveloping her. The shadow battered her mercilessly, and she strained to pump as much magic as she possibly could into the paper-thin shield that was the only separation between her and the wrath of the empty-one.

Her one salvation was that the empty-one's blast had been meant only to kill the human, not a realm-dancer. Empty-ones were not known for their reserve, but it hadn't been using all its strength to wipe away the mere irritation that had irked it. Despite that slight reprieve, Fali's shield was shakily constructed at best, and the flaws in its design strained past bursting point.

With a last gasp of effort, she pushed forward against the darkness and drove it back, shield shattering from the action.

Breathing hard to gain back her strength in her reprieve, as the shadow before her cleared into wispy tendrils, she saw the empty-one's maw open once again. It had used the time she had fought the initial blast to prepare a grander one. Immediately a far greater force tore across the room towards her. This one was designed to eradicate her rather than the person she protected. The air crackled as it streaked towards her, tearing the very fabric of reality.

This time there was no chance for even the sketchiest of spells, and all she could do was throw all her power into her defensive aura and pray the light, her light, could hold back the darkness.

Chapter Sixty-One

Hopeless

Sinking dread nearly overwhelmed Olyra as Fali stood before her, braced against the storm about to hit them.

Even without the ability to sense magic, Olyra could tell this blast was far greater than the last.

The air itself felt like it was being torn apart in its path, and the floor buckled and groaned as shards of earth sheared in its wake. This time there was no shield to save Fali. Olyra watched hopeless, powerless to resist the death that was coming for them.

A shining, glorious aura erupted around Fali, bathing Olyra in light. Despite the imminent peril, an exultant singing rang in her ears, and the doubts and cruel whispers dissipated as the divine light immersed her.

Then the blast hit.

The shadow roiled and writhed around her protector, dissolving with an angry hiss against the blazing light. But even as it was destroyed, it enacted even greater retribution as it tore gashes throughout. The shadow spread like a ravenous beast devouring all that stood before it.

Fali cried out in resolute protest and pain. In an intense burst, her light decimated the shadow around it for one brief, glorious moment of triumph.

Then it went out.

The dark crashed against her once more, and now she was completely and utterly unprotected from its force. She had held out for the brunt of the attack, but the last crash of its thunderous advance met her entirely without opposition.

With a bone-shattering explosion, the realm-dancer was flung violently across the room, careening into the far wall with enough force to knock the great stones loose.

She landed in a heap. Unmoving. Broken.

Ryheart watched in horror as Fali was slung like a ragdoll, landing in a heap of rubble. Vicious shadows clung to her skin like tiny termites, eating away at the fading remains of her light, casting the room into darkness. Only the faint glow of the magical dome around them remained. That dome was feeling increasingly more like the roof of a tomb.

He felt numb and hopeless, and it was all he could do just to stay standing, still hidden as he was behind his pillar. His instinct was to cry out to the realm-dancer, to cling desperately to the last bit of dying light. But that would let the empty-one know of his presence. That thought both paralysed him with fear and would give away his last desperate hope of somehow saving the situation.

They needed Fali; that much was abundantly clear. Without her, the last faint flickers of hope in his heart were gone. The only thing that could save them was to stall somehow to give her time to recuperate, if she could recuperate. If she wasn't dead. The large chunks of stone mostly obscured her, but he couldn't see even the slightest signs of life from her still body. Possibly, her still corpse.

He snapped his head back up as the empty-one let out a throaty, horrid laugh. It was a guttural, horrific sound that no human could have made, and it chilled him to his core. The vile abomination rested a moment to gather its strength, now that all left in its way was seemingly one insignificant human who knelt unmoving before it.

Then, it started to breathe in the paltry remaining energy from the room. Enveloping them in darkness once again, it was savouring its victory now that nothing was left to resist destruction.

Ryheart steeled himself, blocking out the whispers paralysing him. Fali hadn't asked for his help, but she was no longer in a state to do so. This was his best, his only, chance to help. He had sworn to help her. He had sworn to become strong enough to be of use to her. If he couldn't do so now, well, he would never have another chance. The spark of light inside him that she had bequeathed to him might be the only light they had left.

The empty-one stood braced to fire, to snuff out the last flickers of resistance before it.

Jumping from his cover, Ryheart charged. The empty-one was so focused on its triumph that it didn't notice him until he was virtually close enough to touch it. It was too embroiled in its attack to disengage immediately. It closed its mouth and then opened it again to let the power loose. As it did, with all the might he could muster, Ryheart channelled his talent, the blessing bestowed upon him by his fallen friend. He smashed the empty-one in its open jaw. The stored power was violently expulsed, and he felt a sickening crunch under his fist as the empty-one's jaw shattered and hung limp. Its decimating surge streaked violently off course, crashing into the side of the chasm in an explosion of stone.

The empty-one howled, lashing at its attacker with its arm. Ryheart, however, was on the side with the stump Fali had left it, and its blow was clumsy, giving him time, if only barely, to back out of reach.

It stooped over slightly as it stood, arm still dribbling a slow ooze of darkness. Firing three powerful blasts in quick succession had weakened it considerably. Ryheart had dealt far more damage than he could have otherwise. It no longer presented quite the absolute unstoppable force it had first been in his mind.

However, he was under no allusions. Even weakened and crippled, he knew he was still hopelessly and utterly outmatched.

With all the strength he could muster, he had only barely dislodged its vulnerable jaw. He doubted he would have even managed that if the explosive power it had been gathering hadn't backfired on itself. The chances he could do much further to it beyond superficial damage was low.

As if that wasn't quite insurmountable enough, the degree of protection he had absorbed from Fali against the empty-one's corruptive, vile touch would only protect him for the briefest of contact. After that, even a faint connection would eat away at him. After just his single blow, he could already feel a fizzing against his hand like it was fighting to remain in existence.

He had, however, no other choice, and no way out. He set his jaw grimly and advanced warily to the horror before him. If he was going out, he was at least going out kicking and screaming.

Chapter Sixty-Two

Gambit

Olyra knelt in a numbed stupor, sagged on the broken ground as whispers and angry accusations filled her mind. She glanced blankly at the realm-dancer, motionless and still. Then, she turned to the empty-one.

She felt hollow and lost. She had doomed all of them. The air around her felt palpably heavy and thick. She was sure if it could have pulled her through the ground itself, it would have done so.

The numbed but still functional part of her mind watched in barely registered surprise as Ryheart smashed the maw of the beast and violently redirected its final blast.

She had to move to avoid the falling rubble, her finely trained and honed instincts kicking in through her dull haze without conscious thought. The sudden movement roused her from her plagued stupor, and she got to her feet.

Tactically, she knew it was hopeless now the realm-dancer was dead. Even the pair of them couldn't hope to beat the creature. But, she told herself as she banished the whispers from her mind, *going down in battle is better than dying paralysed by my failures.*

Rising to her feet and prepared to make her last charge, a voice carried to her. It was quiet, barely more than a whisper, but it was unmistakable.

It was Fali.

"Olyra," she called in a voice much weaker than her usual commanding tone, "to me."

Olyra noted the empty-one's concentration was fully engaged by Ryheart's valiant last stand, then span around in surprise to see the realm-dancer struggling to a knee. "You're alive?" she exclaimed, startled.

"We have one chance at this. One chance only," the realm-dancer told her with an absolute urgency in her voice, ignoring her question. "Come here."

"Ryheart won't last a second without my help," she cautioned.

"He is more competent than you know," Fali said. "He has never failed to do what was needed, even when he did not win. Besides, if he cannot last long enough, we are all dead anyway. Now come."

The whispers were still flurrying through Olyra's head, unable to banish them, but she drowned them out and ran to the realm-dancer.

Fali commanded her to turn around to face the empty-one, and the realm-dancer's tiny hand touched her shoulder as she brought herself to her feet. The touch quieted the whispers in Olyra's mind, and a calming wave washed over her. Her mind cleared, and while a niggling voice entirely her own still told her she'd doomed them all, her training took hold.

"Orders," she asked crisply.

"How confident are you about hitting the empty-one with your rifle?"

"Moving at full speed? I'm not sure I could."

"Assume it is temporarily still."

"If the shots clear, no issue," she said confidently. This was a time for clear answers rather than false modesty, and if there was one thing she was rock-solid on, it was her aim. "I doubt my shots will do anything to it. They didn't work at close range, and that was in its eye."

"Yes, but you did not have me acting as a power source. I will pour all the power I have left into you, and convert all the artificial magic you can muster yourself into pure creation on top of that. Channelled through you, mundane as you are, the empty-one will not sense it until it is too late. Then we are going to blast the vile thing into oblivion. All you need to do is hold until I say so, and then pull the trigger."

"Alright. Go."

Olyra readied herself and started pouring her artificial magic into her gun, every bit she could muster. For a moment, she felt nothing at all other than her own steady trickle of power. She gasped as energy suddenly flooded into her. This was the realm-dancer's magical power weakened? Every hair on her body stood upright as if it were trying to escape the flow of pure magic streaming through her. Her dark skin started to glow, and the faint smell of singed hair met her nostrils. The very air startled to crackle around them.

She swore as another surge of power nearly jolted the firearm from her hands, and tightened her grip.

"What happens if I can't contain all the energy?" she asked grimly, through gritted teeth.

"You will explode," Fali said bluntly, well past the point of sugar-coating. "But if it is any consolation, me and Ryheart will be following you shortly."

"I'm sure that'll comfort me in oblivion," Olyra said dryly.

"You have been following us all this time ostensibly to protect people. You are not going to back down when you have a chance to protect all of them, are you?"

"No, ma'am," she asserted, without a hint of hesitation.

"Good girl," the realm-dancer said. "Now prepare to aim, and fire on my command."

Chapter Sixty-Three

Stand

Ryheart was stalling for time. Desperately stalling for time, and doing little else. All for a cavalry he didn't even believe was coming.

All he had to drive him forward was faith in Fali, of which he didn't even truly know the origin. As far as he knew, she was dead, and he didn't dare take his attention from the creature even for a moment to check. All he had was hope.

Hope, and one last gambit. One last gambit he didn't have any way to capitalise upon. Even with the empty-one severely hampered by its injuries and fatigue, he was just barely managing to keep himself alive. Staying in the dead spot of reach created by its severed arm gave him just enough time to dodge its attacks as it angled awkwardly. Even with that, he was scarcely keeping himself standing, with little opportunity to strike back. Each blow he dodged brought him that bit closer to exhaustion, and inevitably to his demise.

When he did strike back, he kept his powered blows weak, late and clumsy, as they had been when he had fought with Olyra. This was his one last gambit. His holdout, his one-use weapon that once spent would be done. His one trick to pull on the empty-one. But even if it worked and the empty-one was underestimating him, he had no way to make use of it.

He was already growing exhausted, and he knew he had maybe one solid, full-powered attack left in him. Once he used it, he wouldn't have the energy to repeat it. Even if he could unleash it and connect, he had no follow-up. But he'd at least do some damage before he went out. Maybe, in the long run, that would do some good for someone in the future, somewhere. Maybe it would do nothing at all.

Either way, it was all he had, and he started to inwardly prepare for a last burst of talent, when he felt it. Fali's presence. It filled his heart like the ring of a church bell, carried via the intimate link her blood had bestowed to him. It was weak, scarcely reaching him over the cacophony of demonic whispers coursing through him. But it was unmistakably her.

He got the feeling all her faith was in him, and that he needed to hit it with everything he had when she called. This was their last, best chance.

Even the brief distraction trying to feel her suggestion caused was immediately exploited, and he felt a searing pain as claws razed across his stomach. The glancing blow hit him hard, and his wound hissed and sizzled as the corruption of its touch rejected his existence. His protection against the creature was severely depleted from his prolonged close exposure. He had maybe protection for one last hit, and then he was a goner.

But he had a plan now. Fali needed him. She needed him. She was alive, and he had hope. And sometimes, that was all you needed. Sometimes that was all you had. He kept his power held under the surface and waited for the signal.

"I don't know how much longer I can hold this," Olyra protested, forcing the words through her now firmly clenched teeth. Her entire being felt like it was going to rip apart, the faint glow behind her skin now built to a shining light. She held on despite every fibre of her being screaming at her to release the energy storming inside her. This was far beyond her capacity to store and release artificial magic through her rifle. It was barely even comparable.

"Just a few seconds longer," Fali insisted. "We need everything we can muster. This has to end it."

"What if it doesn't?"

"It has to," she repeated grimly.

Olyra held braced and ready, every cell in her body screaming in protest as they barely kept a force they were never meant to have contained.

"Ready," Fali said softly to her, and inwardly Olyra sighed with relief. Her veins were burning. She was lighting up the rubble in front of them now.

Aiming, though, that was something she was equipped to deal with in any situation, natural to her as breathing.

Even as she was burning with the power, she couldn't help analysing the tactical situation now that she was calm. She would follow her instructions to the letter, but she wasn't above making an observation.

"Ryheart's never going to hit the creature. Not with any decent impact," Olyra said clinically. "He's far too clumsy with his power; he telegraphs too much."

"He will come through when I need him," Fali said confidently. "In fact, I am rather betting our lives on it."

"He's in the way of my shot," she advised. "I presume you don't want him dead?"

"He knows to move," the realm-dancer explained softly. "Eyes on the prize, Olyra. Aim, and on my command, fire."

Olyra snapped her attention back, clearing her racing thoughts and focusing solely on her target, her singular purpose. She aimed, making minute adjustments, and braced.

Ryheart fought desperately now, keeping his punches pulled, luring the empty-one while trying with all his focus to avoid its deadly touch. He stepped too far, just slightly out of step, and he paid for it severely.

The empty-one caught him with its fist. Even with only a light blow, the empty-one ripped through his defence like paper and doubled him over, his skin screaming in protest at the contact with the unholy creature. That was the last hit he could take. He could maybe last a second more, and then it would be over.

'Attack! Retreat!' Fali's presence rang in his mind, and he grinned despite the pain. The empty-one kicked to swat him away to nothing. As it thundered towards him, he brought his fist down towards the extended and exposed joint.

The empty-one saw this as a futile attack, unpowered and weak, and made no move to change its course.

At the last second, Ryheart let his power burst forth to the surface as his fist came down. He unleashed everything he had. Smashing into the empty-one's extended kneecap, halting its assault. He screamed in desperation and pain as he connected with a loud crunch. His hand blistered at the contact, and he dived clear as far as he could.

"Fire!" Fali commanded.

Olyra squeezed the trigger and poured everything they collectively had into the hunk of engineered metal and wood in her hands. For a moment, it hung there, paused between herself and the rifle, almost like the weapon couldn't quite process how to deal with the energy. Then with a deafening crack, her weapon exploded into shards of jagged metal, but not before the blast fired true.

The shining light pierced the air so bright it burned her eyes, and the shadow tore like paper in the wake of its reckoning. If the empty-one's blast had torn up the ground in its aftermath, this one razed it. Ryheart scarcely flew clear as a small precise beam – the prelude of the attack – hit the empty-one squarely through the centre of its bulk. Then the rest caught up, engulfing the empty-one in its entirety.

There was a horrific blood-curdling howl, and the shadow in the room seemed to draw into the empty-one and congeal itself into a shield desperate to hold back the light.

It fought back furiously, and for a moment, it held. Then it cracked. Then it shattered. The power annihilated the shadow and the empty-one along with it in one final shriek.

Nothing happened for a moment as if the world itself was figuring out what had occurred, and then the magical shield softly fell with a tinkling sound. The unnatural shadows dying on the ground gave way to natural patterns, relinquishing their irregular twisted forms. The room was cast in the soft blanket of darkness now; the only light left was that which radiated from Fali, pitifully weak and reduced to scarcely a flicker.

There was a long, long moment as the three stood in total silence, content just to exist, until finally, Fali spoke.

"Well," she said glibly, "that was rather exciting, was it not?"

Chapter Sixty-Four

Miracle

Ryheart felt the strength leave him as the immediate danger passed, and his screaming muscles reasserted that they were really *very* tired and would be most obliged to him if they could rest now. His hand and chest still burned with pain, but the unnatural fizzing eating away at him had faded with the empty-one.

"Next time you tell me I should or shouldn't do something, remind me of this, and I might listen," he said with an exhausted but joyous laugh.

Fali smiled wanly, leaning precariously on the hilt of her recovered sword, the warmth returned to her visage. The red fire drained from her eyes, but the pink that replaced it seemed muted as if even the colour was tired. For the first time since Ryheart had met her, she looked utterly exhausted.

"Do not promise things you are not going to stick to, dearest Ryheart," she said, warmly reproachful. "If there is one thing you humans truly excel at, it is not doing what you are told."

"We're done here, right?" Olyra asked, also looking as spent as Ryheart felt. She stood covered in debris, her hair frazzled. "For some reason, I have a distinct urge to see the open sky again."

"Not quite," Fali replied, then clarified immediately at their slightly panicked looks. "We are done with everything dangerous, yes. But this," she gestured at the spell-work on the floor, "while dormant, is not destroyed, and there is still a moderate amount of magic left in it. I need to clean all this up before we go."

"Can't it wait?" Ryheart asked with concern in his eyes, holding out a hand to help her fully stand.

Fali ignored the hand, still so proud, and pushed herself up to her full height with her sword, then slotted it into its scabbard. There was a satisfying-sounding click as the guard settled into place, and then the sword promptly disappeared, leaving behind only an empty sheath once more.

"I swore to our dragon friend I would clean this up as soon as I possibly could, and despite how we met, I do take my oaths seriously. Besides, I can repurpose the magic left in the spell to do most of the work. Now that it is inactive and both its recipient and creator are indisposed, it will not be that much trouble breaking and realigning it to my purpose. I just have to redirect it." As she spoke, she walked into the centre of the circle. She bowed her head. "Besides which, the spells left the fabric holding reality in place a little strained. I would rather not risk any other empty-ones trying to capitalise on that right now."

She stood before the central altar and began to glow with her incandescent light once again, though it was weak, scarcely shining past herself. Then, the lines of magic before her started to shift and rearrange as if alive, restructuring to her will. The spell's glow began to add to hers, and flowers bloomed first upon the altar her hand laid upon, then onto the rock under her feet. They spread outwards until the entire cavern filled with vibrant flowers glowing with a faint white light, softly illuminating the cave.

The glow subsided, and Fali panted deeply, a faint sparkle of colour in the air before her like misty breath in the cold. Ryheart hadn't even been sure she breathed at all until now, let alone seen her out of breath.

"It's a miracle," Olyra said under her breath, staring in awe at the mesmerising growth around them.

"Just a small one," Fali said modestly. "The spell did a lot of the work. Now our scaly friend can rest peacefully."

"They're beautiful," Ryheart said, "but there's not exactly much light for them here."

"They do not need it. They magisynthesise rather than photosynthesise, and they will purify any stray bits of the void I have missed. This place will never be abused again."

Fali led them out of the cave via a circuitous route, back to the small cabin. The forest immediately around it looked vibrant with fresh saplings and growth. No longer able to contain himself, Ryheart ran outside laughing, and the open sky and stars were about the most beautiful thing he had ever seen.

The cabin looked strangely mundane, given the magnitude of what had occurred under it. A reminder that the witch had once just been trying to survive a world that had rejected her.

"I know the house is probably fine, but can we sleep outside instead?" he asked, peering back in.

"Yes. I just need to find the witch's grimoire. The spell was too complicated to be constructed from memory. It was a touch too stiff, as if copied. This was all clearly the witch's doing, but something nudged her in this direction."

They watched as she searched for a few moments, then, with a soft click, pulled a stone away, a heavy leather book behind it.

She opened it and frowned.

"What's the matter?" Ryheart asked warily.

"It does not want me to read it," she said, showing him a page, the letters all jumbled into nonsense. "I will have to break it, but it will take time. I believe the spell that corrupted the Nemean was designed by the same hand that the spell below came from. Such an intricate and powerful spell explains how it shattered the Fae barrier, and they had a similar 'handwriting'. The empty-one we just fought might have provided her with it, but I doubt he authored it. For now, though, let us rest."

After quickly setting up a rough camp a short distance from the cabin, Ryheart immediately fell asleep, the soundest he had slept in a long while.

Chapter Sixty-Five

Return

Sleeping until the sun heated his tent like an oven, unsurprisingly, Ryheart awoke to find Fali already up. Less expected, Olyra too, seemed to have only just arisen.

"First thing a good soldier learns is to sleep well when you can get it," Olyra said in response to his surprised expression. Fali's wings seemed to have disappeared again, though he had a faint awareness that, unlike before, they were still present, just hidden from his sight.

Fali's familiar had returned, and he crouched before it and waved fondly, unable as he was to touch it.

After a light breakfast of the farm produce they had brought, they set off back towards the village. The vibrant life gradually toned down as they moved from the epicentre, until the forest was primarily dead trees with only weak new growth. However, they didn't carry the air of absolute desolation that they had before, and it seemed in time, they would regrow.

Upon returning to the village, they found a small commotion in the centre. A dozen regal-looking soldiers were flanking a wizened-looking man who held a glass globe in his palm. They seemed to be quizzing the locals, who were pointing in the direction of the forest. Clearly, they were looking for someone, and Ryheart had the distinct impression he knew who.

He turned to Olyra, a sinking feeling in his stomach. "You didn't," he accused.

"I swear this isn't my doing," she assured, before frowning. "That is a wizard, though, and those are the royal guard."

Before they could discuss further, the old man held the globe up and swung it towards them, pointing excitedly. Straight at them.

The guards marched towards them at pace, and Ryheart tried to calm his frayed nerves and take small comfort in the fact their weapons weren't drawn. Less reassuringly, they filed either side of the trio and effectively surrounded them.

"That's her! That's her without a doubt," the wizard said excitedly, holding his globe out towards Fali like he was appraising some rare antique with a magnifying glass. "This matches the reading my colleagues measured at the phenomenon in Londaya. It's the same one that flared up last night."

One of the guards, his armour more embellished than the others, stepped forward. "Fali Lightflower, and Ryheart of no family name, the King requires your presence immediately. We are to escort you to him at once."

Ryheart felt some slight relief. They at least weren't being thrown in chains, but he couldn't help but note that their previous invitation had now become a demand.

"As it happens, we were just on our way to visit him," Fali said, just a tad blasé for his comfort. "Can I ask why he wishes my company?"

"I'm not privy to the Kings reasons, ma'am. I am simply here to carry out his will."

"Oh, very well, since he asked nicely. What about her?" Fali asked, gesturing at Olyra.

"Any within your company are to come with me," he said, nevertheless nodding respectfully to Olyra, evidently recognising her position. "This is to take priority over any current operations you are undertaking."

"Very well, Major," Olyra acquiesced. "Lead the way."

They were escorted to the stables, which, not used to so many guests, had horses tied to fences scattered around the small village square. Olyra retrieved their rented horses, and with that, finally, they were on their way back to Londaya, albeit not quite in the circumstances Ryheart had hoped.

Whether it was a consideration for their guests or the size of the riding party, Ryheart wasn't sure, but they seemed not to be riding over hard. The soldiers rode on all sides of them, and despite Olyra's assurances that this was standard practice when escorting anyone, he couldn't help feeling like a prisoner. The guards were courteous but refused to answer any questions about the exact circumstances of their being taken into custody. The wizard was slightly chattier and seemed positively giddy about Fali, but he too either couldn't or wouldn't tell them why they had been picked up. However, he did tell them that the guards had set off searching for them some time ago without an exact idea where to look. The sudden flare of Fali's immense magical presence at the start of their fight with the empty-one had been sensed even from miles away, and they had ridden overnight to find them.

They made good time on the major roads and stopped overnight at royal way-stops, guards posted at their doors. Fali seemed quite nonplussed by the situation, but Ryheart couldn't help feeling increasingly anxious about the constant monitoring. There was a brief but welcome distraction from his worries as they arrived at the way-stop they had stayed in before, and the rude guard almost bolted at the mere sight of Fali escorted by an entourage of soldiers.

Eventually, they made their way to the capital. Rather than proceeding to the south of the city where the gate to the residential area was, they proceeded to the north gate. That was the only way to access the city's government district, and through it, the royal grounds in the city's centre.

Small crowds of officials unlucky enough to live outside the district they worked in congregated by the gate. The guards pushed their way through to the front, where they were ushered through.

Grand buildings far vaster than Ryheart was used to seeing in his less wealthy home district towered around them. They were taken to an enormous gateway, through which the royal castle lay.

Even the royal guards had to present their identification at the gate. They were verified by various means, both magical and mundane, before they passed into the castle's courtyard. The castle itself dwarfed all other buildings, and he felt more uneasy with each step. Finally, they entered the castle itself, a vast hall with thick carpets, the emblem of Brittaya plastered on virtually every surface and decoration available.

The guards spoke for some time to an impeccably dressed butler. Before Ryheart had a chance to talk to his companions, a pair of inner guards flanked him. Olyra and Fali had guards assigned to them, and they were all separately escorted away. He hoped the next time he saw them, that they wouldn't be in chains.

Chapter Sixty-Six

Hierarchy

Ryheart was escorted down a long corridor, where the guards opened a wooden door and gestured politely for him to enter without a word.

He did so with mild trepidation, only to find a smartly appointed room, and a maid sat by a freestanding bath. She took one look at him and wrinkled her nose.

"If you present yourself to the King in that state, he's likely to die from the smell. His Royal Highness isn't used to the smells of us common folk."

He started to protest, but she pointed imperiously at the tub in a manner not entirely unlike Fali. Evidently, she wasn't about to accept excuses.

"We haven't got much time, and we don't want to keep the King waiting, do we? Strip, boy."

Feeling very awkward, he peeled his armour and clothes off and hopped into the tub as quickly as possible. For the next half-hour, she attacked him with a scrubber so thoroughly he felt like his entire skin had been removed. She scurried out of the room while he dried and came back with a neat stack of clothes.

"Get these on you, young sir; they should be your size. Everyone gets to present themselves to the King looking their absolute best. Your clothes smell as much as you do."

He dressed in the brightly coloured embroidered doublet that he was reasonably sure was more expensive than every possession he owned added together, and she ushered him out of the room.

"Come along now. These gentlemen will see you on your way," she said, waving to the guards.

He was escorted back to the main hall. To his relief, both Fali and Olyra were also shepherded into view. Both wore opulent gowns, Fali's a royal blue and Olyra's a vibrant green. Both had had their hair coiled upon their head in an elegant pile, the current fashion with ladies of high stature. Fali wore it so comfortably she might have been born in it. Olyra looked palpably unimpressed, if resigned.

Fali smiled warmly at him as he approached, and some of his trepidation fell away. At least they were facing whatever this was together.

"Well, after all those delays, we are finally here," Fali murmured. "Let us go see what this is all about, shall we?"

Their procession went up a wide staircase to an ornately carved door, and they came through it to a spacious throne room, brightly lit by what looked to be magical light. Plush red and gold carpets flanked by pillars led to the end of the hall, dominated by the golden throne that stood there. Within it was seated the King. He wore only a simple circlet instead of a crown, for his true badge of office was hanging upon the wall behind him. The sword of Brittaya, said to be bequeathed to each King by the spirit of the land itself.

The King himself wore a bright red doublet laced with gold and had jet-black hair that ran to his shoulders. As he stared at them, his unwavering grey eyes spoke of a patient but firm temperament.

"My liege," a finely dressed servant proclaimed. "I present to you Fali Lightflower, Valkyrie Agent Olyra Holloway of the OPMC and Ryheart, ah, of no family name." He turned to the guests. "You are all in the esteemed presence of His Grand Majesty, King of all Brittaya."

Olyra and Ryheart both dropped to a knee and bowed their heads low to the ground. He nearly had a heart attack as he noticed from the corner of his eye that Fali stood at her full height, unbent.

"You will pay fealty to the King!" one of his attendants nearly screamed, eyes bulging.

"I shall not," she replied simply and definitively.

Ryheart groaned internally. It was like she wanted them all executed!

The royal attendant was practically frothing at the mouth now. "Remove her at once!" he yelled.

"Would you care to listen to a song, Your Majesty?" Fali asked out of the blue, ignoring the attendant's shouts.

The guards moved to detain her, but the King commanded them to halt. "I hope, for your sake, it's the right song," he intoned in a sombre voice.

In answer, she tilted her head and sang. Her voice was rich and pure, carrying a depth and grace Ryheart could barely comprehend. She didn't sing in Anglasan, but the very sound seemed to impart the meaning within it. As she sang, she opened her palm, and a small spherical ball of fire lit up. The fire froze into ice, broke apart into a small gale of wind and then solidified into a flower. Finally, the flower shone until it was a white light of pure, unadulterated creation. It was a greeting from beyond this realm to those who recognised it. As she did so, her wings and familiar appeared fleetingly, too. They glowed softly with the same beautiful light, shining with myriad colours.

The King's face paled slightly as he watched, and then silently, he stood from his throne. Then, to the absolute amazement of the room, he sank to a knee before the diminutive figure before him.

"Your Grace," he said reverently.

A slight smile lit her face. "Ah, you have taken your studies of the old ways to heart, I see. Your 'grandfather' was not the most studious man, and he had his sword at my neck before he recognised me." Brittayan royalty was unique in the world. Rather

311

than biological lineage, the successor was chosen by the sword upon the wall, and the new royal renounced any other family name they might have had. In its place, they took the surname Brittaya to signify their loyalty to the country. From her speech, Ryheart inferred she meant his royal grandfather, rather than biological.

"I study them yearly, Light Mother."

"Oh, you are a good boy, are you not," she said, beaming even more extensively. "I have not heard that form of address from a human in a long time, and I am rather partial to it. Now that that is out of the way, please, let us talk as equals."

The King rose and gestured to the human pair still kneeling before him.

"Rise," he commanded, then turned his attention entirely back to Fali. "Now, I heard tell of your presence, Your Grace, and wished to see whether the signs reported were true. I had no idea where you were, but I heard you had taken the young hunter into your confidence, hence my invitation. I was content to let you return in your own time, then learned that the OPMC had taken a less genteel interest into you and already had an agent in the field with hostile intent. At that point, I thought it best to detain everyone to avoid any irreversible action from either party. I pray they acted fairly with you?" he asked, glancing at Olyra.

"We were able to make amicable arrangements," Fali said smoothly, and Ryheart heard Olyra let out a nearly imperceptible breath of relief.

"Grand. I would like to discuss why you have graced us with your presence after an aeon, but first, outstanding matters. I pray Ryheart has acted honourably as a representative of his crown and country?"

"You could not have asked for better," she said solemnly, then added, less regally, "I trust you will compensate him fairly for his service?"

"Ryheart?" he addressed.

"Yes, Your Majesty?" Ryheart croaked out, mouth dry.

"You have my true gratitude. I'll make arrangements to see you paid as agreed."

"I'm honoured, Your Majesty," he said, heart thumping.

"Grand," Fali addressed the other royal, and it truly hit Ryheart for the first time that she was just that. Royal. "Now then, I have rather a lot to fill you in on about some of the things that have occurred within your kingdom. Would you care for a long walk, Your Majesty? I prefer to talk surrounded by greenery, do you?"

"Whatever you wish, Your Grace," he said, holding out his arm for her.

"Why, thank you," she said, taking his arm lightly as they strode from the room, leaving a stunned court behind them. "Tell me, Your Highness, before we get to business. Are you courting anyone? You are such a polite boy, and bachelors sometimes develop unpleasant habits."

Chapter Sixty-Seven

Parting

Two days after their audience, Ryheart had seen nary a peep of human King or Fae Queen. Scratch that, realm-dancer Queen. A hard knock rang on his door, and he hoped to find Fali behind it. Instead, he found Olyra, which was still a welcome sight given his seeming abandonment.

"Alright?" Olyra asked, laconic as ever, now back in her armour.

"Grand. You?"

"Leaving. I'm not built for this poncing around."

"Oh. Any word?" Ryheart asked.

"If you mean about our diminutive flame-haired warrior, not a peep. I've been fully debriefed by the royal court, though. So now I get to be debriefed all over again by OPMC command."

"Ah. Fun," he said with a grin.

"It's what I live for," she said dryly. "I can't wait around here, but... tell her it's been fun."

"Ooh, I don't know. A bit soppy for you, isn't it?" he joked.

"I think that's the effect she's had on me," Olyra answered, taking his comment at face value. "Oh, by the way. I'm going to report that Fali performed all the magic I saw in our group. No one else did anything remarkable," she said, staring pointedly at his still slightly burnt hand where he had punched the empty-one with his talent. "No one's going to see anything inside the city to suggest the contrary, are they?"

"No, ma'am," he said, holding his hand out for her to shake. "If I don't see you again, I'm glad to have fought alongside you."

"Oh, don't worry," she said with the smallest of grins, "I know exactly where to find you if I want you."

A further two days later, Ryheart was still in his guestroom in the castle, and he still hadn't seen so much as a glance of Fali. He was beginning to think the place was simply so large that he had been forgotten. He was surprised on his walks in the guest wing and accessible parts of the castle to find a surprising amount of Fae within, as guests, engineers, servants and envoys. The vast majority of beings he encountered were still human, but compared to the near-complete absence of Fae in the residential part of the city, it was notable.

He had received an official letter stating all debts with the guild were squared. He should have felt ecstatic, and he was to an extent. However, this was the final answer to the very first letter that had set him and Fali off on their fantastic adventure together in the first place. Receiving it without her by his side felt a little hollow, incomplete. He sighed. Clearly, Fali fit in here, with people far more important than him. He was pretty sure even the maids were of a higher class than he was. Maybe she had just outgrown the need for him. It made far more sense for a queen, an otherworldly one at that, to be surrounded by royalty and power rather than being in the company of a simple, common hunter. He was lucky she had spent any time with him at all, on reflection. She'd never wanted his company in the first place originally, after all. He decided it was probably best to leave and get on with his life, since he'd seemingly been abandoned. She could always find him if she wanted to look in on him.

It had been fun while it had lasted. Well, it was terrifying some of the time. A lot of the time. But it had been an adventure. For a

315

little while, he had been a proper, genuine hunter. He had done, maybe, some good for the world. Just a little. And now he had his debt paid; he was a free man. He could start again.

The feeling was bittersweet, but at least it wasn't just bitter.

Packing his things and dressing in his armour, he set off to leave the castle. He had a seal to allow him to leave the district.

Following passages to the winding staircase that led to the visitor's hall, he stepped towards the entrance to leave.

"Why, Ryheart," a rich voice called behind him, "you were not about to go and abandon me, were you?"

He whirled around, and Fali stood before him in her usual, less opulent attire.

"Fali!" he exclaimed. "Where have you been?"

"Sorry, dear-heart. I have had a lot to discuss with Arendeth," she said, using the King's first name oh-so-casually. "I had several arrangements to make with numerous people. King's assurances or no, his people were quite adamant they test me with all their various trinkets to ensure I was not controlling his mind or something. I hope you have been well?"

"Fine, just, listless. I figured this was the better company for you anyway."

"My people's concept of a queen is somewhat different to yours, Ryheart, and I am not over-fond of all this pageantry. Besides, we have some absolutely vital business to attend to."

"Oh? What?"

"Why, I promised you I would help pay your debt, did I not?"

"Done. Wiped clear already."

"Yes, by the King. But do you not remember how I said I would help pay you?" she said with some small amusement.

He frowned. "Err...?"

"I said I would help you get a bounty, did I not? We can hardly say we are finished until we cash it in together, can we?"

He stared a moment, then chuckled. They had been so rolled up in events he had virtually forgotten he still had the Nemean bounty to collect from the guild. He wouldn't just be clear of debt. He, for once in his life, would be up.

"And afterwards?" he asked hopefully.

"Well, I need somewhere quiet to study this grimoire. As I say, the summoning spell was far too complex to have come from the witch herself. Someone had to teach it to her, and there may be more than one person who received a copy of this grimoire. I do not think I am entirely done here. Nor is your training. Besides, since we more than paid your debt, it is only fair you extend your offer of sanctuary to me for longer, really. I put all that work into enchanting the place, and it would be a waste not to use it. It would be extraordinarily rude of you to kick me out now, would it not?"

Ryheart couldn't help but let a dopey grin spread over his face. Whatever Fali discovered in that book, wherever fate was about to take him next, he knew the only thing he needed to. He would be facing it by her side.